Being
Me

Being Me

Lisa Renee Jones

Gallery Books

New York London Toronto Sydney New Delhi

G

Gallery Books

A Division of Simon & Schuster, Inc.

1230 Avenue of the Americas

New York, NY 10020

First Gallery Books trade paperback edition June 2013

GALLERY BOOKS and colophon are registered trademarks of Simon & Schuster, Inc.

For information about special discounts for bulk purchases, please contact Simon & Schuster Special Sales at 1-866-506-1949 or business@simonandschuster.com.

The Simon & Schuster Speakers Bureau can bring authors to your live event. For more information or to book an event contact the Simon & Schuster Speakers Bureau at 1-866-248-3049 or visit our website at www.simonspeakers.com.

Designed by Ruth Lee-Mui

Manufactured in the United States of America

10 9 8 7 6 5 4 3 2 1

Library of Congress Cataloging-in-Publication Data
Jones, Lisa Renee.
Being me / Lisa Renee Jones.—First Gallery Books trade paperback edition.
pages cm
1. Secrets—Fiction. I. Title.
PS3610.O627B45 2013
813'.6—dc23
2013003126

ISBN 978-1-4767-2721-9
ISBN 978-1-4767-2723-3 (ebook)

To Diego for his enduring belief in me and this series

Acknowledgments

I have so many people to thank for helping this series find its audience. First, Louise Fury, my agent, for reading *If I Were You* and feeling passionate enough about it to sing its praises from rooftops, and she really did pretty much jump on rooftops.

To Lori Perkins for jumping on those rooftops with her. Then Micki Nuding joined them and magic was created. Also, thank you to Shari Smiley, who has done such great things to bring the series to an entirely new audience. I also cannot say enough about the entire Simon & Schuster team. Everyone has taken such care with the series and shown great excitement.

I also want to thank the many bloggers, readers, and reviewers who read *If I Were You* early and told the world they had to read it, too! And continue to tell the world they need to read the series! Thank you so much!

And to my street team, The Underground Angels, for all your love, support, and efforts, to spread the word about my books. You really are my angels!

Darkness surrounded me, a complete absence of light that left me shaking inside. No. It wasn't the darkness that had me shaking. It was him. I could feel him, even if I could not see him. Oh yes, I could feel him. In every pore of my body, every nerve ending I owned, I could feel him. Stalking me. Claiming me, even though he hadn't touched me yet. I was completely at his mercy, naked and on my knees, in the center of a soft wool rug. Tight bands held my calves to my thighs, while another set of ties wrapped my chest and held my arms behind my back. It hurt in a bittersweet, arousing way, and while I felt exposed and vulnerable, I've come to know those things arouse me in ways I never thought possible. It isn't logical really, how I can feel scared of where he will take me next, and still quiver with arousal. And I was scared as I knelt there in the darkness. Scared of how little control I have over my own body's response, how much he controls me when I do not. How much I need him to control me. I do not recognize this part of me now, as I write this, but when I'm with him, I become what he wants me to be. I become his willing slave, even though I've come to know I am only a token in his games. He's promised me nothing other than to possess me. He will never belong to me as I do to him. I will never control him as he does me. I play by his rules and I never know how they will change, or what, or who will be part of the new game each of our encounters become. And last night, when a spotlight suddenly shone down on me and me alone, when he stepped out of the darkness to stand before me, it was the man standing by his side that jolted me to the core. Two of them, one of whom I despise being with us and he knows it, yet he still invited this person to share me. I wanted to object. I should have objected. But there in that room, I wasn't Rebecca. I was just his. Sometimes, in the morning light, when he cannot touch me, when we are apart, I think I want to just be me, to be Rebecca again. Only I'm not sure who that is. I'm not sure I know me anymore. Who is Rebecca Mason?

One

❦

I am suffocating in a tunnel of complete, utter darkness created by the unexpected power outage in the storage unit I've been digging through in hopes of finding clues to Rebecca's whereabouts. I have been thrust into the middle of a dreaded horror movie, the kind I hate watching, and I instantly picture myself as the girl who makes all the wrong moves and ends up bloody and lifeless. I, Sara McMillan, am a logical person, and I tell myself to reject my fear as irrational. This is simply one of the random power outages San Francisco has experienced in the past few months, and a mouse at my feet is the worst of my worries.

But then, isn't that what the girl who gets killed in the horror movie always thinks, too? It's *just* a power outage. It's just a mouse. I was stupid to come here alone at night as it is and I try not to be stupid. I knew from a prior encounter that the attendant of this place was creepy but I dismissed him as a concern. I'd just been too darn desperate to feel I was doing something to find Rebecca, and desperate to take my mind off Chris's silence since our text exchange this morning, when I'd confessed to missing him. I fear his trip out of town for a charity event has given him time to decide he doesn't miss me. After all, he'd dared to show me one of his darkest secrets the night before and I'd done exactly what he'd said I would, and I'd sworn I wouldn't, by pushing him away. *Running away,* I add silently, thinking of the words Chris had used quite often to predict my behavior.

Another popping sound permeates the eerie silence and I am officially freaking out about more than Chris's silence. My mind struggles to identify the sound, with no results. Oh yes, indeed, I am so flipping stupid for coming here alone. And while I like to think I'm not stupid often, tonight proves that when I am, I do it in a big way.

I don't dare move, let alone breathe, yet I can hear low, raspy pants and I know they are mine. I will myself to silence but it doesn't work. My chest is tight, and air becomes harder to draw into my lungs. I need air. I need it desperately. I'm hyperventilating, I think. Yes. That's it. I remember this same, almost out-of-body sensation, from the moment a doctor exited my mother's hospital room five years ago and told me she was dead. Even knowing what is happening to me, I continue the damnable shallow gasps certain to give away my location. I do not understand how I can know what is happening to me and still not be capable of controlling it.

Somehow, I am standing and I don't remember standing. Papers fall from my hands that I don't remember holding. Panic rises inside me and tells me to scream and run. So right and real is this "fight or flight" sensation that I take a step forward, but another popping sound freezes me in place. My gaze jerks to the door, where I see nothing but more darkness. Nothing but this deep, black hole threatening to gobble me up. Another pop. What is that sound? Another noise—a shuffle of a foot, I think—sounds closer to the doorway. Adrenaline races through me, and I don't consciously think, I just act.

I launch myself across the room, in a direction I think is free of obstacles. Door, door, door! I need the door. Where is the damn door? My fingers find empty space and more empty space until, finally, I hit cold steel and relief washes over me as I slam the door shut. I hold my palms against the surface. Now what? Now what?! Lock the door. But I can't. Reality hits hard. The lock is outside and—oh, God—whoever is outside could lock me inside. Or . . . what if the person I sensed in the hallway had made it inside with me before I shut the door?

I whirl around at the terrifying thought and flatten myself against the door. I remember my phone in my jacket pocket and dig for it. I can't see anything. I clearly cannot even think straight. How had I not thought of my phone before now? I grab it but it slips from my hand and drops to the ground. Frantically, I fall to my knees on the ground to scrabble for it, relieved when my hand closes around the slick plastic, but I struggle without success to get the lock button off.

As I dart to my feet, afraid I'll be slashed to death while trying to dial—and this time nothing is stopping my escape. Running might be another stupid move, but at this point not running feels pretty darn stupid, too. I yank the door open and more darkness greets me, but I don't care. I run and pray that I don't charge into whoever is inside with me or trip over my own feet in the black hole that is everything around me. I just want out. Out. Out. Out. It is all I can think of. It's what drives me forward in the direct line to the exit. I am an explosion of fear and adrenaline that has dissolved the logic I'd had moments before.

I search for the exit, for light, but the exterior door that had been open is closed, and I hit it with a force that rattles my teeth. The iron taste of blood spills into my mouth where my teeth have ground into my tongue, but I don't let it shake my resolve to escape in one piece. I feel for the handle and let out a breath of relief when it gives and the door opens.

Within a split second I am out of the building, the dim streetlights and cold San Francisco night air a welcome escape from the suffocating darkness of the building as I bolt for my car. My muscles flex and burn as I fear someone is at my back but I do not dare waste precious seconds to confirm or deny this possibility. The delicate skin of my palm is pinched between my keys where I have squeezed the metal into the flesh, and I struggle to find the electronic clicker to unlock my car door. Time seems to stand still as I fight the urge to look behind me again and, instead, I tug the door open.

Certain someone is about to grab me from behind, I throw myself into my seat and yank the handle, sealing myself inside and clicking the locks into place. Frantically I look out my window and see no one, but I expect shattered glass any second. My hands shake with such fierceness I have to steady one with the other to get the key in the ignition. The instant it's in, I start the engine and throw the vehicle into reverse. Tires squeal and my heart thunders. I shift the gear into drive and instantly stomp on the brake, jerking myself forward with the impact. The sound of my heavy breathing fills the eerily silent car as I stare at the open door of the building and see nothing spectacular or scary. It's just . . . there. And I'm here and no one else seems to be around.

It doesn't matter. The longer I sit here the more I feel exposed, vulnerable, a target. My foot hits the gas. I need out of this parking lot and I need out now.

I'm barely on the side street leading to the highway, my hands clutching the steering wheel, when it hits me: the storage unit is unlocked. I've left it open and I'm driving away. I cut the car into a gas station and park beside the building. I just sit. It could be a minute, or two or ten. I can't be sure. I can't seem to form coherent thoughts. I let my head fall to the steering wheel and try to focus. The storage unit. Rebecca's secrets, her life. Her death. My head jerks up. No. She's not dead. She's not dead . . . and yet, I know in my gut there is a secret about her in that storage unit that someone doesn't want me or anyone else to discover.

"I have to go back and lock the unit," I whisper. I could call the police to meet me. They won't arrest me for being afraid of the dark. They might laugh, they might be irritated, but I'll be safe and smart this time.

My cell phone rings from the seat, where I don't remember tossing it, and I jump, balling my fist between my breasts. "Good grief," I murmur, chiding myself. "Get a grip, Sara."

I glance at the number. *Chris.* My chest burns hot with emotion. There is so much between us that is unsettled, so many reasons why we are wrong for each other. Yet, despite this or perhaps because of it, I have never needed to hear someone's voice as much as I need to hear his now.

"Sara," he murmurs when I answer, and my name is a soft rasp of silky male perfection that radiates through me and settles in the deep hollow of my soul only he seems to fill.

"Chris." My voice cracks on his name, because damn it, my eyes are burning. How have I gone from living the past few years so unaffected by what is around me to the opposite in a matter of weeks? "I . . . I wish you were here."

"I am here, baby," he says, and I think, I hope, I hear a note of his own emotion etched deep within his words. "I'm at your front door. Open up."

I blink in confusion. "I thought you were in L.A. for the charity event."

"I was and I have to fly out again in the morning, but I had to see you. Open up and let me in."

I am stunned. I've worried all day over his silence. Feared he'd shut me out, as I had him last night. "You came home just to see me?"

"Yes. I came just to see you." He seems to hesitate. "Are you going to leave me outside?"

More of that emotion I try not to feel erupts inside me, and the burn in my eyes threatens to become tears. He came to see me, went out of his way, to fly here from another city, even after the way I'd reacted to his confession at the club last night. "I'm not home." My voice is barely audible. "I'm not and I want to be. Can you please come here?"

"Where is here?" he asks, sounding as urgent as I feel.

"A few blocks away. At a Stop N Buy store by the storage unit I told you about." I can't bring myself to say Rebecca's name and I don't know why.

"I'll be right there."

I open my mouth to give him directions, but the line goes dead.

Two

I'm out of my car the instant I see Chris's Porsche pulling into the parking lot, and the chill I feel when I step outside has nothing to do with the cold air blasting from the nearby ocean, and everything to do with what had happened back at that storage unit. I hug myself and watch him drive toward my silver Ford Focus, and my heart thunders in my chest. Suddenly, I am nervous and insecure, and I hate this part of me I cannot escape. What if I've read his visit wrong and he's here to end what's between us? What if my reaction to his big reveal last night at Mark's club has convinced him of what he's so often declared? That I don't belong in this world, in his world.

The 911 slides sleekly into the parking spot next to mine, and I try not to think about it being the same car my father drives. My father is the last person I should have on my mind, yet he's been in my head these past few weeks and I don't know why.

I'm off-kilter, my mind all over the place, shaken by the night's events and my fear of what will happen with Chris.

I watch Chris exit the car, and just the sight of him towering over the roof of the Porsche sets my pulse to racing all over again. He rounds the trunk, and dressed in black jeans, biker boots, and a leather jacket, his blond hair spiking to his collar, he looks rumpled and sexy, and oh so ruggedly male. His long strides mimic the same urgency I feel, and I launch myself in his direction.

The few steps between us feel like an eternity before I am finally in his arms, wrapped in the warm cocoon of his embrace, his powerful body absorbing mine. The battle of the night before is gone as if it never existed. I melt into the hard lines of him, sliding my hands beneath his leather jacket, and inhaling the wonderful sandalwood and musk scent that is so wonderfully Chris.

In an easy move, he maneuvers me to the side of the car, where the wall hides us from the sight of the people coming and going into the store. "Talk to me, baby," he orders, studying me in the dim, barely there glow of some kind of parking lights on the Porsche. "Are you okay?"

My eyes meet his and even in the deep haze of the shadows I feel the connection between us, the depths of his feelings for me. Chris has layers I don't pretend to understand, but he cares about me and I want him to see what I failed to show him last night. I want to understand him. I want him, all of him, including those parts I made him feel I can't deal with.

"Yes," I whisper. "Now that you're here, I'm okay."

I've barely spoken the words when his mouth closes over

mine, and I can taste his urgency, his fear, which I recognize now as my own, a fear that after our visit to Mark's club, we'd never be here, like this, again. I arch into him, drinking in his passion, instantly, willingly consumed by all that he is and could be to me. A dark seed of something that started back in the storage unit, or maybe last night in the club, tries to surface, something my mind refuses to accept. Desperate to escape what I do not want to face, I do what I never dare, and lose myself in the moment. I feel myself sinking deeper into passion, lost in the heat burning low in my belly, the desire spreading slick and hot, between my thighs. There is nothing but the slide of Chris's tongue against mine, the taste and scent of him, the feel of his hands molding me possessively against his body. I need this. I need *him*.

I shove my hands under his shirt, absorbing the hot feel of taut skin over hard muscle, pressing closer to him. A rough sound of desire rumbles in his chest, and I revel in his pleasure, his desire for me, at the way his hands slide down my back, over my backside, before he pulls me hard against his groin. I lick into his mouth as I feel his erection thick against my stomach, and something just snaps inside me. I don't care where I am. I don't know where I am. I just want Chris. I cannot stop touching him, tasting him. We are all over each other and I am lost. And still, it's not enough to keep that dark seed at bay. I need something . . . more. I need . . .

"Sara."

I gasp as Chris tears his mouth from mine and my name is a rasp of heat and desire torn from his throat. With no concept of how much time has passed, I'm against the wall and I don't remember how I got there, nor do I care. I try to kiss Chris again. His fingers tunnel into my hair, holding me back, and he is breathing as hard as I am. "We have to stop before I get us arrested. And right now, it wouldn't take much to risk it just to be inside you."

Yes. Please. Chris inside me, filling me. I crave that more than my next breath. I blink up at him, dazed but not confused about what I want, which is him. Now. Here. But the sound of an engine, and the laughter of a child, blast through me with a jolt that stiffens my spine. Everything that's happened in the past hour rushes over me and balls into a tight knot in my stomach. I am appalled that I have forgotten where I am, and the urgency of needing to secure Rebecca's things.

I splay my hand over the warm heat of Chris's chest. "I forgot the time." I'm panting. How can I not be with this man's hips ground to mine, promising the kind of sweet escape I know he can give me? I push thoughts through the haze of lust. "I forgot to lock the unit. I have to get back before the main building is locked and I can't." I *want* to tell him everything that has happened. He's the only person I can talk to about my fears for Rebecca, but I instinctively know he will flip out and ask too many questions when I have no time. I have to get to the storage unit quickly. "Can you follow me over? I need to hurry." I don't wait for an answer. I slide along the wall to make my escape and ineffectively try to dart around him.

His hand settles on the wall by my head, caging me in. "What do you need from Rebecca's storage unit this late at night?" His jaw is set in that stubborn way I am coming to know, and despite its meaning, a part of me revels that I am coming to know him.

12

I brush my hand over the dark blond stubble on his jaw responsible for the delicious rasp on my cheek. "Can I explain on the way over? Please, Chris? I really don't want to get sealed out of the main building."

His keen stare cuts through the darkness and, damn it, I was right in my assumption. He's steel, unmoving. Unwilling to let me escape without explanation. "What haven't you told me, Sara?"

"In case you don't know, you can be very overbearing, Chris. I'll tell you on the way over."

"Tell me now."

"They'll lock the building, Chris."

He doesn't move. Right. Of course not. Chris is always in control. *Not always*, a voice in my head says, and I remember him offering me his shirt to keep me from feeling insecure about my nudity when he was still dressed. In small but important ways he shares the power with me.

"I stopped by to see if I could find anything else that might tell me how to contact Rebecca." I intend to say no more, but he stares at me and my tendency toward nervous rambling kicks in. "I lost track of time and then all of a sudden the power went out and it was pitch black. I felt like I was suffocating and I couldn't see anything and I got spooked. I heard this weird popping sound and I felt like I wasn't alone."

"What do you mean you felt like you weren't alone?"

"I just know I wasn't alone. Someone was inside the building. It felt like they were stalking me. I didn't know if I should hide or run and I couldn't see my damn phone to dial. I finally ran and when I got to my car I drove here. That's how

I ended up leaving the unit unlocked. I'd just pulled in here when you called."

He stares at me for another intense moment and then pushes off the wall, cursing under his breath as his hands settle on his hips, under his jacket. "What the fuck were you doing at the storage unit after dark alone in the first place?"

My defenses flare, made worse by the fact that I know it wasn't the smartest thing I've ever done. Stupidity is not an easy thing to face. "Don't curse at me, Chris."

"Don't make decisions that put yourself in danger and I won't."

My feathers are ruffled further. "I can take care of myself. I've been doing it for years."

"Is that what you call tonight?" His anger is palpable, crackling off him like the hum of electricity. "Taking care of yourself? Because if it is, you're scaring the crap out of me, Sara. I told you I'd have someone look into Rebecca's whereabouts and that means you leave it the hell alone."

I'm more than defensive now. I'm pissed. I don't need another man to tell me I don't know how to take care of myself. I lash out. "We've had this conversation, Chris. Fucking me does not give you the right to run my life."

His jaw flexes, and while the shadows hide the green of his eyes, I'm pretty sure they'd be burning with red–hot anger. "Is that what we're back to, Sara? I'm fucking you? Is that where last night took us again? Why you are all over me in a parking lot? Because if you want me to fuck you, I'll fuck you until you can't remember your damn name and you never forget mine."

Heat rushes over me because I know how capable he is of

making good on his words. But in their depths is the inference I'm not already there, that he doesn't know I will never forget him, and more so, that I don't want to try. I open my mouth to say as much, but I don't get the chance.

"Decide now, Sara," he demands. "If I'm with you beyond a few fuck sessions, I'm damn sure going to do everything I can to protect you and you're going to have to deal with it."

My mood shifts instantly with his ultimatum. I'm already in old demon territory and I can suddenly taste the poison of the past in every word I hiss. "Protect me or control me, Chris?"

I wait for him to react, to try to smash me back down, to demand of me whatever he sees as his right. Part of me wants him to rise to this challenge. Another fears he will. But at least if he does, I know how to deal with it.

But this is Chris, and he doesn't do anything I expect, now or ever. He just stares at me, his expression unreadable, his jaw set in a hard line.

Long, tense seconds tick by, and he reaches into his jacket and snatches his keys from his pocket. "Let's go lock the damn storage unit."

He turns away and I feel my stomach sink to my feet. I don't want to fight with him. And I'm not fighting with Chris, anyway, I realize. I'm fighting with my past and I refuse to let my old demons come between us.

I dart forward and put myself between him and the car, my hand settling on his chest. He doesn't touch me. He stares down at me and I see no emotion in him. I've seen this Chris, back at the winery, when he'd been given something of his father's, when he was shutting down emotionally, and I am not going to let him do that now. Not with me. Not because I let some damnable past demon get in the way.

Emotion claws at my chest and my lashes lower. "I'm sorry." I draw a heavy breath and meet his stare. I'm scared to death of being vulnerable with this man who, without even trying, has more power over me than anyone before him did, but I remind myself that coming here was his olive branch, his act of vulnerability. "I needed you to be here and somehow you are, and it means more to me than you can possibly know. I don't know how I've made such a mess of this, Chris. Please don't let me screw this up again like I did last night."

For a moment he is stiff, unyielding, staring at me with hooded eyes I can't read, but suddenly, his fingers curl around my neck in that familiar way and he pulls my mouth to a mere breath away from his. "I'm not sure I know the difference between protect and control. You need to know that."

On the surface his warning is all alpha male, but beneath it there is something more. He is not stone and granite, at least not with me, and like so much with Chris, this speaks to me. "As long as you know I'm going to tell you when you cross the line."

He brushes his lips over mine, soft but somehow possessive. "I'm looking forward to it," he assures me, the furthest from resistant he could be to me claiming my piece of control. The soft rasp of seductive promise in his voice tingles down my spine and sizzles every nerve ending in my body. Like many times with Chris, I sense there is a meaning beyond the words yet to be revealed, and I want to understand it, and him.

He leans back and stares down at me, and something shifts

between us and expands. Something I can't name, but my sex contracts and I crave whatever it is in a deep, aching way. Something I have yet to discover about myself and I know that Chris can show me. And I know that I am willing to go places with him I wouldn't go with anyone else. No. It goes deeper than willingness. It is a physical need.

Three

Chris parks the 911 in front of the building, right by the door, rather than in the empty parking lot. "I'll go lock up," he says, putting the car in idle and turning on the parking lights. "What unit number is it and do I need a key?"

"One-twelve and it's a combination lock I left hanging open on the door," I reply, my gaze having settled on the storage facility. We appear to be the only ones here and the building is still dark. Chris starts to exit and I grab his arm. "The door is open, Chris."

"Isn't that the idea? Getting here in time to lock the unit?"

"Yes," I say, glancing at the clock on his dash. "But it's thirty minutes after closing. It shouldn't be open." I glance at the door again, and to the black hole beyond it. I remember how suffocating it had been inside, and I shiver, hugging myself with the certainty that someone had been in there with me.

"What's wrong, baby?" Chris prods, gently tilting my chin to search my face. "What are you thinking and not saying?"

My mind replays the moment I had burst from the door to freedom and my heart is once again in my throat. "The door was open when I went inside, and when I ran out of the building it was shut. Someone intentionally shut me inside." I cut him a look. "And please don't lecture me. I already know I was stupid to come here alone at night. Believe me, I know, Chris. I paid the price a hundred times over in fear inside that building."

His eyes soften instantly and he strokes a hand down my hair. "I know you did, baby. And you can bet I'm going to have a talk with the office about security. They're liable for the security of everyone on the property."

"The guy who works here is creepy, Chris. I don't have high hopes for this place providing security."

His brow furrows. "Sara, damn it, you say that, yet you tell me you came here late at night alone."

I grimace. "You're cursing again."

"You keep giving me reasons to wonder what you were thinking tonight."

"The lady who works the morning shift at McDonald's by my school is cranky but I still went there for my coffee."

"Deflection will get you nowhere with me, Sara, besides a little extra of my certain wrath in store for you when we get home."

Home. The word hums through me because I know that with Chris nothing is unintentional. My heart races with the intimacy implied and how . . . right it feels.

"Wrath?" I ask. "What exactly does that mean?"

He tilts his head slightly, and his voice turns dangerously tight. "Use your imagination. Or maybe we should use mine. Unless that scares you now."

He's testing me again, reminding me of the club the night before, making sure I don't forget the woman I watched being bound and flogged. Of his confession that he has given and received pain. I lift my chin defiantly. "I'm not scared. Not of you. Not . . . with you."

He narrows his stare on me and I know he is weighing my claim. "You've said that before."

"And nothing has changed."

"Hasn't it?"

"It has actually. I now know the deep, dark secrets you said would make me run and here I am."

"You did run, and baby, you only think you know my deep, dark secrets."

"Show me." I sound breathless.

"Show you." It's not a question. His gaze slips to my mouth and I am instantly aware of how deliciously brutal it can be as he adds, "There's a price for not taking care of yourself as you claim you do so well." His eyes lift to mine and there is mischief in their depths. "I'll have to punish you."

I glower at his reference to how well I take care of myself. "Don't be a smart-ass. I can take care of myself."

"So you say." His lips quirk, his eyes twinkle, and his dark mood has lightened in a flash as it often does. "I'm just looking out for us both. I need you alive and well if I'm going to fuck you until you can't forget my name."

I feel myself heat from the inside out and I seize the opportunity to say what I had not earlier. "You've already done that, but if you want to be an overachiever, feel free."

"Your wish is my command," he assures me.

"I somehow doubt that."

"Don't doubt, baby," he says, and the laughter between us fades as we stare at each other with the promise of dark, erotic pleasure between us and so much more.

My chest tightens and I touch his cheek. "I'm really glad you're here."

He traces my bottom lip and kisses me, a quick slide of his tongue that has me moaning with the taste of his hunger, with my own. "Let me go lock up so we can get the hell out of here."

I grab his hand as he tries to move. "You can't see in there to lock up."

"I have a flashlight in the trunk."

"What if whoever was in there with me is still inside?"

"If they make a wrong move, I'll hit them with the flashlight." He wiggles a brow. "I'm efficient like that, especially when I have better things to do." He grins. "Like you." He's out of the car before I can stop him and I can't stand the idea of him going inside that black hole. I get out, too, and meet him at the trunk.

"Woman—"

"Save your commands for another more enticing time, Chris. I'm not staying in the car. Haven't you watched *Friday the 13th*? Michael slashes the girl in the car."

"Michael is from *Halloween*. Jason is *Friday the 13th*."

"Whoever he is, he slashes the girl in the car. I'm not staying in the car."

He slams the trunk shut, and he's now holding a long, silver flashlight. "And you think going inside the dark storage room with a guy and a flashlight is the safer bet?"

"I'm staying with you, Chris."

"Sara—"

Lights flicker behind us and we both turn as a utility truck pulls into the drive. "Looks like the repairman has arrived."

The truck pulls in beside us and the sound of steps on gravel draws my gaze to a man in an orange maintenance uniform walking from the office building down from this one. "The guy you don't like?" Chris asks.

I shake my head. "No. That's not him." This man is a good twenty years older, and though he looks grumpy, he doesn't ooze creepiness. I glance at Chris. "I guess I should have gone to the office in the first place." I begin to doubt myself. Have I created this danger in my mind? Did I make this more than it had to be?

Chris pulls me around to face him, and I slide my arms under his jacket. He is warm and the wind is cold. "Don't do what you're doing," he orders.

"What am I doing?"

"If you felt that you were in danger, if you ever feel that you're in danger, don't ignore that feeling."

"And if it is a random power outage?"

"How do you define random?" he asked.

"I don't know. It's not a city-wide thing like I thought it might be. I just . . . I don't know what I think."

"We'll figure it out together." His fingers brand my hips, and the possessive way they splay there makes me believe him.

"Can I help you folks?"

We turn to find the maintenance man behind us and I'm amazed at how fast he's arrived, or maybe time just goes by quickly when Chris is holding me. I suspect that is the case when Chris releases me, and I wish he hadn't.

Chris indicates his flashlight with a lift of his hand. "The power went out before we could lock up. We just want to get it sealed up and then we're on our way."

The man scrubs his jaw. "I wasn't aware we had anyone inside when the power blew. I went inside and checked for anyone who needed help."

"I was inside," I say. "And it wasn't fun. Someone shut the outer door and I couldn't seem to get out."

The man frowns. "The door's open, ma'am. It was open when I went inside."

"Because I opened it," I say, pointing out the obvious, and I can't keep the defensiveness out of my voice.

"You have cameras in this place?" Chris asks.

"We do," he said. "But no power means no camera."

"Surely the remote security has its own feed," Chris argues.

"We aren't sophisticated here, mister. It's all us."

Chris's brows furrow. "Then maybe you should get more sophisticated. She could have been hurt."

"We've never had anyone hurt on site," the man argues.

Chris looks like he's going to argue but then clamps his lips together. "We just want to lock up our unit and be out of your way."

"What's the number?" the man asks.

"One-twelve," I tell him.

He scrubs his jaw. "Oh right. I was the one you talked to on the phone. I see that unit is on my pending auction list again. It's past due."

"But the office manager gave me a one-week extension."

"Almost two weeks ago," he said. "And that was me."

24

"We'll pay for another month," Chris says, and I cringe.

I turn to face him and he pretends not to notice the objection in my face when I know he does. He focuses on the maintenance man. "Let us lock up and we'll come to the office and pay."

"That'll be fine," the man agrees.

Chris takes my hand. "Don't argue."

"I don't want you to pay my bills," I say softly as we walk toward the building.

"I know."

"I don't need you to take care of me, Chris."

He glances down at me. "Questionable after tonight."

"I'll pretend you didn't say that, because I'm sure you wouldn't want me to keep feeling the sting of my decision over and over again. That would be downright not nice of you."

"I want you safe."

"I am. I'm safe. And I have a check from the gallery coming soon to pay the rent here. I planned to beg for more time and pay them then."

"Now you don't have to," he said. "And what are you going to do about your job at the school?"

"You're changing the subject."

"You aren't answering the question."

"I have time to decide." I don't know how in tune he is with the school system and the new mayor's budget cuts since he's in Paris half the year. "This is the second year that the public high schools have shorter years and longer days. I don't start back until October first."

We stop at the door of the building and Chris turns on the

flashlight. "You know you aren't going back. You should tell them now so they can replace you."

"I can't talk about this now," I say as we stop at the doorway of the building, and the darkness starts to creep me out. I move closer to Chris and wrap my arm around his. "I just want to get in and out of here."

Chris flips on the flashlight. We take several steps forward and I hear that noise that had freaked me out in the dark alone. *Pop. Pop.* I stop dead in my tracks. "What is that?"

Chris slowly moves the flashlight around in the darkness and there is a crackling sound and another pop. He settles the glow on the wall by the floor and leads me forward. He squats next to a light socket and I follow him down into the beam of the light to stare at the outlet. There is a paper clip shoved inside the hole of one plug.

My chest tightens. "I guess we now know how to define random." I meet his stare. "I need to make sure nothing obvious is missing in the unit."

Chris pushes to his feet and takes me with him and we find the unit door shut. "I suspect the guy we just talked to shut it."

Right. Of course. That makes sense. "I still want to look inside."

He pulls open the door and shines the light around the room, focusing on the papers on the floor. "I dropped those," I tell him, reliving my panic.

"Do you need whatever they are?"

"No," I say, just wanting out of here. "Not now."

"Then everything else looks in order?"

"Yes. It doesn't seem like whoever was here touched anything inside." Unless they knew exactly what they wanted and where it was, a voice in my head says. Perhaps more journals? There are many pieces of Rebecca's life, including how she arrived and left the gallery, that are missing from what I've read. I don't know why this hasn't hit me until now. Rebecca was too consistent with her writing to skip long periods of time. If I'm right, there has to be at least a few more journals, and it would make sense for them to be in the unit. Or they were, until tonight.

Thirty minutes later, I am leaning against the wall of the small, boxlike office of the storage unit, remotely aware that Chris is in deep conversation with the manager. My Dark Prince can pretty much do or say whatever he wants right now if it gets me out of this place sooner. I manage to stay present in the conversation long enough to hear Chris secure a month of free rental, but then that's not surprising since Chris all but flattens the office manager with a promise of a lawsuit over the danger I'd been put in.

Danger. That word has me checking out and into my own head. I tell myself Chris is excessively protective, and while it feels good to have someone care, he's also blowing up the fear in my mind that I'm quite capable of exaggerating without his aid. My thoughts go on a roller-coaster ride of wicked possibilities that has me in knots. If I was in danger in that storage unit, am I in danger now? What have I gotten myself into? And what did Rebecca get herself into? I cannot help but relive the events in the darkness, replaying alternate endings, and none of them are happy. How does everyone just say she's off with some hot man and not miss her?

My gut twists and my mind goes to Ella. I've dismissed her

silence as a happy honeymoon and a friend who's forgotten me in the midst of passion and newfound love. This isn't so hard for me to believe of Ella. She's alone and hungry for the sense of belonging this man has given her. But isn't that hunger a vulnerability the wrong man could take advantage of?

Suddenly, I need to hear Ella's voice, and if she's forgotten me for wedded bliss, I will happily scold her. I just need to know she's okay. I'm the only one Ella has to miss her. Ella knowing I am there for her, that if she ever isn't okay someone will care, is important to me.

I shove off of the wall and grab my phone from my jacket and head outside, but I am quick to plant myself against the glass by the door where Chris can see me and I can see him. Stupid once tonight, not twice. The night air is not my friend, but I ignore the chill.

Punching in Ella's number, I pray for an answer and get a fast busy signal. I shove the phone to my forehead. Why didn't I get an alternate number? Why? I have no idea what to do. I don't even know the exact day she is due back into town, and I decide calling her new husband's medical practice tomorrow is my best option.

The door opens and Chris appears. I do not know how it's possible, but each time I see him it is as if it's the first time, as if he slides inside me and fills what is empty.

He leans a hand on the wall above me, sheltering me from the wind, from the world. He is quiet power and strength and he speaks to the woman in me in ways no man ever has. "How are you doing?" he asks, studying me with probing, pale green eyes that always seem to see too much. "You okay?"

I brush my hand over his cheek, letting the soft rasp of his dark blond stubble stroke my fingers. "I will be when we get out of here." I let my hand drop away. "What did the manager say about the paper clips?"

"He claims they've had problems with kids messing around the building. Vandals."

I feel a stab of anger and indignation. "So that's his explanation? Kids did this?"

"He's protecting his ass, Sara." He slides his hand down my waist and around my backside, caressing me intimately. "And I plan to protect yours." He brushes hair from my eyes. "You're staying at my place until the private investigator tells us there's nothing to worry about. That way no one but me can get to you." His voice lowers, turns rough. "You'll be all mine."

The possessive way his body cradles mine, the way he says the words, sends a tingling sensation spiraling through my body. I refuse to think of the consequences of giving myself to Chris, a man I know will consume me, perhaps destroy me, but right now he feels as if he is saving me. I am willingly all his.

Four

After a quick stop by my apartment, I am glad to be in my car, following Chris to his place. I have no idea why the stop to get my things made me uneasy, but it did. Maybe it was the tiny space and my feeling of claustrophobia after being in the storage unit in the darkness. I couldn't pack quickly enough. Chris hovering by the door, just as eager to leave, hadn't helped, either. It was as if we both sensed something was off.

Just beyond the driveway to Chris's building, he stops at a light, and I halt behind him and use the opportunity to try for the fifth time to call Ella. Once again, I receive only a fast busy signal. I am helplessly incapable of reaching her and I'm rattled.

I contemplate all that might have befallen her while I was safely back here in the States. I am all doom and gloom tonight, but then, I've been locked in a dark storage unit and scared shitless. I am giving myself tonight to wallow in it. I decide that might not be a good idea, when I blink and realize I don't remember pulling into the driveway of Chris's place, and the doorman is standing beside my car.

With my purse strap over my shoulder, I step out of the car and hand the twenty-something doorman I don't recognize my keys. I glance up at the high-rise that is more luxury hotel than apartment and am reminded of how rich and powerful Chris is and how humbly he wears his success. "Thank you," I murmur.

"We need your bag from the trunk," Chris reminds me, and the bellman pops the trunk. Chris's leather jacket slides open to reveal the stretch of a black T-shirt over his incredibly hot body, and I decide the heck with wallowing in doom and gloom. I'm going to wallow in Chris tonight.

"I can bring it up," the doorman offers.

"I got it," Chris says and quickly grabs my bags, and I know this is because Chris doesn't want to be disturbed once we are upstairs. I approve. Oh yes, I do.

I fall into step with Chris, and I am not surprised by how comfortable I feel by his side. He has a way of making me feel alive and at ease that I have never felt before. It's a big part of what drew me to him from the beginning. It's also why I know I can go places with him no one else could take me.

We stop just inside the lobby, where fancy marble glistens under our feet and expensive furniture decorates a sitting room to our left. Jacob, the building security officer, whom I've met on a prior visit, is looking as I remember him, all *Men in Black* in a dark suit and earpiece, where he stands by a counter. He is impressively capable of pulling off the stone-faced serious persona but his eyes light on me with approval. "Welcome back, Ms. McMillan."

"Ms. McMillan will be staying here all week while I travel. I'll need you to ensure she's well looked after."

Jacob's expression is back to stone but his gaze meets mine and he gives a small nod. "Anything you need, just ask."

"Thank you, Jacob," I say, and I mean it. He has a way about him that makes me feel I can trust him, and I think it's because I sense Chris trusts him, and I have a sense that Chris doesn't trust easily.

The two men exchange a few casual words, and when finally Chris and I step onto the elevator, I am suddenly, ridiculously nervous. It isn't like this is my first time at Chris's apartment but much has happened in the past few days. I do not know what to expect besides the unexpected with Chris, and while this excites me, it is hard not to feel some trepidation.

I lean against the wall and our eyes meet, and no matter how hard I try to stop rambling when I'm nervous, I never seem to succeed. "When you're in Paris, if I try to call you, will I be able reach you?"

His eyes narrow and darken. "I'm not planning on going anywhere anytime soon, Sara."

His reply hits an instant nerve, and I know it is partly because staying with him is a shift in our relationship. It's taking the vulnerable theme of the night to a whole new level. I do not want him to see this in me and my gaze drops to the ground. I try to fight what I am feeling but his words play in my head. Anytime soon. Eventually he will leave. We need each other right now, I tell myself, two broken people who have connected in the depths of all our fucked-upness. I wonder why it feels that it isn't enough when only days ago it was exactly what I wanted.

The doors open to reveal his apartment and my gaze jerks to Chris's. He is watching me with an unreadable expression. I cut my gaze and walk from the elevator into his apartment. The entire front wall window of twinkling city lights is one big erotic memory of him pressing me against it, of the danger of it breaking, and even more so of trusting him, while he fucked me senseless. I want to be senseless right now in an almost desperate way.

"Sara," he says softly from behind me.

I turn to him, and I launch into the obvious deflection he is too smart not to see for what it is. "My friend I told you about, the one who is in Paris. I can't reach her. I just get a fast busy signal."

He hesitates a moment, and I know he's contemplating pushing me to talk about what just happened in the elevator, but he doesn't. "Sounds like she's in one of the more remote areas, which isn't uncommon when people take tours."

We are still standing by the elevator and it feels awkward but I don't know where to go. To the living room? To his bedroom? "I guess that makes sense," I say, hoping the logical answer is the right one. "It's her honeymoon, so seeing the country would be logical while there."

"What has you worried about her all of a sudden?"

"It's not all of a sudden, but . . . nobody is worried about Rebecca, and Ella, she has no one but me to worry about her."

Seconds tick by and I want to rip a reply from him before he says, "You have me. You know that, right?"

I swallow hard against the lump that forms in my throat. "I know." But a voice in my head rejects my reply.

Awareness flickers in his eyes and I know he sees what I do not want him to see. He pulls me to him and kisses me. "I'm going to make you believe that the next time you say it." He runs a hand over my hair. "And before this night is over. Now off to my bedroom, where I've wanted you all night." He turns me and swats my backside.

I revel in his primitive order, and that hand on my backside, promising something erotic and thrilling, and I grow more intrigued. I do not understand this feeling I have when I've spent years fighting to be independent, free of controlling men.

I'm out of my head and back into the fiery storm of nerves as we enter his bedroom. This isn't our first time together. I stare at the massive king-sized bed, set on top of a pedestal, which promises seductive pleasures, and some kind of buzzer sounds in the other room. I think it must be the delivery chute in the kitchen, which is much like that of a bank drive-through.

"Most likely my messages," Chris says from behind me, then sets my bags down on top of the pedestal. "I'll be right back." He motions to an open door by the bathroom. "That's the closet. Take whatever space you like. Nothing is off-limits."

Nothing is off-limits. Isn't he telling me that by having me stay here while he's gone, he's inviting me into his life, his secrets? It is more than an olive branch. It's an entire tree.

I squat down next to the expensive Louis Vuitton suitcase Chris had bought me for our Napa trip the weekend before, and I unzip it. I shrug my purse off my shoulder and set it on the floor next to it. I flip open the case, and there lying on top of my things are the journals and the box I'd taken from Rebecca's unit. I wasn't about to leave them at my apartment, where I felt they might fall into the wrong hands. They hold her secrets, and I wonder if they hold someone else's as well. I intend to stack them in Chris's closet but a passage I'd read suddenly burns into my mind.

I reach for the top journal that is bookmarked and walk to the pedestal at the side of the bed, out of view from the doorway, and sit down. Pulling my knees to my chest, I begin to read the familiar passage and the words ripple through me with painful clarity. This is Chris's world.

Suddenly, he is in front of me, towering above me. I feel him in every pore of my existence even before I dare to lift my gaze to his. I know what I must do but I am scared. I told him I wasn't. I told myself I wasn't. But I am.

Chris kneels down in front of me, and though he doesn't look at the journal, it is the white elephant between us. He's removed his jacket and my gaze catches on the bright coloring of the dragon tattoo on his right arm. I reach out and touch it. It is a part of him, his past, his pain. I want to be a part of him, to truly understand.

"Whatever you read in that journal has nothing to do with you and me."

Emotion tightens my throat and I do not look at him. I trace that tattoo, the bright red of the wings that flex as he grips his knee. "But it does," I whisper.

"It doesn't."

Reading him the passage seems the only way for him to understand. I force my gaze from his arm to Rebecca's writing. "Like the thorns on the roses he loves to give me, I welcomed the pain of the flogger biting into my back. It is the escape from all that I have lost, all that I have seen and done, and regret doing. He gives this to me. He is my drug. The pain is my drug.

It ripples through me and I feel nothing but the bitter bite of leather and the sweet silk of the darkness and pleasure that follows." My gaze lifts to Chris's.

Tension crackles off him and he takes the journal from me and sets it on the nightstand. "If not for those journals bringing you to me, I'd curse the day you ever found them." He slides his hands to my face and forces my gaze to his. "You aren't Rebecca, and we don't have, nor will we ever have, the kind of relationship she had with Mark."

"Mark."

"Yes, Mark."

"How can you be sure?"

"Because he can't just be happy with those who invite this lifestyle and welcome it. He has a thing for bringing in innocents who don't belong in this world and training them as subs. He gets off on the power of it."

In the back of my mind, there are questions about Mark, but there is only room now for where this takes me with Chris. "You've trained . . . subs?"

He scrubs his jaw and then runs his hands down his jean-clad legs. "Don't do this to yourself or to us."

"That's a yes." My voice is barely audible. And is that what he wants me to be? Am I confused about where we are going? Do I really have any idea at all where we are headed?

"It's a no, Sara. I'm not Mark. Master and sub was too much commitment for me. I do not want to be responsible for someone's well-being. Not beyond one session. I got my fix and then quickly moved on."

His fix. I hate this choice of words. I barely know the man

who uses them, who lived them. But it is Chris and it confuses me. "What does that even mean?"

His jaw clenches.

"I need to understand, Chris."

His lashes lower, the lines of his face hardening. "There are rooms you go to," he surprises me by explaining. "You can choose to be masked and I do. I don't want faces and names."

My mind goes crazy with what might happen in those rooms. "Never?"

"That was my style, Sara. No commitments."

He didn't say "never" and I press for more, for how his past affects us now. "And yet I'm here."

"I told you. I've broken all my rules with you."

"Why me?"

"Because you're you, Sara. There is no other answer."

The part of me that is never confident, that is never completely convinced this talented and famous man can really want me, struggles with this answer, but yet, I feel this way about him. He has become my escape and my sanctuary. I think he is telling me he sees me the same way, but I know we are lying to ourselves and each other if we think nothing else matters. "You can't just shut this all out, Chris. You can't just meet me and be who you were before. I need to understand it and be a part of it."

"No. You don't."

"But you took me to that club last night. You wanted me to understand."

"I wanted you to understand where Mark would lead you and why I wasn't going to let that happen. Rebecca didn't belong in this world and you've read how it tormented her to be here."

"You told me I don't belong in this world, either," I manage, choking on the words.

"You don't." His jaw clenches. "Which is why I tried to warn you away and why I tried to walk away."

My stomach knots. "You still can." I start to get up, suddenly needing an escape, and this time Chris can't give it to me.

He shackles my wrists in his hands and pulls me to him, between his legs, on my knees. "That's just it. I can't and I don't want to even try. And I don't want you to, either." His expression softens and he brushes his knuckles over my jaw. "You're inside me now, baby. All the rest was how I stayed outside myself and I'll be damned if I let it tear us apart."

I soften instantly at his confession and my hand slides to his face. "It's the unknown that scares me, Chris. It's what you need, the pleasure inside the pain, that I can't possibly understand, and that terrifies me. I need you to make me understand."

"You do understand, Sara. More than you know. More than I wish you did." His mouth closes down over mine, hot with demand, and I know he believes this conversation is over, that he means to end it with the wicked caress of his tongue against mine, the possessive splay of his hands on my body. But I refuse to be this powerless, to be silenced with the very passion that drives me to need to understand this man.

"No," I gasp, and shove against him, breathless as I meet his gaze and demand, "Make me understand, Chris." And on some level I know this is that unknown place I've craved to go with him, that place he hides from me, that place he wants to take me. This is where we have to go, where we've always been headed.

Five

"You want to understand?" he asks, his voice low, his eyes ripe with challenge.

"It's not about want. It's about need, Chris. I *need* to understand."

He considers me, his expression impassive, but his pale green eyes shimmer and then burn. "Stand up and take off your clothes, Sara."

After a moment of hesitation, I decide his command is as close to an agreement as I'm going to get. It's enough. I stand up and walk to the bottom of the pedestal and Chris shifts to sit against the bed. In spite of this power play he is using on me, or perhaps because of it, there is something wickedly erotic about standing before this man and undressing. This brings my vulnerability back to the forefront. It is an act of trust, and my chest tightens at the implications of giving myself to him, of why he might need me to do this. I think . . . I think he needs to know that I'm not holding back, that he's shown me his dark side, and I am still willingly his.

Yes. I am *willingly* his. Suddenly, I want him to know this more than ever.

With a lift of my arms, I peel away my T-shirt and toss it away. My hair catches on my mouth. I tug away the long, dark brown strands and Chris's gaze settles on my mouth. My sex clenches because I know he is imagining my mouth on his body and I very much want my mouth on his body. But he is always in control, deciding what I do and don't do. I vow right then that he won't tonight. Now, yes, but not all night. At some point before he leaves for Los Angeles again, my mouth is going wherever it damn well pleases. I cannot be naked quickly enough. He will leave in the morning for a week. There is much unresolved between us. Too much.

I strip away my clothes in seconds, and I'm pretty sure the art of the seductive, slow striptease is really not my forte. I'll work harder at it when I want to tease him and not me. I just need Chris right now. I need to be naked with him, all barriers gone. I need him to know that I want to understand him because he matters, because *we* matter. Because life made me believe that what is blossoming between us wasn't possible, but maybe, just maybe, it is.

"Come here," he commands urgently as I toss aside my panties, his voice gravelly, affected, and I revel in the impatience in him that matches mine. It is still hard for me to believe I affect him sometimes. He is so many things that I aspire to be: strong and powerful, confident and in charge of his life, his destiny. It moves me to know I make this man as hot as he makes me. It makes me stronger. He makes me stronger.

I go to him, letting him pull me to his lap, straddling him, his thick erection settling between my legs. I do not like that he is fully dressed, but I know this is about control to Chris. I know on some level I have taken it from him and he needs it back.

"Lace your fingers together behind your back," he orders.

Adrenaline rushes through me instantly and my heart thunders in my chest. Yes. This is about control with Chris, but in his control he's revealed far more than he knows. He has to have it and that says much about him. That I have some deep burn to let him have it says just as much about me, I know.

Watching his face, I search for a reaction I do not find as I slide my hands behind my back. His hands settle firmly on my upper arms, branding me with his touch, even as his gaze rakes over my breasts. The air crackles with a charge I feel in every inch of my body, before his eyes lift to mine and his voice is rougher now, tighter. "Lace your fingers together, baby."

I do as he bids and the instant I comply, he lowers his mouth to linger above mine, his hands still holding my arms, his breath warm, teasing me with the kiss I burn for, but he withholds. I am breathless when his mouth brushes mine, and shocked when his teeth nip my bottom lip. I yelp with the sting and my fingers loosen behind me. Chris holds my arms in place, so I can't reach for him, and his tongue snakes forward. He licks the wound before he delves deep into my mouth, stroking me into a compliant moan.

"Pain," he explains moments later, his arms still wrapping my shoulders, "that becomes pleasure." His eyes burn into mine. "Lace your fingers again."

Shaking inside, I nod, afraid to speak, afraid I'll somehow do something to shut this window he is opening for me. His hands caress a path up my arms and down my shoulders. His path travels downward, over my chest, and he fingers my nipples, sending a rush of sensation through my body with the delicate, sensual caresses that become rougher and rougher. He tugs the stiff peaks, and this time I squeeze my eyes shut against the bite of tension.

"Look at me," he orders. "Let me see what you're feeling."

I force my lashes to lift and the amber glint in his green eyes is as wicked as his touch. It is not just *what* Chris does to me that is enticingly erotic, but how he commands and claims me with every action, every reaction.

He pinches my nipples, tugging roughly at the same time, sending conflicting sensations of pain and pleasure through my body and straight to my sex. I pant with the delicious roughness and arch against his hips, against the thickness of his erection straining against his zipper.

His lips press to my ear, nibbling on the delicate lobe. The gentleness of the touch is a startling contrast to the way he continues to pinch and tug my nipples, and I can hardly stand the way he is teasing me. I want to reach for him, to touch him, but I am afraid he will stop what he is doing and I cannot bear the idea. I want more, not less, and I am wet and achy and I think . . . oh . . . my sex clenches and I think—no—unbelievably I am almost certain I am going to come.

Seconds before I tumble, his hands leave my breasts and slide down my arms, holding my hands behind my back, and I know this is no accident. He has intentionally taken me to the edge and pulled me back. I am panting and I want to scream with the pain of needing release and having it denied.

He leans back, putting intolerable distance between our lips, our bodies that makes me want to scream. "Pain that's about pleasure," he repeats huskily, "and sometimes, baby, that pain is so intense that it becomes the pleasure."

I understand. Right now, I understand oh so well. "And clearly you know how to make someone feel just that." There is accusation in my voice. I can't help it. He knows what he just did to me. He knows he took me to the edge but not over.

His shift in mood is instant, the game we've just played ending abruptly. He reaches behind me and unlaces my fingers, settling my hands on his shoulders. "Yeah, baby. I do. But I have never *hurt* anyone. And I won't ever hurt you."

Guilt over what I've made him feel slams into me. "I know that. *I know,* Chris."

"You didn't know that last night." His voice is tight, strained, the torment I've caused him etched in his words, in the tight lines of his face.

"I was scared and confused."

"And when you feel that way again?"

"I won't." I barely contain the urgency to tell him I love him, but I fear I will scare him and he will reject me, maybe reject us. *"I won't."*

He studies me a long moment, his expression impossible to read no matter how hard I search for a clue to what he is thinking. I'm still trying to read him when suddenly his mouth is on mine, and he is kissing me, tasting me, testing my words on his tongue. I cling to him, meet him stroke for stroke, trying to answer him, trying to show him that I am here. I am not going anywhere.

I feel the moment he snaps, the moment he needs to claim and possess, rather than question. He picks me up and carries me to the bed, a man with a mission, and I am that willing mission. He sets me down on the edge of the mattress and reaches up and yanks his shirt over his head. I barely have time to admire him when he's pulling me forward, spreading my legs. He sinks to his knees and his mouth closes on my clit and he suckles and licks. I gasp and fall back against the mattress, my fingers curling around the black comforter. I pant and try to hold back but his fingers are inside me and his tongue tantalizes me in all the right spots. I shatter with ridiculous speed that screams of him owning me. He owns my pleasure. He owns me. It is a terrifying thought because I'm not sure I will ever have that power over him. Not the way he does over me. I scoot up the bed, grappling with my emotions, but he is already undressed and pulling me beneath him, and I am helpless to resist. Of course I am. He owns me. Damn it, he owns me.

My arms wrap his neck, and he comes down on top of me and his weight settles on me. I am suddenly, intensely aware that we have never been like this, in a bed, with him on top of me. We've fucked all kinds of ways, but never in a bed, never in his bed. Awareness rushes over me, the reason I'd been nervous. We are in new territory, the intimacy of this night taking us to a new place.

"I'm going to make love to you now, Sara."

It is the last thing I expect, and everything I both want and fear. My world is spinning out of control and I'm not sure if it will stop in a place where I will have even footing. "What happened to fuck and get fucked?"

"Baby, the ways I'm going to fuck you are too many to count, but not tonight. Tonight, I'm going to make love to you." His lips part mine, his tongue delving deeply, exploring, and the demand of minutes before becomes a sultry, sensual caress. He has torn down every wall I possess and I cannot fight him, or this.

He spreads me wide and settles between my thighs, thick and pulsing, parting me with the promise of finally filling me. I feel him press into me and my arms tighten around his neck. I lift my hips and meet him, urge him to go deeper, to give me more, when I know it is him demanding more of me, taking what I try to hold back but cannot.

He sinks into me, buries his cock inside me, and we lie there, foreheads touching, breathing together. I have never felt as part of a man as I do in that moment. Never felt so a part of another human being. I do not know what to do with the emotions inside me. I do not know how to be this close to someone and still hold on to myself.

"Chris?" I rasp desperately, afraid of this, of him, of where I am spiraling and will never be found.

He moves then, the thick ridge of his shaft caressing a path backward until I think he is going to pull out, to move away. I arch forward, desperate to bring him back, and he answers me with a hard thrust. I cry out and wrap my leg around his, lifting my body, moaning as his hand slides under my backside and pulls me closer, drives him deeper. He pumps into me over and over and I feel him shaking, or maybe it is me who is shaking. I don't want this to end, and I sense he, too, is fighting it, as if we both fear the moment after, and what comes next. But the pleasure is too intense, too overwhelming, to be sustained. My sex clamps down on him, spasming with the most intense orgasm of my life. He growls low in his throat and thrusts deep into me, before I feel the wet, hot heat of his release. And then we are there, in the moment after, him on top of me in his bed. I don't know what to expect. I don't know what to do with this ball of emotion threatening to explode in my chest.

Chris moves first, shifting me to lie in front of him and pulling the blanket over the top of me. I feel the wetness clinging to my thighs but I don't care. Chris is wrapped around me, holding me in his bed. For long minutes, we lie there in silence and I don't want to sleep. I just want to feel him here with me.

"Come with me to Los Angeles."

For a moment I consider saying yes and my reasons are many. Chris somehow steadies the shaky ground of uncertainty in my world.

"I bought you a seat on the plane."

"Chris," I say, rolling over and feeling defensive, and more than a little pressured. "You know I can't. You know I have a job. And when did you even have time to buy me a seat?"

"Before I even knew about the storage unit power outage. I came here tonight determined to convince you to come back with me, and before you start to argue, getting out of town gives the private detective time to check on what happened last night and gives us some peace of mind that it was nothing to worry about."

My stomach flutters wildly. "You think I'm in danger?"

"I just don't want to take any chances, Sara."

"You do think I'm in danger."

"I'm not trying to scare you, but I also told you I want to

protect you and I meant it. That means being cautious." He teases a tendril of hair at my forehead. "And I want you with me. I'd want you with me even if this wasn't going on."

He wants me with him. These words please me deeply and I yearn to say yes but my fear for my job holds me back. "I want to go, but I can't. I have to stay. And I'll be fine thanks to you. I feel safe here."

His expression darkens. "You won't be in the apartment around the clock."

"I'll be at the gallery and it's safe."

"That's a matter of opinion," he says dryly, and I know he's talking about Mark's presence there, not the security. He runs a hand over the back of his neck and casts me a wry glance. "I'm about as likely to change your mind about this as I am likely to get you to watch *Friday the 13th* with me, aren't I?"

"Less." I cup his cheek and plant a quick kiss on his mouth. "Buttered popcorn and the promise of a chick flick to follow might convince me to watch the movie." I roll back over and he leans away from me and turns out the light before pulling me close, and yes, we are spooning. It's wonderful.

"You really are making me crazy, woman," he murmurs, nuzzling my ear.

"Good," I say, smiling into the darkness. "Because you make me crazy, too."

"Is that right?" he challenges.

"Hmm," I assure him, feeling the heaviness of emotional and physical exhaustion begin to settle deep in my limbs. "Yes. You absolutely make me crazy." And it's crazy good, I add silently, letting my lashes lower and the groggy sensation of sleep claim me.

• • •

Blinking awake, I am instantly aware that Chris is gone. For a moment, I fear that morning has come and he's flown off to Los Angeles and hasn't given me a chance to say good-bye. But there's the soft hum of a light beyond the door, and it gives me hope he's still here. The sound of muffled music slides into my awareness, and relief washes over me. I know I am not really alone and I am eager to seek out Chris.

I sit up and the blanket falls to my waist, the cool air chilling my naked body. Still, I toss away the comforter and find Chris's shirt on the floor, and glance at the clock to find it's almost five in the morning. I wonder how early his flight leaves and hope it's not the early bird, but it must be since he's awake. It is odd to imagine being here without Chris, and I am shocked and pleased at his willingness to allow me such a freedom.

Pulling his shirt over my head, I inhale the delicious scent of the man who has come to fill such a big part of my life, and I decide I'll keep this shirt to sleep in until he returns.

I pad in bare feet to the doorway and stare at the empty living room. The music pulls me to my left and down a hallway that is long and narrow, and I pass several closed doors. The one at the very end of the walkway that serves as an endcap is open several inches, and I rest my hand on the surface. I am certain this is Chris's studio, which I have longed to see, and I know the crack is an invitation. The music changes, and the song, "You Taste Like Sugar," a sexy Matchbox Twenty tune, begins to play. I remember Chris saying he paints to music and I wonder what this song inspires, and I am almost nervous to find out.

The door opens, taking me off guard, and Chris stands there

wearing nothing but low-slung jeans and looking like *he* tastes of sugar. My eyes travel the rich reds, blues, and yellows of his dragon tattoo, which covers hard muscle and taut, tanned skin, and my mind plays something he'd said to me not that long ago. *Do you know what happens when you push a dragon? They burn you alive, baby. You're playing with fire.* I've played with fire tonight with Chris, pushed him to be that dragon, and the way he's looking at me now, the way he sees what I do not want him to see, is burning me alive. I know in that moment that I cannot keep asking Chris to show me who he is and not be willing to show him all that I am. My gut twists with the biting possibility that holds because it means confessing something I haven't been completely honest about, something I don't want him to know. Something I wish I could forget forever but it is carved in my chest like a brand that only seems to get deeper when I try to wash it away.

Chris draws my hand into his and my eyes lift to his and there is mischief dancing in their depths. "Come into the 'man-cave,' baby."

Laughter bubbles from my throat and I am amazed at how he takes me from somber to lighthearted. I love this about Chris. "The 'man-cave'?"

"That's right. Are you scared?"

"I guess it depends what kind of man-cave we're talking about. Wasn't the room you took me to at that club called the Lion's Den?"

"Don't worry. I'll be gentle." He wiggles a brow and pulls me forward and I instantly forget man-caves and Mark's club. I am standing inside a massive room carved into a circle and windows surrounding me on all sides, the twinkling lights of the city enclosing me like a glove. I have this sense of being at the railing of a massive ship, about to tumble into an ocean of never-ending discovery.

"It's amazing," I whisper, my gaze brushing his.

"I told you," he says. "This is why I bought the apartment."

I nod. "Yes. I understand."

He releases me, silently giving me the freedom to explore on my own, and I walk deeper into the core of this magnificent studio. Random easels sit on stands, all covered in cloths, and I am excited at the prospect of uncovering them and seeing what is beneath. My gaze catches on the splattered paint here and there beneath my feet, and I smile at the remnants of his work, his frustrations, his excitement to get paint on canvas.

"I've been known to get a little messy while I work," Chris informs me, stepping behind me, his hands settling on my waist, and I am instantly aware of him in every inch of my body. The sultry words of the song filter through the air—*I just want to make you go away but you taste like sugar*—and Chris leans down and murmurs something in French in my ear.

I shiver with the erotic way the words roll off his tongue and twist in his arms to face him, wrapping my arms around his neck. "What did you say?"

"I said," he murmurs softly, "that I want to make you melt like sugar on my tongue like you did earlier." He tugs the T-shirt I'm wearing up my hips and cups my bare ass, pulling me against the thick ridge of his erection. "And if I didn't have a flight in two hours, I'd lick all that sweetness until you begged me to stop."

"I don't beg," I declare, though I have no idea how I've formed what could be called a sentence when his fingers are tracing the crevice between my cheeks and promising delicious exploration.

"Oh, you'd beg, baby. I'd bet on it and if you tempt me much more I might just have to prove how fast. In fact"—he starts leading me toward a stool sitting in front of an easel—"I have time."

Yes. Please. "Two hours and you still have to drive across the bridge to the airport? You don't have time."

"I have time." He sets me on the stool and his hands settle on my waist. "Now, about the begging."

I smile. "You're going to miss your flight. You do know that, don't you?"

He turns me to face the easel and tugs the shirt over my head. I brush hair from my eyes and suck in a breath at the painting I'm now staring at. It's me, and I'm sitting in the middle of the floor of the "man-cave" on my knees with my hands bound in front me. "What's that wrapped around my wrists?" I ask, my throat rasping with dryness when suddenly my hands are behind my back and I feel the tug of them being wrapped and bound.

Chris steps in front of me and holds up a roll of tape. "Very efficient."

"Chris," I whisper. "You're going to miss your flight."

His lips curve seductively. "You clearly underestimate my efficiency." He goes down on a knee in front of me and spreads my legs. "Now. On to the begging." His hands, those talented, artistic hands, travel up my thighs and his thumbs stroke my clit. "I'm on a timer, right? I'd better get busy?" His tongue drags slowly, sensually over me. "Like sugar, baby, and I'm going to melt you like honey."

My body sways. "And I'm going to fall off this stool."

"Not if you lean into me," he says, and slides two fingers inside me. "Lean."

I arch forward and slide. "I'm going to fall."

"I have you, Sara." His fingers splay on my thighs. "Trust me. I have you." His eyes hold mine and the depth of power and heat I find there are as limitless as what he makes me feel. His voice softens into a caress. "Relax into me."

Relax into him. Like I had in bed. I nod. "Yes."

Slowly, he lowers his head and I feel the warm trickle of his hot breath a moment before his mouth closes down on my clit. I gasp as his hand leaves my leg and my body shifts forward, but then his fingers are inside me, and that arch of my body is like sweet, unbearably necessary pressure. I am on the edge in a flash of seconds and Chris is wrong, so very wrong. I won't beg. There isn't time. I'm going to come and there is no question, none whatsoever, that this man owns me and I can't think of a single reason why that's a bad thing.

Forty-five minutes later, I'm still wearing nothing but Chris's shirt and standing in the kitchen, watching while he downs the cup of coffee I've poured him as if it's not scalding hot. His hair is damp, finger tossed, and sexy, and he's wearing a light blue T-shirt with Spider-Man on the front that one of the kids he's seeing at the hospital gave to him, with black jeans. I'm eager to discover what has inspired such fierce dedication to this charity and wish I had more time to ask him about his involvement.

"Did you sleep at all?" I ask, and I try not to let my insecurity run wild. But if he wanted me in his bed, why wasn't he in it with me?

"I don't sleep much at night. That's when I paint." He reaches for the cup I'm holding and sips some of my coffee. "I had something I wanted to paint for one of the kids. He's a bit of a movie fanatic like I am so we've bonded over a few favorites."

"How old is he?"

"Thirteen."

"Cancer?"

He nods, his expression tightening. "Leukemia. Late stages. It's destroying his parents. They're good people forced to watch their child die."

My chest pinches painfully. "You're sure he's going to die?"

"Yeah. He's going to die. And believe me, if there was an amount of money or medicine that would change that, I'd make it happen." He runs his hand through his fast-drying hair and turns away, walking to the phone and calling for a cab. I can see the tension ripple along his shoulders. I can't imagine what it must be like to know someone you love is dying and be powerless to stop it, but I think Chris does. I mean, didn't he watch his father slowly drink himself to death? I suddenly wish I was going with him and decide right then to try to get Saturday off, even if I have to use the charity event as publicity for the gallery to make it happen. And I'm darn sure going to make Mark open his thick wallet for a big fat donation.

Chris hangs up the phone and turns to me and I don't get the chance to ask why he's taking a cab. "Come with me," he says. "I didn't cancel your reservation."

Knowing more about the charity only makes my reply harder. "Not this time."

He does not look appeased by my inference that I would accept a future invitation. "That's not the right answer."

"It's the only one I have."

He scrubs his jaw and turns to the counter directly beside me and presses his hands to it. His head falls forward and he just hangs there for several seconds, tension rolling off him in waves.

I reach over and run my hand through the spiky blond of his hair. He lifts his head, and the concern in his pale green eyes glistens in sunlight beaming from the bay window behind us. "I'm going to be out of my mind with worry. Do you have any idea how hard it is for me to leave you like this?"

"It's hard for me to let you leave."

He registers my words, and I know I've pleased him, but his mood shifts, his jaw tenses. "I need you to do something for me, Sara. I need you to lock those journals in the safe in my closet and leave them there. I'll give you the combination."

My heart begins to race and I lean against the counter to see him more fully. "You're worried someone will try and take them? I thought you said the apartment was safe?"

He rotates around to face me. "It is safe. That's not what I'm worried about or else I wouldn't be trying to talk you into going with me. I'd be insisting instead. What I'm worried about is you reading the damn things and then reading into them. I'm asking you to put them away while I'm gone. Save your curiosity until I'm present and have the chance to explain whatever you read if you somehow relate it to you and me like you did last night."

"It's not about curiosity, Chris. It's about finding Rebecca."

"Let the private detective do his job. I'm going to put a call into him this morning to talk about what happened last night and see if he can get anything from the storage facility about the incident that we couldn't." His hands slide down my hair. "Please, Sara. Lock up the journals."

I swallow hard against the refusal that wants to spurt from my lips. This is important to him, and there is nothing in the journals I haven't read at least once before. Reluctantly, I nod. "Yes. Okay. I'll lock them up."

Approval crosses his face. "Thank you."

My lips curve at his thank-you.

He arches a brow. "Why are you smiling?"

"Because most macho control freaks don't say 'thank you.' I like it."

"Enough to agree to fly up to Los Angeles Saturday after work and help me survive being stuffed in a tuxedo at a gala that evening?"

I wiggle an eyebrow. "I get to see you in a tuxedo?"

"Better. You can help me take it off."

"Deal," I say with a laugh. "Though I want a picture before the undressing begins."

"I'll give you the picture if I can talk you into bringing the painting I did last night with you. It's not dry enough for me to carry with me."

"Of course. I don't mind at all."

"Great. There's a small room in the back of the studio with a high-tech dryer. It's sitting back there. I'll call you when I get settled and work out the travel arrangements."

The phone buzzes on the wall and he grabs it. "Be right

down," he murmurs and replaces the receiver before reluctantly announcing, "My cab is here."

"Why aren't you driving?"

"I want you to take the Porsche."

"I have my car."

"The Porsche has top-notch security. It knows where you are at all times."

A flash of a past I prefer to forget slips between us, sharpening my tone. "In other words, you want to know where I am at all times?"

He appears unfazed by my reaction. "If I had to find you I could, but that's not the point. If you were in trouble, you'd be found and found quickly. If you need help, you just tell the computer and it will get you help. It's peace of mind for us both."

His reasoning isn't horrible and the past begins to slip away, replaced by another, rather obvious potential motive. "And as a bonus me driving your car makes a statement to Mark."

He crosses his arms over his chest. "As a bonus, yes."

My hands go to my hips. "I don't want to be in the middle of the war between the two of you. I'm not a game token, Chris."

He backs me against the counter, his legs framing mine, and in my bare feet and only his T-shirt, I feel tiny and he is larger-than-life. "It says you're mine," he informs me, his voice low, intense, "and I want him to know you're mine."

I'm thrilled when I should be objecting. "And you, Chris?" I challenge instead. "Are you mine?"

"Every bit of me, baby, good and bad."

I am shocked at how easily this declaration has rolled from his lips. My own lips part and no words come out.

"Take the Porsche." His voice is softer now, rough and seductive.

He was right earlier, I conclude instantly. I melt like honey for this man when he wants me to. "I'll take the Porsche."

Chris's hand slides to the side of my face. "That's the right answer, baby," he murmurs, then slants his mouth over mine, his tongue pressing past my lips. The ripe taste of his approval mixed with the sweet nuttiness of hazelnut coffee floods my taste buds, and consumes me. I am happy for the first time in a very long time.

Six

⁓

Watching the elevator doors close on Chris leaves me hollow inside. I'm alone in his apartment and the happiness of the last few minutes has waned with the sensation of being lost. I know that distance does not have to create separation between us but our newfound closeness is fragile.

For several seconds I face those steel doors, willing them to open again, but they do not, and with good reason. Chris has a flight to catch and a good reason to leave. I on the other hand have several hours until I have to be at work and way too much time to think. I tell myself to sleep, since I've done little of it, but I know that isn't going to happen. There is simply too much weighing on my mind. Besides, I need to unpack and shower.

I quickly head to the bedroom and find my nearly dead phone and dig the charger out of my suitcase. Once I've plugged it in and set it on the nightstand by the unmade bed, I glance at the closet. I've never actually shared a closet with a man before and I fight a wave of discomfort. I fight off the feeling. I am crazy about Chris. I am thrilled with the evolution of our relationship. So why am I fighting a sensation not so unlike what I felt in the storage unit, a sort of claustrophobia?

"This is ridiculous," I scold myself, then zip my case back up and snatch up the handle. "You want this man. You want to be close to him." I roll it to the closet and flip on the light and my eyes go wide at what I find. The closet is amazing, a girl's dream, the size of a small bedroom with racks for clothes that line each of the three sides that don't have a door, only two of which are being used for Chris's clothes.

Once I've settled the case on the floor, I squat down and unzip it. My eyes catch on the safe embedded on the right wall and I find the door open. Chris hasn't given me the combination yet and it's unnerving to lock Rebecca's things away without a way to get back inside.

My teeth scrape my bottom lip and I stare down at my open case, at the small keepsake box and the journals lying on top of my things. I made a promise to Chris to lock the journals up. I gather the three journals and the box and carry them to the safe, and shove them inside, but I do not lock the door. The fourth journal is by the bed somewhere, where I've left it the night before, and I push to my feet and head to the other room to find it. I spot it on the floor by the bed and reach down to grab it but my hand slips and it falls open. I grab it and sit on the bed, staring at the open page. I know this entry. My knowledge of the contents makes the urge to read almost unbearable. I draw a breath and promise myself this is the last time I'll touch any of the journals before Chris returns. I'll call him before he's in the air, get the combination to the safe, and lock them away. Air trickles from my lips and my gaze drops to the book.

I woke this morning to the dull ache of my raw backside, proof of his punishment. I did not wear panties when I dressed for work. I cannot bear the touch of anything on my skin. The dull ache eased as the day went on but the memory of my punishment did not.

I did, however, have several large sales today and my evening ended with a private showing of a famous artist's collection. My clients were thrilled to meet the actual artist and I understand why. He has a gentle strength about him that carries through to his brush. He is passion personified and I wonder what it would be like to have a man like that feel passionate about me. I wonder what it would feel like to wake up my passion for life again, instead of just wondering what the new game will be. The games are no longer fun. They are not the escape they once were. He is not the Master he once was. I feel as if I am spiraling into darkness and I hunger for the kind of passion this artist has for life again. I hunger for more . . . but isn't that what brought me to the gallery in the first place? A hunger for more? Maybe it's the "more" that is the danger . . . because more just never seems to be enough.

I slam the journal shut and my mind is on one thing. The artist Rebecca has written about. It's not Chris, I tell myself. Chris would never invite strangers into his home and studio for a showing. It has to be Ricco Alvarez, who is meeting with me about some private showings; he apparently used to do them with

Rebecca. So why am I still thinking of Chris? It's insane. "Inherently private" is how he described himself. And even if Rebecca was talking about Chris, there is nothing in this entry, or any other, that suggests Rebecca's lover had been an artist. My gut tightens and I shove to my feet and rush back to the closet. I drop down on the floor in front of the safe, before setting the journal I'm still holding inside. I pull out the velvet box and lift the lid and stare down at the paintbrush and picture of Rebecca that is torn in two so that I can't see who was in the photo with her.

"It's not Chris," I whisper. "It's not."

My cell phone begins to ring and I shove the lid down and stick the box back inside the safe. I give the journal a glare and shove it inside the safe as well, and then I shut the safe and twirl the combination dial into place. I'm making myself crazy and I have to stop.

Afraid I'm going to miss my call, I push to my feet and run toward the bedroom, certain it's Chris, and reach it just as it stops ringing. A glance at the caller ID tells me it was Chris. I'm about to punch REDIAL when it rings again.

"Chris," I answer urgently, sitting on the edge of the bed, hoping to hear something in this call to erase the journal entry and how it's made me feel.

"If this was any other trip for any other reason, I wouldn't be leaving."

"I know." As insecure as I can be, in this moment, I feel the connection between myself and this man. "I also know that what you're doing at the hospital is important. Where are you now?"

"We just started to cross the bridge. I had to push my flight back an hour but I should still make all my scheduled events."

"I knew you were pushing it to make the flight." Guilt over the journal entry twists inside me and I can't hold it in. "I'm weak, Chris," I blurt out. "I read another journal entry after you left, but I'm done now. No more. I locked all four of the journals in the safe and I don't want the combination. Just tell me when you get back."

He's silent for several seconds, which feel like an eternity. "Do I want to know what you read and what it's making you think about us or me?"

"No," I say firmly, trying to convince him, and maybe myself, too. "What matters is they're locked up now." My grip tightens around the phone. "I promised you I wouldn't read anything else until you got back, and I did. I'm sorry. I don't want you to feel my word means nothing."

"You told me when you didn't have to," he says softly. "That matters, Sara."

"You matter. You coming back to see me last night and worrying about me and so many other things, Chris. I'm not sure I really told you how much it all means but it does. It really does."

"If you're trying to make me want to turn the cab around and come back, it's working." His voice softens. "Saturday is going to take forever to get here."

"Yes," I agree. "Forever."

"More so because I'm worried about you. I talked to Jacob before I left. He's going to give you his cell phone number and if you need anything you call him. He'll even take you to and from work if you want, though I know you well enough to know you aren't going to agree to that."

"No, but after what happened at the storage unit, I'm not

complaining about having someone to call if I need to." Had Chris not shown up last night, I'd have had no one to lean on, and it wasn't a good feeling. "Thank you, Chris."

"Thank me by staying safe and make sure you stop and talk to Jacob before you leave. If he's not around have the front desk call for him."

"Yes, okay. I will."

"I'll call you once I get settled in L.A. to check on you." His voice lowers, turns soft and intimate. "Bye, baby."

"Bye, Chris," I whisper, and end the call, falling back on the mattress. I stare at the ceiling, my emotions all over the place. I really don't know what to do with them or myself. I grab my phone, set the alarm for half an hour from now, and snuggle into a pillow, smiling as my nostrils flare approvingly with the heady male scent of the man making me absolutely crazy. "Crazy good," I whisper.

"Coffee's ready."

My head snaps up from the pad of paper where I've been jotting information about Ella's new husband, David, including his work number, and find Ralph, the gallery accountant and ever the comedian, poking his head in the door. Considering "Ralph" is Asian, I can't help but wonder if his parents have the same infectious sense of humor I adore about Ralph. "Thank you," I say, eager to pick Ralph's brain about Rebecca and her relationship with Alvarez before my visit with him the next evening.

"I suggest you fill your mug before 'Bossman' drinks it all," Ralph whispers conspiratorially, using one of his random, ever-changing nicknames for Mark. "He looks like he had a long night." He tips back an imaginary glass and makes a comical face. "A bit too much wine for the Wine Master, I do think."

I wave off this notion and glance at the clock, remotely registering that it's almost nine and David's office should be opening any minute. "Mark's way too in control to let that happen."

Ralph snorts. "You haven't seen him today."

He grimaces and disappears around the corner and my brows dip. Mark looking anything but perfect is hard to fathom, and since Mark seems to have quite the impact on my future, I'm curious about this development.

I push to my feet in pursuit of Ralph while he's in willing informant mood, and find him sitting behind his desk in the office next door to mine. "I scored a meeting with Ricco Alvarez tomorrow," I say, claiming the chair in front of his desk, not wanting to be obvious about my interest in Mark.

He arches a regal brow. "Did you now? Does Bossman know yet?"

"Not yet."

"I'm sure he won't be overly surprised. Alvarez has a thing for pretty women who tell him he paints like a Mexican god. And since you ooh and aah over his work, I assume you did. Stick to that strategy and you should do well with him."

"A Mexican god?" I laugh.

He shrugs. "I call it like I see it. His ego is only exceeded by 'the one' who writes our checks."

"I recall Amanda saying she thought Alvarez was worse."

He shoved his glasses up his nose. "I guess that's a matter of opinion. Actually, Amanda is right. Bossman rules with an iron fist but he does take care of his employees. And he'd never curse us for a mistake big or small. Of course, he'd flatten you with a look, and successfully. Alvarez once cursed me out over a one-dollar error in his payout."

"Actually cursed?"

"Profusely."

"Unbelievable," I say, and in my mind, I'm replaying the journal and how Rebecca had said the artist she wrote about had a gentle strength about him. Suddenly, this doesn't remind me of Ricco Alvarez at all. It reminds me of Chris. I shake off the ridiculous notion, trying to focus on what Ralph is saying.

"The only person with love for Alvarez—aside from admiration for his work, that is—is gone. Rebecca had a soft spot for him, and he for her, and for whatever reason when she left, he pulled his work from the gallery."

"But he did the charity event?"

"Set up by Rebecca before she left."

"Right. I remember Amanda saying that, too, now." My brows furrow. "You have no clue at all why Alvarez pulled his work?"

"The man went off over one dollar, Sara. The possibilities are innumerable."

"And he was working with Mark before Rebecca arrived?" I ask, confirming what I think I understand.

"For years."

I wonder if Alvarez could be the man she'd been dating, but of course, that didn't add up, since he was in town and she wasn't. But maybe at some point they had? "Were she and Alvarez dating?"

"I don't think so. She never talked about any man that I know of, and I don't know how she'd have had time for one. She had two jobs when she started here—"

"Two?"

"Waitress at night."

My belly tightens. "To pay the bills." Rebecca had done what I hadn't dared until she'd inadvertently led me here. She gambled that she could find a way to turn the dream into an income.

"Exactly," Ralph confirms. "She never slept, and took naps at lunch in a chair in one of the back offices. Bossman didn't like the conflict, though, and she'd done well enough that somehow she negotiated it into commissions."

"Somehow? You were surprised?"

"Aren't you? She was young and inexperienced, barely a year out of college."

"I thought she was a few years older."

He shakes his head. "Nope, so you can see that to snag what many a professional in this business wants and doesn't get was a big deal. But I give her credit. She didn't get bigheaded or take it for granted. She worked like a dog, through her lunches and late into the evenings. She needed her vacation, though this has become a bit extreme. Hard to believe she's returning. Maybe this rich guy convinced her she needed a sugar daddy."

"Did you meet him?"

"Never even heard of him until she was gone. I told you, she didn't talk about the men in her life."

But Ava had heard of this man and even met him, hadn't she? Rebecca must have kept her new man away from the gallery, and Mark, but she was evidentially closer to Ava than I realized.

My brain hurts every time I try to unravel the mystery that is Rebecca, and Mark, too, for that matter. I glance at the clock and see that it's already after nine. It would soothe me in all kinds of ways to reach David's office, hear Ella is doing great on her honeymoon, and get one thing off my mind.

"I'm going after that coffee," I announce, standing up, intending to get my caffeine fix on my way to make the call.

"Refill my cup, chica," Ralph says, sliding his mug toward me. It reads "Numbers don't count but I do."

"Chica?" I query with an arched brow.

"I speak the language of many and the words of none."

"You can say that again," I laugh as I head for the kitchen, waving at Amanda, who has settled behind the front desk and is looking her adorable Barbie doll self in a pink dress and matching hair clip. I think of Chris's claim that Mark is drawn to those who don't naturally fit into his world. Mark's choice to hire Amanda, a college student eager to please and without real life experience, seems to fit this assessment well. But why hire me? I'm no Amanda. I cannot help but wonder if my asking questions about Rebecca wasn't the reason. He wanted me to be close so he could control what I discovered, or know what I was asking, or even who I was asking it of. Or maybe, I silently scold myself, you just impressed him with your knowledge of art and he needed a new employee. I do know art and I do belong in this world. Maybe not the Lion's Den, or that club Mark owns, but the gallery, and the art industry, yes. I have to believe that if I'm truly going to resign my job as a schoolteacher and embrace my intended career path.

I'm busy talking myself out of a fallback into the haze of

self-doubt when I walk into the small kitchen and freeze. Blood roars in my ears at the sight of Mark. He is standing with his back to me, his broad shoulders stretching the gray of his suit jacket just so. It's the first time I've seen him, beyond a quick few seconds in passing the day before, since I visited his club, and I am suddenly a nervous wreck. I start to back out of the room.

"Not so fast, Ms. McMillan."

Damn. Damn. Damn. "How did you know it was me?" I ask.

He turns, and my breath lodges in my throat with the impact of both his male beauty and steely gray eyes. Power rushes off him and he consumes the room, and me, but I've noted he has this impact on everyone, and I believe no one, male or female, is immune to his presence.

"I can smell your perfume," he informs me. "And it's not your normal scent."

I feel a jolt of surprise at his unexpected observation. Mark knows my normal scent? That he's this aware of me takes me off guard, but not as much as the glint in his bloodshot eyes. It has me wondering if he has actually identified the musky scent as masculine, thus assuming I smell like Chris. I decide to do what I've been doing a lot of lately—actually most of my life, if I'm honest with myself. I deflect. "You don't look so good, Bossman." I can't seem to bring myself to call him Mr. Compton.

"Thank you, Ms. McMillan," he says dryly. "Compliments will get you everywhere."

It's impossible to contain a smile at the reference to a comment I'd once made to him. "Good to know something works with you."

His lips twist wryly. "You make it sound as if I'm impossible to please."

I set Ralph's coffee mug on the small table in the center of the room. "You do come across as a bit . . . challenging."

His lips twitch. "I can think of worse things to be called."

"Like rich and arrogant?" I tease, because I'd called him those things a few days earlier.

"I told you, I am—"

"Rich and arrogant," I finish for him. "Believe me, I know." I'm remarkably comfortable in this little exchange and I feel daring enough to question him. "You really don't look like yourself. Are you sick?"

"Sometimes morning simply comes a little too early," he says dryly, before turning away from me to fill his coffee cup, clearly not willing to supply more details.

My brow furrows. I'm certain he's turned away from me to avoid me seeing his expression, and I don't miss the subtle but evident discomfort in him that I've never seen before. I have an irrational need to pull down whatever wall he's just erected and I joke, "Especially after the nights I stayed up studying wine, opera, and classical music so that my boss will believe I can interact with the clientele of the elite auction house his family owns."

He turns and leans on the counter, sipping his coffee. Any sign of discomfort is gone, and his eyes blaze with power. "I'm simply looking out for your best interests."

A sense of unease overcomes me and I know our easy conversation is over. We're heading into quicksand territory and I already feel myself sinking. "And yours," I point out.

He inclines his head. "Your interests are mine. We've had this conversation."

He's referring to our talk two nights before, when he'd showed me a video of Chris kissing me in the gallery and convinced me that Chris had used it to stake his claim on me. I'd felt like a token in a game that night. The same night Chris had taken me to the club. Mark's club. A sudden rush of claustrophobia overtakes me and I reach for the coffee mug and step toward the coffeepot. Somehow, I catch my heel on what seems to be empty air and still I manage to trip. Mark reaches forward and catches my arm. The touch makes me gasp and my eyes shoot to his keen, silvery stare, more primal than concerned, and I feel as if the air has been sucked out of my lungs. I want to pull away but my hands are full.

"You okay, Ms. McMillan?" he asks, his voice etched with a deep, suggestive quality that burns through me with warning. I have the distinct impression that how I handle this moment in time will define our relationship, and perhaps the future of a job I've decided I want to keep.

"I do high heels better post-caffeine," I reply.

His lips twitch and he surprises me by offering me a rare smile. "You are quite witty, aren't you?"

His hand slips away from my arm and I remember all too well Rebecca talking about Mark's games. I wonder if this shift in moods, which feels far more menacing than Chris's, aren't a part of how he plays with people. I set the mug down and reach for the pot.

"We should talk before you fill that," Mark comments, and my hand stills mid-action.

I squeeze my eyes shut a moment and steel myself for what I know is coming, before rotating to face him. He's set his mug down and both of us have our hips aligned with the counter.

"Talk?" I asked. "I thought that's what we were doing already?"

"My world is invitation-only, Sara."

Sara. He's used my first name and I know it's meant to intimidate me. "You hired me. That's an invitation."

"Coy doesn't suit you."

He's right. We both know he means to the club. "I was invited."

"By the wrong person."

"No. Not the wrong person."

"Quite the change of heart from our chat two nights ago, when you were quite displeased with him."

I decide to bypass defending my reasons for being with Chris. It isn't like Mark will approve. He won't even say Chris's name. "I'm good at my job. I'm going to make you lots of money, but my private life is my private life. I don't belong to you, Mark." I use his name intentionally.

"Then who do you belong to, Ms. McMillan?"

Chris. That's the answer he is looking for, the answer Chris would want me to give, but the ghosts of the past roar inside me. My survival instinct refuses to let go of what I've fought hard to achieve these past few years in my independence. "I belong to myself."

Mark's eyes gleam with satisfaction and I know I've made a critical misstep. "A good answer and one I can live with." His lips twist and he turns away, sauntering toward the exit, only to stop at the door and glance back at me. "There's no in between. Don't let him convince you there is."

He's gone before I can reply and I feel my knees quake with the aftermath of his words. Chris had said the same thing to me back in his apartment the morning we'd headed out to Napa Valley. No in between, I repeat in my mind. It is a reality I've had lurking in the back of my mind all morning. A reality that says "all" means not only that I have to embrace Chris's dark side fully, no matter where that takes me, and us, but also that I have to show him mine, and I don't know if I'm ready. I don't know if I'll ever be ready and I doubt very seriously he will be, either. Not for this. Not for his own reasons as well.

I fill the two coffee cups and I'm relieved to find Ralph on the phone, and so make my escape back to my office without conversation, quickly and painlessly. Settling behind my desk, I set my mug down and dial David's office, only to get an answering service. The office is "indefinitely" closed. The choice of words the operator uses sends a chill down my spine. I set the receiver down and stare at the desktop without seeing it.

I'm starting to feel like I'm losing my mind. I can't see danger everywhere. Ella is in Paris on her honeymoon. She's fine. I'm letting this Rebecca mystery make my mind run wild. Actually, my whole life feels like it's running wild whereas only weeks before it was calm and uneventful. I'm standing on a high-rise ledge and walking the edge, and while there is fear and apprehension, there is also a high I can only call an adrenaline rush that I crave more and more each day.

My cell phone rings and I dig it from my purse to see Chris's number on caller ID. "You made it okay?" I ask when I answer.

"I just landed, and you know how I spent the entire flight?"

He sounds a bit on edge, or maybe I'm on edge. Maybe we both are. "Sleeping, I hope."

"Thinking about you and not even about fucking you, Sara. About lying in my bed, with you asleep in my arms."

His confession thrills and worries me. "Why do I feel like I should apologize?"

"Because you chose to stay there and you won't be sleeping with me tonight."

"Oh," I say, and the tension that had curled inside me begins to unwind. Chris is upset that we can't sleep together tonight?

"I'm not used to anyone having this kind of hold on me," he continues, his voice dark and troubled. "I feel like I'm crawling out of my own skin."

I've rattled his deep-rooted need for control and I am still struggling with the idea that I have this power over him that he does over me. It pleases me but I am fairly certain it truly has him unsettled. "Just hearing your voice now affects me," I say, trying to give him the reassurance I would need if I'd just said to him what he'd said to me. "That's how much of a hold you have on me."

"Good." He breathes out and I feel the relief wash over him even through the phone line. "Because it would suck to feel like this alone."

"Yes," I say, smiling. "It would suck." I hear someone shout in the background, and I think Chris is outside the airport, trying to get a cab.

"That would be my cab," Chris confirms. "Or rather someone getting me a cab. I'll call you later. And order in lunch today. I'm worried about you going out." I hear someone, the cab driver, I assume, ask Chris about his bag, and Chris replies before he returns his attention to me. "I'm serious about lunch, Sara. Order in."

"I'll be careful, I promise. Catch your cab and call me when you can."

"Careful isn't the answer I'm looking for and you know it." More voices in the background and I hear Chris issue a muffled curse. "I have to go but this conversation is not over. Did you talk with Jacob?"

"He wasn't around—"

"Sara—"

"I'm fine."

"The point is *keeping* you fine." He makes a frustrated sound. "I'll call you when I get a break and we will talk about your definition of 'careful' and mine." He hangs up before I can answer, another one of his "control" things.

I drop the phone back into my desk drawer and I am warm all over thinking about Chris's confessions, and even his concerns when it comes to my safety. I do not know why it feels wicked and wonderful when Chris pretty much bosses me around, but it does. Chris Merit is my adrenaline rush.

The intercom buzzes and Amanda announces, "There's someone named Jacob on the line for you."

Seven

I've barely hung up with Jacob when I receive an e-mail from Mark titled "Riptide." Tension slides through me at the timing of a message related to the famous auction house his family owns. He knows how much I want to earn the opportunity to work with Riptide and he's too smart not to know how uneasy I am about where I stand. Anxiously, I click on the message.

Ms. McMillan:

Riptide has an auction planned for two months from now and I'm attaching a list of the items to be offered to the public, along with estimated sale prices. This should give you an idea of exactly how including a piece of art in a Riptide auction can impact its value. This should clearly show why you would want a customer, or artists wishing to sell unique pieces of their collections, to use Riptide as an avenue to do so. Furthermore, to have our gallery listed as the sale's agent amplifies our reputation as a prestigious gallery, thus drawing high-end clientele to shop and artists to show their work here.

Consider this an invitation to seek out items that would fit this upcoming auction, and should you succeed, you will be invited to attend the event when it takes place. You will also receive a substantial commission of the sale.

Sincerely,
Bossman

The humor Mark shows in the e-mail by signing it "Boss-man" does nothing to lessen my instant unease at the timing of the message. Mark stirs conflicting feelings inside me. I respect his success, and I've seen him act in protective ways toward me and his other employees that conflict with the man in the journal Chris insists is Mark. My gaze lifts to the oil painting on the wall in front of me, red and white roses by the brilliant Georgia O'Nay, a part of Mark's personal collection that he'd placed in Rebecca's office.

I am reminded of the roses Rebecca's Master had sent her, of her words after receiving them. I do feel ready to bloom, ready to go wherever he leads me. I have the sense that Mark is trying to lead me, and my spine stiffens. I do not know if he is the man from the journal, but I do know that I am not his slave or submissive, nor do I intend to be. I do, however, fear that is where he intends to take me. I feel like this Riptide offer is about Chris, about me not saying he owns me. Mark is trying to own me. I've finally dared to chase my dream of a career in this industry, and he's using it against me. He knows I know that while I could get a job elsewhere, the pay would be too low for me to consider it a viable way to leave teaching behind. I cannot just sit back and ignore what this could mean for me.

My mind is racing as I round my desk and head to the hallway. If I let fear of losing this dream control me, Mark controls me. I've worked too hard to make my life my own to let that happen. And damn it, if this dream isn't going to happen for me, I need to stop teasing myself. The longer I do, the more painful my return to teaching will be. I can't make a living on the pay I'll get without the Riptide commissions. If I could, I'd have been working at this a long time ago.

My worries consume the short walk to Mark's door and I am not surprised to find it shut. It's not like the man invites a warm and fuzzy environment. Lifting my hand to knock, I pause as adrenaline slams into me and this time it's not such a high. Nerves assail me and I hate it. They are a weakness and I am so damn tired of weakness. Grinding my teeth through the very real fear of this meeting ending my dream job and mocking my bravado, I knock and hear Mark's deep voice resonate a command to come in. Everything is a command with Mark.

After opening the door I step inside. I shut the door behind me before he has a chance to tell me to. Control, I think. I have to claim it. I turn to face him, taking in the oval-shaped office and the spectacular art on the walls surrounding me. Finally, I allow myself to glimpse the man behind the massive glass desk, who oozes power and sex in explosive quantities, and whom I'd dubbed "King" the first time I'd seen him behind his desk. It's hard not to find him impressively male and highly intimidating, and to not be drawn to him. But there is something more compelling demanding my attention. My gaze slides beyond Mark to the giant Paris-themed mural covering the entire wall and my teeth sink into my bottom lip at the delicate, familiar strokes of the brush I see in the work I know belongs to Chris.

"Yes," Mark says, answering my unanswered question. "It's Chris's work."

My attention slides to his face and I try to read him. I don't know what happened between these two men, but I have no doubt it burns deeper for them both because they were once friends. "I assumed as much," I reply when I can read nothing in the carefully schooled expression he wears on his too-handsome face and he seems too intent to say nothing more. "And it surprises me. You two don't seem too close these days."

"Money talks," he says.

My brows dip before I can stifle the reaction, the defensive rise for Chris impossible to contain. "Chris doesn't seem motivated by money."

Mark gives me a deadpan look I think might hold a hint of irritation. "What can I do for you, Ms. McMillan?" Mark asks, clearly diverting the conversation. I get the impression he's not pleased with me defending Chris. It's a good reminder, though, that I'm trapped in a battle of wills between him and Chris, and it renews my resolve to get the answers I came here for.

I do not wait for him to ask me to sit. I walk forward, thankful my feet don't trip on empty space again, and sit in one of the two armchairs in front of his desk, sinking into the expensive leather. "I want to talk about Riptide."

He leans back, rests his elbows on the arms of his chair, and steeples two fingers together. "What about it?"

"You told me I wasn't ready for Riptide. Why am I suddenly now?"

His expression is unreadable, unchanged. If he feels put on the spot, he shows nothing. "There is no suddenly about this."

"You said I had to learn about wine, opera, and classical music."

"I told you," he says slowly. "I was testing your dedication. And I'd still like you to learn those things. I thought you'd be pleased. Unless . . . you don't plan to stay here after the summer ends?"

"I haven't been offered a job beyond filling in for Rebecca." A thought slams into me with my own comment. I barely contain the urgency in my voice as I ask, "Has she resigned?" And would he tell me if she has? Or would he think I'd be less motivated to create a new spot for myself out of assumed stability?

"I haven't heard from Rebecca in weeks," he informs me. "If she decides to come back, I'll make room for her, but I cannot operate a business with an absentee employee dictating my moves."

I study him and look for some hint of discomfort, of a lie, but see nothing. I do not believe he has heard from Rebecca. "Did you expect her return, or at least some communication, by now?"

"Yes," he replies without hesitation.

"Are you worried about her?"

"Displeased," he says, and the tone is that and more. He is not worried about her. He's furious that she has disobeyed him. In that instant, I am convinced he is the man in the journal, who has lost his submissive to another man. And I believe he would punish her on her return for misbehaving. Certainly disappearing is misbehaving.

"You say you can't operate like this, but you still haven't offered me a full-time job," I comment, testing him, trying to see if he shows me any sign he has talked to her, that he does know she is returning.

"Because I don't offer what I feel will be declined. Chris will have offered to get you another job, but you're still here. I'd assume that's because you refuse to be controlled; however, I've gathered you want the security Riptide commissions can offer you. Which consequently is another sign you are all about maintaining control by way of supporting yourself. I'm simply giving you what you want."

"Translation," I say. "This is about what you can give me versus what Chris can give me." It is a crushing blow to believe this has never been about my work, both to my self-respect and my plans for the future. I can't leave teaching for a career that exists only as a pawn of their play for power, and I am suddenly angry enough not to need wine to speak my mind. "It's about the damn cockfight you two can't get over."

He leans forward, his eyes dark, the silver color turning a deep gray. "This is about me wanting you. Nothing else. And I go after what I want, Ms. McMillan."

Right. He wants to fuck me. Because he knows Chris already is. And because there is an inherent weakness in me that draws men like Mark. A voice in my head adds, "like Chris," and I crush it. Chris is not Mark. Not even close.

"Stop it, Ms. McMillan."

My gaze jerks to Mark's with the sharpness of the command. "Stop what?"

"Doubting yourself, which makes you doubt me. You're

destining us for failure and I do not fail. Either decide you won't fail or you will, in which case, any talk of Riptide or this job full-time is a waste of both of our time."

Air freezes in my lungs. I'm stunned that this man who I have compared to others I believed to be like him has just challenged me to believe in myself rather than shoving me back in a hole. I don't know how to compute this new information. How to relate this to a man, a Master, who forces women into submission? He doesn't force them, is the only answer. They choose to give to him as freely, as I do Chris.

"Choose success," he says, and my eyes go wide at the word he seems to have plucked from my head.

"I do. I am."

"Then stop questioning why you're here. I hired you because I watched the video of you with the two customers you helped the night of the Alvarez show. You knew your art and you persuaded them to make a purchase and you didn't even work here yet. You sold them and you sold me. You continue to do so. What happens with your job here is based on performance. Nothing, and I mean *nothing,* affects it. Are we clear?"

"Yes. Thank you."

"Thank me by continuing to make sales, starting with a close friend of mine coming in later this morning. He has deep pockets I fully expect you to empty."

A smile breaks unexpectedly over my features. "I'll do my best."

"From what I've seen, your best works quite well."

I beam under his praise and it scares me how much I seem to need his approval, but I've done enough self-reflection over the past few years to know it's more about me than him. About a past with powerful men that I haven't quite erased, no matter how much I've tried.

"I set a meeting with Alvarez for tomorrow evening."

"We have an event here at the gallery tomorrow night," he says, and I do not sense pleasure at the announcement of the Alvarez meeting I'd expected.

"I really think I can get him to do the private showing our customer wants and place more art here if I do this."

He leans back in his chair and steeples his fingers again. "Do you remember what I told you about Alvarez?"

"That if I got this meeting, I'd impress you. And from what I hear, I assume that's because he pulled his work when Rebecca left. Are you going to tell me why?"

"He wanted her contact information after she left and I told him I didn't have it and even if I did, I couldn't legally give it out. He wasn't pleased. He likes to get his way, which leads me back to—what else did I tell you about Alvarez?"

I replay our previous conversation in my mind. *We do not beg, and you do not let yourself get manipulated. Period. The end. These artists know I don't tolerate that crap and as long as they believe I own you, they won't believe you will, either. So when I say I own you, Sara, I mean I own you.*

Own. Mark likes this word far too much. However, in analyzing what I've learned of him as a boss, I'm beginning to believe he has some odd sense of ownership equaling protection. He owns you and thus he is responsible for your well-being. It's not the Kool-Aid I intend to drink, but I think of how he insisted all employees and patrons take cabs at his expense after a wine tasting at the gallery, and I do believe it is how he thinks.

"We don't beg for his business and he doesn't own us."

He arches a brow, but thankfully, before he can push me into some mind game sure to leave my head spinning, the buzzer on his desk goes off and he punches it. He doesn't immediately respond; his steely, steady stare is locked on my face. Adrenaline shoots through my veins and my fingers press into my legs. I do not know what to expect from Mark besides discomfort that is darkly addictive, and I know this is a part of how dysfunctional I've allowed myself to become.

Without freeing me from his scrutiny, Mark punches the button on the phone. "Ryan Kilmer is here," Amanda announces. "He says he has an appointment."

"We'll be right with him," Mark replies, then releases the button, and finally blinks away our connection. "That will be my close friend and your new client, Ms. McMillan. Hurry up front and greet him."

He's dismissed me but I don't move. This conversation about my job has me thinking about the decision before me. Before I talk myself out of it, I blurt, "I have two weeks to resign my teaching job to give them time to replace me for the new year. That job offer has to come by then and so does my sense of a secure earning potential. If that's unrealistic, we should deal with that now."

"It's only too soon if you allow it to be."

"That's a nonanswer," I reply, but what did I really expect? Men like Mark do not allow themselves to be cornered or put on a deadline and I've done just that.

"It's nothing of the sort. It's just not the answer you wanted."

"Right. And why would you give me the answer I wanted?"

"I gave you the answer you needed to hear, not the one that makes your life easy. Easy is not better."

These head games do not sit well. I push to my feet. "I had better go meet my customer." I turn and head for the door, wondering how many times I'll replay "It's only too soon if you allow it to be," while analyzing the meaning in it before the day is over.

"Ms. McMillan."

I stop but I don't turn. I'm frustrated he's ended this meeting with me on edge and him in control.

"I go for what I want but I respect certain limits. Tell me you belong to him and I'll back off."

No in between, he and Chris had both said it to me, but I can't bring myself to say I belong to Chris, like I am his property. I squeeze my eyes shut as Chris's words replay in my mind. *I want him to know you're mine.* It's the same thing really as belonging, but it felt different when it was just us talking and Chris had declared himself mine as well. It was a defining time of commitment in our relationship that shifted the dynamic between us and the expectations we have for each other. *Don't let old skeletons destroy you and Chris. Think of how betrayed you would feel if Chris didn't make your relationship clear in a similar situation.*

I turn and make sure Mark reads how much I mean my words. "I'm with Chris and that's as close as he or anyone will ever come to me belonging to them." I leave, not giving him a chance to reply, and am proud of myself. Now I will know that whatever happens here at the gallery is about my job performance only. And I haven't let the past have an impact on Chris and me. At least not this time.

Eight

Ryan Kilmer nails the tall, dark, and good-looking playboy persona to perfection clear down to his expensive light brown suit, which matches the image and his eye color almost exactly. "So you're Rebecca's replacement," he says in greeting, holding on to my hand a bit too long.

"I wasn't aware I was being billed as her replacement," I say when he releases me. "More as a fill-in."

"Ah yes," he replies, and there is a slight edge to his tone that has me wondering what it means. "Fill-in. Well, I'm hoping you will stay around long enough to fill my needs."

I refuse to read an undertone to the comment, but he's Mark's friend, and I wonder if he's also the other man in the journal. I choose my words carefully. "You have a project requiring artwork?"

"I'm a real estate investor and I'm involved in a high-rise going up a few blocks away. We're ready to put together the lobby and a few show units for viewing. We need them to impress a wealthy audience. Rebecca basically took control of another property for me a few months back." He holds up a folder. "I brought you pictures of her work and the floor plans and pictures of what you have to work with now. I'd like you to come over and see the property as soon as possible."

"Of course. I'd love to see what you've brought. Why don't we head to my office?"

"Excellent."

I spend the next hour reviewing the work Rebecca has done in the past for Ryan, and find out what he is looking for in the future. I am not beyond seeing this man as attractive, but unlike Mark, his lighthearted nature and easy humor are infectious and he sets me at ease. It's hard to see him as a close friend to Mark, but then, maybe it's his differences that make that possible. Maybe Mark and Chris are too alike, too in competition for control.

I close the folder. "I'm excited to see the property." And about the extravagant budget that allows me to place some amazing pieces in the property, but suddenly I'm thinking about Mark and Chris and I wonder what caused the bad turn in their relationship.

". . . and we should have the furnishings staged next week."

I blink; it seems I have missed part of what Ryan is saying. "Ah yes. Staging is helpful. I'll know what I have to work around."

"I'm sure the decorator is going to want to have a say in things," he adds. "But she worked with Rebecca and understands the idea is to impress the visitors with the artist as much as the design work."

I've never worked with a designer and it's a bit intimidating. I wonder if Rebecca had done so before she worked at the gallery. It hits me that I know nothing of her before her time here. How have I missed such an important clue that might help me find her?

"For now," Ryan continues, "you can be thinking through options. The volume of pieces I need may require some outside purchases and I thought you'd need time to coordinate." He rises and I follow, walking with him toward the lobby, but he smiles at Amanda and stops behind her desk.

The two begin making small talk, and I feel my schoolteacher motherly side kick in when I realize he is flirting with Amanda. This man is close to Mark and most likely a member of his club, and Amanda is a young college girl ten years his junior. I hover, unable to stop myself. When he's done with his flirtation, I walk him to the door.

When I return to the office area, I stop at the front desk to chat with Amanda. "He's very sexy," she says, glowing from the attention. "And he's never stopped and talked to me like that."

"He's too old for you," I point out.

"No, he's not," she argues. "An older man is sexy."

There is that word again. "And bossy," I assure her.

She grins. "He can boss me around any day." She lowers her voice. "Unlike Bossman, who makes me hot and bothered, like he does the entire female population, Ryan doesn't scare me at the same time. No wonder Rebecca liked him so much."

"He's likable," I agree, but I also think of how Rebecca saw the other man in the journal as an intrusion into her and Mark's relationship and I cannot help but think it had been Ryan. I can see how Ryan would be Mark's choice in a ménage. A man who didn't threaten his role as King.

"But?" Amanda prods when I say nothing else.

"But remember that sometimes the likable ones have the darkest secrets." And on that note, I'm headed to dangerous territory I decide to avoid. "Is Mary in?"

"She's still sick," Amanda declares. "You're on your own today."

Mary doesn't seem to like me much so my heart isn't broken. I enjoy working the floor anyway. "Not a problem. I'll be on standby in my office."

A few seconds later, I settle behind my desk, and my drawer vibrates as my phone buzzes with a text message. Retrieving my phone, I realize the message was sent some time back and I find myself looking at a picture of Chris with a teenage boy I know is the leukemia patient. The kid looks happy but thin, and pale. And while Chris is smiling, I don't miss the sadness lurking in the depth of his eyes. Being with the boy and knowing he can't be saved is eating him up. Layers, I think. Chris has so many layers.

I text him: You are amazing.

He replies. You can prove you mean that when I see you again.

I smile and type. How?

He answers with Try to use my imagination.

He'd accused me of being afraid of his imagination not so long ago. I'm not. Maybe you need to draw me another picture.

Yes, he types. Maybe I do.

I am grinning when the exchange ends and I begin thumbing through my prospect lists, contemplating lunch. Frustratingly, my mind goes back to Chris's relationship with Mark. They were both control freaks. Both into the club activity. What if they had tried to share a woman and they'd clashed? This idea twists me in knots for all kinds of reasons, and I shove it aside. No. That isn't what happened. That would mean Chris lied to me about his sexual preferences. Or would it? He told me what he favored. Had he ever said he'd never gone other directions? Chris didn't lie to me, but is it possible that he didn't exactly tell me the truth? I swallow hard. Who am I to judge where those lines are? I haven't exactly been completely truthful with Chris and I don't know if I can be. Not without destroying us.

My day is finally nearing an end just before seven and I'm about to gather my things to leave. "You ready to dart out of here?" Ralph asks from my doorway. "I'll walk you and Amanda to your cars."

As much as I don't want to walk to my car, or rather Chris's, alone, I don't have the energy to answer the questions that would come when they discover I'm driving the 911. I regret driving it, for the complications it presents. And thankfully, the parking lot has cameras and Mark is still here. "I have to check in with Bossman on a couple of things so go on without me."

Amanda appears in my doorway. "Tuesdays are supposed to be slow. That's why we don't have more staff scheduled, but today was insanity. What did you do to bring in so many customers? They were all asking for you."

"Mark gave me a prospect list I called down. I guess the calls worked. Unfortunately, not one of them bought anything, but I have high hopes a few will be back."

I chat with them for a few minutes until they finally depart.

I'm beyond ready to leave myself. My cold Chinese food between clients has long ago worn off and no sleep the night before has taken a toll.

"What exactly do you have to run by me?"

I look up to find Mark standing in the doorway, his tie loose and his hair rumpled. He'd had a meeting with several people today that had lasted hours and he seems oddly harried. "The prospect list," I reply. "I was hoping you could tell me which ones own pieces that Riptide might contact tomorrow."

"I emailed you a list of those prospects earlier this afternoon."

"Oh. Hmm. I guess I should check my e-mail. I was slammed with people today."

"And yet we had no sales."

My spine stiffens and I am instantly transported back to my past, when my father, and yes, Michael, were quick to flatten me when anything went wrong. Anger begins to stir inside me and not at Mark. I thought I'd put it behind me, but I clearly have not. Choose success, Mark had said, and yet he's here trying to make me admit to failure that doesn't exist? My anger shifts, twists, and turns inside me. No matter what the outcome, I cannot lie down for Mark as I have others in the past.

"You know," I say, and I am proud of how strong my voice is, how steady my gaze, "if you're trying to get me to 'choose success,' assuming my failure isn't going to help. No sales today might be correct, but I have several customers I feel will buy, and buy well."

His lips twitch. "Good to see you feeling confident enough to put me in my place."

My eyes go wide. Had I really just put him in his place? And he let me, even seeming amused when I barely think he's capable of such a feeling. Self-doubt rips through me and I try to reel it in, to remind myself he doesn't seem upset, but I can't do it. He's my boss. He's my path to financial security. I have to justify my reply. "I'm just . . . trying to make sure you know I don't like failing, either."

"And I approve."

A frisson of pleasure runs through me with his words and the light in his eyes. Pleasing Mark pleases me and it's not sexual. No. Chris has that part of me wrapped up tightly enough that there is no room for anyone else. It's that power thing Mark has along with his role of authority. The pleasure of seconds before begins to ebb and fade at the uncomfortable reminder that even after daring to stand up to him, I did not stand my ground, and I am not in full control of how my past influences me.

"You look tired," he says. "And so am I. Why don't I walk you to your car?"

"I look tired," I repeat. "Compliments will get you every-where, Bossman."

"Ah now," he purrs, his voice low and rough, "if only it were that easy."

I swallow hard at the heat in his stare and quickly reach for my purse and briefcase, and words, oh the words I can never control, tumble from my mouth. "Somehow I doubt anything easy would hold your interest." Oh shit. Had I just issued him a challenge? I didn't mean to. My eyes jerk to his. "Not that I—"

Laughter rolls from his lips, deep and rough like his voice. "Relax, Ms. McMillan. I know you weren't issuing a challenge, though if you have a change of heart that sways in my direction,

I'll be happy to take you up on one." He pulls his keys from his pocket. "Let's get out of here. I'm of the opinion we both had way too long of a night for a long day like this one."

No, I think, as I push to my feet, already feeling the absence of Chris in his own apartment. Mine was too short considering Chris was gone for a few more days.

We exit the gallery, the dim glow of a streetlight illuminating the back of the building and parking lot, where our two cars are the only ones left, and that means by process of elimination, the sporty silver Jaguar is Mark's. He glances at the 911.

"I see he made sure to stake his claim," he states dryly.

"Or he just really hates my Ford Focus."

His eyes narrow sharply. "Don't get used to what he gives you or you won't want to earn it for yourself. And that, Ms. McMillan, would be a problem for us both. I'll see you tomorrow."

He has dismissed me but he does not walk away, and I realize he's waiting for me to get into the car. He's hit a sensitive spot with me and I level my stare at him. I hesitate and consider letting it go, but I don't. "I come from money, Mark. I've had money, lots of it, and I could have it now if I chose to comply with the expectations. So Chris can't get me used to anything I don't already know and am already willing to walk away from. I want to make my own money. And . . . ." He arches a brow at my hesitation and I realize I don't want to say more. I don't need to say more. This is not Mark's business. "And good night." I climb into the car without giving him another chance to speak, and the regret I felt about driving the car is gone. I don't want to hide my relationship with Chris or make apologies or excuses for driving his car. This is my life and I plan to live it.

I pull onto the road, and the adrenaline high is back and I love that it comes from my actions. My thoughts go to Rebecca and how she used the man in the journal for her highs, how easily another man who wasn't Chris could have brought that out in me. My desire to find her and confirm that she has found a path to her dreams, and is safe and happy, becomes more powerful than ever.

The 911 is a smooth luxury ride I am familiar with from my father's preference for the car, but it's been years since I've ridden in one, and certainly I never drove one. That Chris has easily handed me the keys is far more meaningful than he understands. Not that I didn't have a nice car. My father wouldn't allow his daughter to embarrass him in a Ford Focus like I have now. I'd driven a conservative little Audi during both high school and college, traded in every two years, of course. I'd loved the first car, and hated the two that had followed, as I'd begun to see beneath the veil of the life my mother and I led. No veil now, though. I'm on my own and I'm in a 911.

My lips curve and I hit the gas and indulge myself for a blast a short half block long. The instant I ease up my foot, the car goes into an easy glide. The smooth ride after the wicked acceleration reminds me of the extreme shifts I've experienced in Chris's moods and I decide the car fits him well. I also wonder if I've truly seen what lies beneath the surface to cause those ups and downs. I wonder what he would think if he knew what lies beneath my surface.

I shake off the place my thoughts are going as I pull up to Chris's fancy high-rise only a few blocks from the gallery and the doorman opens my door and greets me. "Good evening, Ms. McMillan."

Handing over the keys, I am reminded of Chris teasing this doorman as he had another at a hotel not to joyride in the car. "I didn't joyride." I grin. "Much."

He grins back at me. "I won't tell."

"Thank you," I say, giving him a small nod before I slide the strap of my briefcase over my shoulder and head inside the building, where I find Jacob standing by the front counter.

"Ms. McMillan," he says with a nod when I stop beside him. "I trust the day was uneventful in a good way since I didn't hear from you after our phone call this morning."

"It was," I confirm. "You know, I just didn't want to risk bothering you if you were off duty this morning."

"I'm always on duty," he informs me. "I live on property and I made a special promise to Chris to look out for you. He doesn't ask for favors, Ms. McMillan. He did for you. I don't intend to let him down. You're on my radar but I need you to communicate with me. If you're going out, let me know."

I have a flashback to the many years of my life my mother and I went nowhere without a security guard we didn't need. I didn't understand that in my youth, of course. Not until college, when I'd torn away my rose-colored glasses, did I realize we were like kept animals, pets to my father, controlled, not protected. Sheltered from the many lives he had led and the many women my mother had pretended she didn't share him with.

"Ms. McMillan?" Jacob asks, and I snap my gaze up from the floor to his.

"Yes," I murmur. "Thank you, Jacob." And despite my walk

down memory lane, I mean the words. Contrary to my actions the night before, I don't make a habit of being stupid, no matter what my father might say otherwise. Someone was in that storage unit with me last night. Maybe it was teenagers, or maybe it wasn't, but with my worries about Rebecca, I'm not sure I'm over the fear I felt inside the darkness.

His eyes narrow and glint with understanding. "I don't care what time of the day or night, you call me if you need to. There is no reason too small. Better safe—"

"Than sorry," I finish for him. "Yes, I know." I incline my head. "I'll call if I need you."

A few minutes later, I walk off the elevator and into Chris's apartment, taking in the twinkling skyline. Exhaustion begins to seep into my bones and I head to the bedroom, pausing at the doorway, entranced by the giant, unmade bed.

Baby, the ways I'm going to fuck you are too many to count, but not tonight. Tonight, I'm going to make love to you.

And he had. I have no idea if that means he's falling in love with me, but I am falling in love with him. I have already.

I wet my suddenly parched lips and kick off my shoes before walking to the bathroom and finding Chris's shirt, which I've saved to sleep in. After undressing, I pull the shirt over my body and inhale deeply. The scent of Chris is a little piece of heaven. I head to the kitchen and spend some time exploring, pleased to find a box of macaroni and cheese that I quickly whip into dinner. Once it's ready, I cave in to curiosity and end up at the door of Chris's studio with dinner, my laptop, and my phone in hand.

I flip on the light and I don't see the gorgeous city surrounding me. There is only the roll of tape lying by the stool. I squeeze my eyes shut and I can almost put myself back on that chair with Chris's mouth and hands on my body. I settled my things on the floor by the wall where I intend to get comfortable, but I don't sit. Now, and only now, do I let myself think about what has randomly slipped into my thoughts today, to be dashed away. *The painting.*

Slowly, I walk forward, my pulse accelerating as I near Chris's depiction of me, bound by the ankles and wrists, in the center of the studio. As I bring it into view, my throat goes instantly dry, and heat burns low in my belly. It's a black-and-white image, which he favors, and well developed with fine details, too well developed to be a draft. He's been working on this for a while and he left it in the open for me to see, this morning and now. Chris does nothing without purpose. This is a message or a challenge. I'm not sure which, or maybe it's both. I'm not clear on either. And considering I'm both aroused and uncomfortable, I'm not even clear on what I feel. This is Chris's sanctuary. What does it mean that he's bound me in real life and on canvas?

Nine

‿‿‿

Tearing my gaze away from the painting, I walk to where I've left my things. Knees weak, I slide down the wall and sit there a moment, trying to make sense of what I'm feeling, when a mission for knowledge hits me. Powering up my computer, I google "pain for pleasure" and find myself greeted by an eyeful of bound naked bodies and dungeonlike playrooms. Whips and chains appear to be a predominant theme and the idea of educating myself isn't working. I'm just plain freaking myself out. I try bondage and BDSM and it's pretty darn close to the same results.

Finally, I land on a site that highlights stories like "Toy with your lover" and contains links to products such as a pink fuzzy paddle and a pair of butterfly nipple clamps. Picturing Chris with anything involving the words *soft, pink,* and *butterfly* is almost comical.

My cell phone rings and with his usual perfect timing, it's Chris. I punch the answer button. "Hi."

"Hi."

The instant I hear his voice, the unease of moments before begins to uncurl and disappear, and I know it's simply because he is Chris. It's the only explanation I require anymore. My lips curve and I can tell he is smiling, too, and alas, that knowledge tears down any wall my unease over my Internet searches might have erected.

"What are you doing?" he asks.

My hesitation is all of two seconds, and considering how uneasy I'd been minutes before, my confession falls freely from my lips. "Eating macaroni and cheese and searching a site called Adam and Eve."

A low rumble of deep, sexy laughter fills the line and sets my blood to simmering. "Adam and Eve and macaroni and cheese. I wish I was there. See anything there you like?"

There is mischief in his voice and I can imagine the wicked dancing in the depth of his green eyes. "So you know the site?"

"Yes. I know the site."

This surprises me and I wonder if some other woman tried to soften his dark side by presenting him with the softer side of BDSM. Maybe one of the L.A. actresses I'd read about him dating before meeting him. It's an unpleasant thought for too many reasons to count and one that doesn't fit the puzzle that is Chris. "I find myself the least intimidated by pink furry paddles and a pair of butterfly nipple clamps. Nothing quite in your league."

"Don't decide for me," he orders, his voice going all low and rough, but still gently seductive. "Let's discover what works for us together. What made you start looking up sex toys anyway?"

"The painting."

"Of you in my studio."

"Yes. Of me. You wanted me to see it this morning and to-night." I don't phrase it as a question.

He's silent a moment, and I sense one of his shifting moods, the subtle edge of one of his many layers. "Yes. I wanted you to see it."

"To scare me?"

"Does it?"

I hesitate too long and he presses. "*Does* it scare you, Sara?"

"Is that what you're hoping for, Chris? To scare me away?"

Now he is silent too long and I am about to press him, when he dodges the question with a surprising revelation. "The painting isn't about bondage to me. It's about trust."

A lump forms in my throat at the thought of my secret, and the poison I cannot escape. "Trust?"

"The kind of trust I want from you and have no right to ask."

But I want him to ask. I want him to trust me. "I want the same from you."

More silence follows, too much silence, and I hate the distance that prevents me from reading him. "Where are you?" he asks finally.

"In the studio." And I tear down one of my walls to try to reach across one of his. "I wanted to be in the place that felt the closest to you."

"Sara." His voice is hoarse, like my name is an emotion, a raw burn, ripped from his throat. This is the intensity of what I create in him, and I am not sure he fully understands he creates the same intensity in me.

"Where are *you*?" I ask softly.

There is a moment of hesitation in which I sense he is relieved to have something to focus on instead of what he is feeling. "I'm in my hotel room, finally. Have you looked at the painting I did for Dylan, the kid I was telling you about?"

"No, not yet. You want me to?"

"Yes. Go look."

Any excitement I feel at discovering a new Chris Merit work is dashed by the solemness of the request. "Okay. Headed there now." I push to my feet and head to the back room, flipping on the light to the small fifteen-by-fifteen room where a few easels sit with clothes over the top. There is only one canvas uncovered and I laugh when I see it.

"Am I really looking at a painting of Freddy Krueger and Jason from *Friday the 13th*?"

He laughs but it's strained. "Yes. The kid is a horror freak. Do you know which one is which?"

"Aren't you funny? Of course I do."

"You didn't at the storage unit."

"Okay, so I mix up Michael and Jason sometimes, but I know Freddy by sight, because he scares the crap out of me. I have to say you've done a fine job of re-creating the reasons why in vivid color." I shiver at the sight of the cratered red and orange face. "Who knew you could craft a monster like you can a cityscape?"

"Apparently Dylan. I've drawn him a collection of those things on paper. This is the first on canvas." Any hint of the lighthearted Chris I often enjoy fades from his voice, turning to pure grim discomfort. "I think he likes horror movies because he's trying to seem brave. But I see the fear in his eyes. He doesn't want to die."

His words scrape a path down my spine, and I ache with this man who I am coming to know is so much more than pain and pleasure. "Just know you're helping make this part of his life better."

"But I will never erase the torture losing him is going to be for his parents."

A powerful rush of certainty washes over me. While I don't understand the depths of where his passion for this charity comes from, I am confident that Chris is trying to make up for some perceived sin of the past, be it subconsciously, or maybe, knowing what I do of him, consciously. And while it is an amazing cause that he is making a difference with, I fear where the pain he's experiencing is driving him. Will that pain, together with all the rest he has inside, drive him to the brink of disaster?

We end our call a few minutes later, and I lie back on the floor and stare at the tiny white stars painted on the ceiling, but I see the painting of me, and I hear Chris's claim it is symbolic of trust. He asked me if it scared me. Could it be that this powerful, confident, talented man is scared himself? And if so, of what?

Morning, and my 9 a.m. starting time at the gallery comes way too early despite my love for my new job, considering a second night of no sleep. Fortunately, Mark isn't in early, and my several stops by the coffeepot come without encounters.

By ten o'clock I'm jittery and on cup number three but the heaviness in my limbs persists. The "Master" has yet to show up to work. I'm reviewing information on Alvarez to prepare for the evening meeting when an e-mail from Mark hits my box, proving he's not sleeping late after all. Or he just got up, one or the other. It's short and sweet. I snort, Mark is anything but "sweet."

He's sent me a cheat sheet of topics and answers to wade successfully through small talk related to wine, opera, and classical music and allow me to impress clientele. The information is actually quite good and I wonder why he didn't give me this instead of insisting I had to learn these extensive topics in record-breaking time.

In contemplating this answer, the journal entry I'd slipped and read before locking them away in the safe comes to mind. I wonder what it would feel like to wake up feeling that passionate about life again, instead of just wondering what the new game will be. I don't want any part of his games and I hope this switch in Mark's approach to my work indicates I've established this with him.

By ten thirty, I've done a light review of the information from Mark and tried calling Ella three more times but I only get the fast busy signal. I take it a step further and call David's office again, frustrated when my needling the operator for information is unsuccessful. On top of that, I haven't talked to Chris. I have no idea why this bothers me. It's not like he has to call me when he starts his day and again I think maybe he hopes I'll call him. Or maybe he'd think I'm overbearing. I'm a mess when Mary stops by my door, looking as pale as her blond hair and my white suit-dress, but no less hostile as her gaze falls on me.

"You're not coming to the event tonight?"

"I have an off-site meeting."

"And I have the flu. What if I can't stay?"

Mary has snubbed me up to this point but she's never been

hostile, and my brow furrows. "It's with Ricco Alvarez about a large sale. I'd reschedule if I could, but I'm not sure he'll agree. If you're still sick and want me to try, I can."

"Ricco Alvarez," she repeats, and her lips thin. "Of course it is." She walks away.

I frown. What the heck?

Ralph walks into my office and puts a packet of papers on my desk. "An inventory listing with the price lists I create monthly." He lowers his voice, saying, "Steer clear of Mary when she's sick. She's been known to rip heads off and leave you bleeding."

"Thanks for the warning, but it's a little too late," I hiss softly.

"Better late than never."

"Not in this case, and why did she act funny about me seeing Alvarez?"

"She's ambitious and competitive and he wouldn't give her the time of the day before Rebecca or after."

"Why?"

"Her personality just doesn't jibe with certain people."

"But everyone says Alvarez is difficult."

"I guess that's why Bossman hires charmers like Rebecca and yourself. To get past the difficult to the payday. He knows Mary is a personality time bomb."

"Then why keep her?"

He glances over his shoulder and then back at me. "She was close to being fired after a blowup with Rebecca but she did some kick-butt scouting and found a couple of unpriced pieces Bossman snatched up for the next Riptide auction. She earned a safety pass."

"Wait. She's working with Riptide?"

"Oh no. Remember, I said she's a personality time bomb. She was told to hand over all the management of the pieces to Rebecca."

Amanda appears in the doorway. "The Riptide accountant is on the line for you."

Ralph pops to his feet and gives me an apologetic look. I watch him leave and my thoughts are going to bad places. How much did Mary hate Rebecca? How certain was she that getting rid of her would lead her to her career goals? I don't want to think about what that might mean for me.

My fingers press to the tightness at my temples and I massage. I'm worried about Rebecca. I'm worried about Ella. I don't know how to locate either of them. Heck, for the longest time, I don't think I even knew how to find myself, even when I was staring at myself in the mirror.

One thing I do know, though, is that all these things seem more doable with Chris in my life. I can't sit back and wait for us to crash and burn, but I feel like we are headed that way. I draw a heavy breath and accept that I have to talk to Chris, to lift more of the proverbial veil, and do so before I lose my courage.

Snatching my jacket from the back of my chair, I shove the papers into my briefcase, grab my phone and purse, and head out of my office toward the reception desk. I bring Amanda into focus and keep walking past her. "I'm going next door to get a mocha and study some work I was given, if Bossman is looking for me."

I start rehearsing different ways to approach Chris about what's on my mind before I've ever left the gallery, but the biting wind blasts coherent thoughts into oblivion. I push through it and enter the coffee shop, where I have mixed feelings about the young college guy behind the counter who takes my order, indicating Ava's absence. Picking her brain about Rebecca and Alvarez before tonight's meeting is on my agenda today, but at this moment, I can't think of anything but Chris anyway.

With more coffee I don't need, I settle into a corner table, slide out of my jacket, and retrieve my phone from the pocket. I take a deep breath and dial Chris. My pulse beats about ten times for every ring until his voice mail picks up. I don't leave a message and I'm officially sick to my stomach. I'm not touching my coffee.

My cell vibrates in my hand and I look down to see a text from Chris.

Hey baby. I had an early breakfast and didn't want to wake you up. At the hospital. Is everything okay?

My entire body feels lighter with his message and I type: Yes. Just wanted to talk. Call me when you get a break?

His reply is instant. Already planned to. Call you in about an hour.

Thanks, I reply automatically.

Thanks? You sure you're okay?

Yes. Too much caffeine. I hesitate and decide there is no in-between. Not enough you.

I'll make you prove that over and over when I get back.

I plan to, I respond and set my phone down, not expecting a reply or getting one.

My pleasure at the exchange should calm me down a bit, but it only sparks a heavier dose of nerves. Can I really tell him?

Ten

I'm staring at the clock, waiting for Chris's call, when Ava walks into the coffee shop. Needing a distraction from the circles I'm running in my head, I watch her pause by the coatrack at the door and peel off her jacket. She's in slim black slacks with a red blouse, and her tousled long, dark hair is striking as it cascades down her back. Maybe it's the numerous tables and displays separating us, but her skin, even just out of the harsh wind, appears a flawless milk chocolate.

Spotting me, Ava waves and heads toward my table. There is a casual confidence and grace about her that I admire immensely. I am confident that Ava would not spill her coffee as I had the first day I'd encountered Chris here at the coffee shop.

Ava slides into the seat in front of me and we exchange greetings. My laptop is occupying the small round table and I shut the lid, drawing her gaze to the papers in front of me. "More assignments from Mark?"

It hits me that she has just called him by name, and it throws me for a loop since no one else but Chris does. But then, what else would someone he's acquainted with, but not having sex with, call him?

"Yes," I confirm, and try to find an angle to discover how well Ava knew Rebecca. "I wonder if Rebecca went through this or if he's reserved the fun for me. He does seem to enjoy the irony of the schoolteacher doing homework."

Her lips lift. "Men do seem to have little schoolteacher fantasies, don't they?" she asks, leaving Rebecca out of the picture.

I grimace at the familiar comment. "In my experience, all the wrong men."

"I think you'll discover at least one man worthy of a fantasy or two. How's a certain sexy artist we both know and lust over?"

The sting of her question is instant. Silly as it might be when she's probably just making girl talk, saying the things girls say to each other about a hot man, jealousy flares inside me and I try unsuccessfully to squash it.

"Actually," I comment a bit hoarsely, eager to change the subject, "today I've got an artist on my mind all right. Have you met Ricco Alvarez?"

"I know him, yes. He used to stop by quite frequently and make small talk."

"Then you know he's not working with the gallery anymore?"

"Didn't he just do the charity event?"

"Yes, but apparently that was set up before Rebecca left. When she left, he left."

"Ouch. I bet Mark isn't happy about that, but Rebecca coddled Alvarez. I assume this is his form of throwing a fit."

"Rebecca coddled him?" I ask, hopeful I'm leading her to real answers.

"Well, that's what I gathered. I'm everyone's bartender during working hours. They grab some coffee and ramble. In Rebecca's case, she'd come in excited about this sale or that sale, which led us to talk about Ricco. She was protective of him, and seemed to get his artistic temperament when no one else did." She shivers. "It seemed a little weird. Almost like she had a father syndrome for him, when you know a man that, despite being in his forties and twenty years her senior, wasn't seeing her as a daughter."

She doesn't have to explain what she means. My father has a thing for women in exotic places not much older than I am. "I'm meeting with him tonight to try to talk him into some private showings. Anything I should be concerned about?"

Her big, dark brown eyes, a shade darker than mine, go wide. "You talked him into seeing you?"

"Yes, I—"

My phone rings and I forget everything else but checking the number and confirming Chris is calling. "I need to get this."

Her brows furrow and she seems a little put off. "Sure. We'll chat later."

"Thank you. I'm sorry. It's important." I push the button to accept the call but I glance at Ava, who is still a little too close. "Hold on one second, Chris." A quick look around and I'm excruciatingly aware of nearby customers, the small environment, and I wonder why I thought this was a good place to do this.

"Actually, I need to go somewhere I can talk freely. That is, if you have a few minutes?"

"Yes. Of course, I do." The deep, rich tone of his voice radiates through me, and despite my anxiety over the call, I shiver with awareness. This is the power this man has over me, and the prospect of losing him if this talk goes poorly is piercing.

I glance toward the door and quickly nix the idea of focusing in the chill outside, instead making a beeline for the single-stall bathroom, where I lock the door behind me. "Okay. Can you hear me?"

"I can," he says, "and why do you sound about as flustered as the night I called you and you'd just left the storage unit?"

"Because in a different way, I am," I surprise myself by confessing. "Are you somewhere you can talk?"

"Yes. What's wrong, Sara?"

"Nothing." I'm pacing the small space. "Not really. I just don't want there to be anything wrong, Chris. And I better warn you that I'm going to ramble. That's what I do when I'm nervous."

"You don't have to be nervous with me. Not ever. Just say what's on your mind, and sooner than later, before you're making me insane trying to guess what's going on."

"I will. I am. I—well, I've had pink paddles and butterflies on my mind and—"

"We don't have to do anything you don't want to do."

"I know and that's the point. Or not really the point." Here comes the rambling. "The real point is that you'd take me to pink paddle and butterfly land, but you aren't pink paddles and butterflies. You're leather and pain and darkness."

"That's how you see me, Sara?"

"That's who you are, Chris, and I like who you are and that means I need to be those things, too."

"Sara—"

"Please let me finish before I can't." My knees wobble and I lean against the wall. "I've let fear of failure hold me back for all kinds of reasons that are too complicated to explain at this moment, and I'm not sure I really understand fully myself, but I'm trying. I don't want to let it hold me back now, so I'm just going to say what's on my mind without even taking a breath here. I know I said I'm not about white picket fences, and I'm not, and never will be, but I can't imagine being without you, either. What that means to me is that I need to go where you need me to go. And don't tell me you don't need anything but me. I wish that were true and it means a lot when you say it, but you have a way you deal with life, a place you go to escape. Everything from the painting, the club, the way you are in general, tells me that. I don't want someone else to be there when you need those things. I want it to be me. I want you to trust me not to run." I stop talking and the dead space afterward is unbearable and I can barely contain an urge to fill it with more words. "Chris, damn it, say something. I'm dying here."

"And what if you can't handle it?" No denial of what I've said.

There is a sudden, crushing pressure in my chest. This is what he is scared of, what he fears. That I can't handle all that he is. "We both need to know if I can. I don't want us to unravel and have to wonder if it's because I didn't try."

"You can't."

"Okay," I say hoarsely, and the pressure intensifies painfully. "Then I guess that's that."

"What does that mean?"

"It means you already know I'm not what you need. I know I'm not what you need. Let's not drag this out any longer than we have to. I'm going to pack, and—"

"No. You are not going to pack. You are not going to leave. Not after the storage unit incident."

My insecurity sends my hand to my throat. Had he meant to break it off with me but the storage incident stopped him? "You don't owe me a safe place to stay. I don't need charity protection, Chris."

"That's not what I meant. Damn it, Sara, I don't want you to leave."

I hurt. He is all about pain and now I am, too. "Want, need. Right, wrong. They all just make me one big mess and I am tired of being one big mess, Chris. We, this, us—it's all going to destroy me if we go on like this."

"You are going to destroy me if you leave me, Sara."

More pain. His pain this time. It radiates through his words and insinuates itself deep in my soul, like he has. And in that moment, I believe he needs me as I do him. "I don't want to leave," I whisper.

"Then don't." His voice is a soft plea, exposing the rare vulnerable side of him I find so impossible to resist. "I'll come home tonight and we'll figure this out together."

"No," I say quickly. "Don't do that. That you want to is enough. I'll be here when you get home. I promise. I'll be here."

"I can fly back there tomorrow morning."

"No, please. Don't. What you're doing there is too important and I work late tonight anyway."

"I'm coming home." A distant voice calls his name and he adds, "I have to go. I may not be able to call you again but I'll see you when I get there."

"I'm not going to talk you out of this, am I?"

"Not a chance."

We say a short good-bye forced on us by someone calling him again, and when I hear the phone go dead, I let my head fall backward to the wooden surface of the door behind me. I am far too happy that Chris is putting himself through hell to see me tonight, and he is far too willing to let it happen. What are we doing to each other? And why can't either of us stop?

After pulling myself together, I step out of the bathroom and a prickling of awareness brings me to a halt. My gaze lifts, seeking the source. My throat tightens at the sight of Mark standing in profile to me at the counter to the right of the register, talking with Ava. I can't see his face, but Ava does not look happy, even less so when Mark leans in closer, intimately close to her ear, to finish whatever he is saying. There is more to their relationship than I had thought and I wonder if I know any of these people at all.

Ava's eyes lift and find mine, and I realize I'm not only staring, but have been caught. I tear my attention away and rush to my table, feeling Mark's gaze on me, intense and heavy. I wonder if everyone else here understands that the power charging the air is him claiming the room simply by existing, or if they just feel the unidentified crackle I did upon exiting the bathroom.

I gather my things at my table, preparing to explain why I'm here instead of at the gallery. It should surprise me that Mark doesn't approach me at my table but it doesn't. Of course, he's building the tension, ensuring I squirm for his enjoyment. It's a familiar method of control to me, or rather, used on me, that fits Mark like a glove. It used to fit me as well, but not anymore. I've come a long way toward understanding and even seeing the positive in Mark today. Understanding doesn't mean liking all that I see, though, and I don't right now.

It's not until I am almost at the door of the coffee shop that he appears at my side. Towering over me, he opens the door; his eyes dark, filled with the never-ending challenge he offers me. "I was afraid you'd gone MIA like Rebecca, Ms. McMillan."

I blink up at him and the past few weeks have done something to my self-censorship. I seem to have none left in me. "I told Amanda where I was going. And besides, I'm not that easy to get rid of." I push open the door and steel myself for the wind that smacks me in the face as I step outside. Mark steps to my side about the same time the double, or even triple meanings that could be taken from my words, hit me. If he'd killed Rebecca, he might think I was saying he couldn't kill me off, too, but I don't think that Mark killed Rebecca. He just fucked her. In all kinds of ways. I've potentially just undone all I established with him by issuing him an invitation to give me a try and promising I won't run.

I stop walking and turn to face him. "I didn't mean that the way you might have taken it."

His dark stare lightens with amusement. "I know, Ms. McMillan. But do remember it's a woman's prerogative to change her mind."

"Somehow, I find it hard to believe you'd let any woman think for herself enough to do that."

"You might be surprised what I would let the right woman do."

Heat rushes to my cheeks. "I don't intend—"

He laughs, low and deep, and I'm taken off guard. I'm not sure I've ever heard him laugh. "I'm aware you don't intend to do many things I'd like you to."

I open my mouth to protest even having this conversation, but he cuts me off by adding, "And no, I'm not going to pressure you." He turns me toward the gallery. "Let's get back to the gallery. I left you a little gift on your desk."

Thankfully, my back is to him, so he can't see me react to his words. Mark has succeeded in doing what only Chris has done before this. He's sent me into an adrenaline rush of anticipation and I can barely keep my pace slow and even. I don't know what to expect. A rare piece of art? An official job offer? The possibilities are many.

I expect Mark to follow me to my office, but again, he is unpredictable. I'm relieved, certain that the less Mark sees me react and the less he knows what makes me tick, the better. The instant I walk into my office, I freeze. Lying on top of my desk is a journal that matches the ones I've locked away in Chris's safe.

Eleven

The journal Mark left for me is sitting in my lap as I drive to Alvarez's Victorian mansion in San Francisco's ritzy Nob Hill area, sometimes referred to as Snob Hill. Just ten minutes from the Allure Gallery, it's here that the rich and famous are plentiful, and aside from mansions galore, the nearby shopping and theater districts cater to the elite. I've gone from avoiding the things that remind me of the money I left behind to drowning in it.

I maneuver into the driveway, which is remarkably unre-markable, but with a city less than forty-seven square miles, even here it's expected. What space doesn't allow on the outside is made up for with glamour on the inside. Since my Google search for directions brought up references to a renowned architect, I'm quite certain this one is not the exception.

Once I kill the engine of the 911, I stare at the red door of the house, my teeth worrying my bottom lip. I am not drown-ing, I remind myself. I'm taking control of my life. I'm no longer hiding. I'm no longer in denial. I have a meeting with the famous, talented Ricco Alvarez. So why the heck am I not hopping out of the car, when it's five minutes until my meeting and being early makes a good impression?

My fingers wrap around the journal I've found to be both a treasure and a disappointment. It is far from the dark and revealing view into Rebecca's soul that are the other journals. It's a detailed accounting of every piece of work she ever sold or evaluated for Riptide. The most revealing things are her short insights into the staff, buyers, sellers, and artists that she has encountered and their personality quirks, interests, and history.

Her notes about Chris are scribbled out and no matter how I try, I cannot make them out, though I'm not surprised about the various art he's sold through Riptide to benefit the children's hospital. I can't think about that now, though. I have to conquer this meeting with success, despite the unease inside me I have no real reason to feel. Rebecca's notes were positive on Alvarez. Generally misunderstood, and while motivated by money and success, he has proven generous in tremendous ways.

I'm close to the gallery. I'm supposed to call Mark after my meeting. People know where I am. But . . . I don't want to be stupid. What if Mark and Alvarez are the two men in the journal?

I grab my phone out of my purse and hit the auto-dial I've programmed for Jacob. He answers on the first ring. "Everything okay, Ms. McMillan?"

"Yes. Completely fine. I just . . . want to make sure it stays that way. I'm probably being paranoid, but . . ."

"Paranoid is better than careless."

I have no idea how much he knows about Rebecca or what

I have going on, but I don't think it matters anyway. "I'm headed into a business meeting and my boss knows where I am, but in light of recent incidents, I'd like someone else to know as well."

"What's the address?"

"It's the private gallery for the artist Ricco Alvarez," I explain after reciting the address. "I'm not sure how long the meeting will be. It could be fifteen minutes or two hours. If it's short I'll head back to an event going on at the gallery."

"Can you check in in an hour to let me know you're okay?"

"I'll try, but I don't want to be rude in the meeting."

"Just text me if you can. That's discreet."

"Right. Okay. Thanks, Jacob." I hesitate and cringe, imagining the moment Jacob tells Chris where I'm at. "Jacob. Don't tell Chris where I'm at while he's traveling. He'll worry. He's had a horrible trip and I don't want him to stress out any more than he already has."

"If he asks, I have to tell him, but . . . I won't go out of my way to announce it."

"Thank you very much, Jacob."

"My pleasure, Ms. McMillan, and I mean that. Chris seems different with you around."

It is the same thing his godmother had said to me when we'd visited her winery. "Is that good?"

"It is. Be safe."

"I will." *I hope.* I say good-bye and hang up. Not giving myself time to fret, I grab my briefcase, get out of the car, and head for the door. My phone goes in my jacket pocket, where I keep it out of habit.

Several flights of stairs later, I'm standing at the top of the porch, relieved to find two entries, one of which is marked STUDIO. This setup is comforting and feels safer and more professional. I lift my hand to knock on the studio entry and the door flies open to reveal Ricco Alvarez. He is striking, not handsome by any means, but there is this arrogant confidence about him that comes across as more suave than belligerent. His skin is a rich brown, his features sharp and defined, like the touch of his brush, and from what I've heard, his personality.

"Welcome, Ms. McMillan."

"Sara," I say. His teal business shirt, which he's paired with his black slacks, accents eyes the same bright color. "And thank you."

"Sara," he replies with a gracious nod of his head, and the tension in my spine eases just a bit with the use of my name.

He backs up to allow me to pass and my gaze lifts to the massive all-glass ceilings. "Spectacular, isn't it?" Ricco asks.

"It is," I agree, letting him take my briefcase and jacket. "And so is the floor." The pale, shiny wood is almost too brilliant to walk on. "You artists have a way of delivering drama."

He hangs my things on a fancy steel rack mounted on the wall. "Some would say me more so than others."

Considering all the talk about him, I'm surprised at his smile and I like that he can joke about himself. "I've heard that," I dare to reply, my lips curving.

"At least I have people talking." He motions me forward. "Welcome to my studio, Bella."

Bella. Beautiful in Spanish. An endearment should make my unease more powerful. Instead, I instantly believe he tries to romanticize everything from his dramatic home to his conversation.

We walk side by side through an archway at least seven feet high, and he dominates the space, being well over six feet himself. The space comes into view and it's like I'm back at Allure. The narrow, rectangular room has several elegant display walls, and at least six paintings on every wall.

Alvarez steps to my side and motions to the room. "These are the pieces that I have at present and will allow for private sales."

I glance up at him and state what I guess to be the truth. "The ones you're willing to show me at this point in time, you mean."

"You are direct, aren't you?"

"Just eager to see every amazing piece of your work you will let me see." I wave my hand toward the art. "Can I?"

"Of course."

My path forward is instant and it's a beeline for a painting on the far right of the room. I stop in front of the Picasso-like Mediterranean landscape, with sharp lines and dynamic colors, and I'm in sensory overload.

"You like the *Meredith*?" he asks.

"I love it," I say and cut him a sideways look. "Why do you call it *Meredith*?

"A woman I once knew, of course."

"I'm sure she's honored."

"She hates me, but alas, there is a fine line between love and hate."

"Then you and Mark must be darn near in love," I comment, baiting him to tell me about his reasons for pulling his work from the gallery.

His eyes light with amusement. "You are quite the character, Bella. I like you. I see why Mark likes you."

"How do you know he does?"

"Because he trusted you enough to send you here and he wants my business back."

"Why'd he lose it?"

"Why did he tell you he lost it?"

"He said that you wanted Rebecca's contact information and he couldn't give it to you."

Disdain fills his eyes. "There is much more to it than that, and Mark knows it."

"I'd like to hear."

"I'm sure you would," he says, and for the first time I catch a sharpness to his voice that makes me believe he's capable of cutting flesh and blood with words. "But out of respect for Rebecca, I won't be sharing more."

"I'm sorry. I didn't mean to be inappropriate."

I watch the tension slide away from his features, and the steel of seconds before is gone. "Forgive me, Bella. Rebecca is a touchy subject for me. Now, why don't we walk through the paintings and let me tell you about each?"

My moment for digging for information is lost, but I hope to find another one. We begin moving around the room, and I ask questions and gush over his work. In between my questions, I answer questions from him as well. "Who's your favorite Renaissance artist?" "How do you ensure you aren't buying a fake?" "What have been the top five bestselling paintings in the last five years?" After a bit, he looks pleased at my answers and our talk turns more casual.

After I have seen that three of his paintings are named after women, I cannot help but comment on the trend. "You must be quite the lady's man."

"I've been called worse," he assures me, "and perhaps I am guilty as charged. I guess it depends on who is defining what constitutes a lady's man."

The statement strikes me as true beyond its intention. How many of us allow others to define us and thus we become what they want us to be, not what we should be or could be?

We continue to chat about the art and I've lost track of time when finally we have finished our tour of his work. "You're impressively knowledgeable, Bella."

This time I don't try to control the curve of my lips. "Glad to hear you think so. I don't know who drilled me harder about my knowledge of art, you or Mark."

His eyes narrow. "Does he let you call him Mark?"

I cringe inside at my slip. "Ah, no. Mr. Compton."

"Of course he doesn't." The snideness to his tone is hard to miss. "My friends call me Ricco, Sara, and so shall you."

"Does this mean you will let me show your work to my client?" I ask hopefully.

"You may show my work. Mark may not. I'll give you a private commission of twenty-five percent. Mark I will give nothing."

I blanch and every muscle in my body locks up. He's using me to get back at Mark for some sin he perceives he's committed against him. "I can't do that. I work for him. That wouldn't be right."

"Mark is out for Mark. You'll learn that soon enough or

you'll end up crushed like everyone else around him. Don't let that happen, Bella."

I'm desperate to get this meeting back under control and reach for a way to mend his and Mark's relationship. "Didn't you do a charity event with Mark? That was a good thing you did together. What if we started out with something like that again?"

"Rebecca set that up, and I can donate my work for a good cause through many venues. I chose to do it at Allure because Rebecca asked me to." He changes the subject back to his offer. "Let me show you how to scout and sell on your own."

"I appreciate the offer, but—"

"Don't let him suck you into his world. It's dangerous and so is he."

What is it about artists warning me off Mark? "Unless he brings a machete to work," I joke weakly, "I can handle him.

"Men like Mark do not need machetes to dice your independence and self-respect. They mind-fuck you."

No matter how true his claim might ring, I feel it like a slap, and I barely stop myself from taking a step backward. "I should go, but please know that I love your work. I mean that. I'd be honored to represent it."

"And you can. You and you alone."

"I'm not going to do that."

He studies me for several tense seconds and waves me forward. "Very well. I'll show you to the door and let you go home and think on this."

We walk side by side again, and when I'm ready to exit the studio, he reaches for my coat and helps me put it on. Immediately I feel my pocket vibrating. Oh crap. How much time has passed? I slide my briefcase onto my shoulder and my hand slips into my pocket. I close my fingers around my cell, cringing because I've failed to communicate with Jacob.

Alvarez pauses with his hand on the doorknob. "It's been a pleasure to meet you, even if the outcome wasn't what either of us had hoped for."

"I'm going to try to get your business again, you know."

"I know."

He opens the door for me and I step outside, and we say a quick good-bye. I'm about to start for the stairs when a question comes to mind that has me hesitating on the porch. The charity event he did at Allure was for the same children's hospital Chris champions, but since they don't seem to be friends, I'm curious about how this came about. I turn to the door to knock and my phone buzzes against my palm again.

I pull it from my pocket and see a text alert and six missed calls. I hit the text from Chris.

Don't go back in that door.

My heart leaps to my throat and I whirl around to scan the driveway. A shadowy movement draws my eyes and I see the Harley parked in the shadows behind the 911, with Chris leaning against it.

Twelve

I start down the stairs of Alvarez's house and my chest is so tight it feels like I have the damn art tape Chris seems to love binding me with around my ribs, and around my control over my own life. I'm furious that he's here. I'm embarrassed that Alvarez most assuredly has cameras and will know about this, if not now, then at some point. The line in the sand between my job and our relationship is beyond blurred. In fact, I'm pretty darn sure I'm the only one who'd imagined it ever existed.

The idea that I've convinced myself he is less controlling than he is has my heels colliding heavily on the driveway. I charge toward the 911, the car I've let myself drive instead of holding on to my own identity. I don't look at Chris but damn him, I can feel him all over, everywhere, inside and out, and in intimate places I can't convince my body he isn't welcome. It's beyond frustrating to know that anger this potent isn't enough to stop the thrum of awareness that just being near him creates.

Not for the first time, I feel Rebecca's words from that first journal entry I'd read deep in my soul. *He was lethal, a drug I feared.* I relate to her, and I understand the inescapable passion she felt and lost herself inside. I don't want to be her. I'm not her. And for the first time since my initial first few encounters with Chris, I wonder if I am drawn to him because I'm self-destructive, and he to me for the same reason.

I reach the side of the car and in my haste to seek the shelter of the 911, I haven't retrieved the key. Without looking at Chris, I fumble with my key. I know he will be standing by his Harley, all decked out in leather and denim, looking like sex and sin and my satisfaction. The key falls on the ground. I squat to retrieve the key and my composure.

Suddenly Chris is there, at eye level, as he had been the first night we'd met, when I'd spilled my purse. My gaze lifts and meets his, and a blast of awareness shakes me to the core. My breasts are heavy, my thighs achy. My skin tingles. A fine line between love and hate, Alvarez had said, and I understand them in this moment. I stare into his eyes and I wonder if he too is thinking about the night we met and the many ways we've made love. The many we have not and I want us to, when I should not. I should be seeking space, independence, and my own identity, which he is threatening by taking over my life. It makes no sense how I feel in these eternal moments. How can I be this furious with Chris and still powerfully, completely lost in him?

"We have a lot to talk about, don't we?" he asks, breaking the spell. His tone is low, and the rasp of anger in his voice is impossible to miss. It jolts me back to reality. He showed up at my client's house and *he's* angry with *me*?

My temper overpowers all other emotions in me and I reach for the key. His hand closes over mine and heat races up my arm and over my chest. "Don't do what you did tonight ever again, Sara."

The sharp command in his voice hits a bull's-eye on every physiological male dominance issue I own, of which there are many. I try to pull my hand back but I am captive to his grip, leaving me with words as my only weapon. "Ditto to you, Chris. And yeah. We have a lot to talk about—somewhere *other* than my client's front yard."

His green eyes glint fire a moment before he releases my hand and helps me to my feet. There is a possessiveness to his touch that has me leaning into him when I should be shoving him away. He notices, too; I see it in the slight narrowing of his eyes, the gleam of satisfaction in their depths that I both hunger for and reject.

"I'll follow you to my place," he informs me.

"I have no doubt you will." I click the key clicker to unlock the 911. I'm about to open the door when his hand comes down on it, and he leans close, so close his breath is warm on my neck and ear. That woodsy scent of him, which I could luxuriate in for a lifetime, permeates my senses, tearing down my already weak defenses.

His hip nudges mine. "Don't think for a minute that when we pull up to my apartment, you're going to ask for your car and leave."

It is all I can do to fight him when he touches me. Purposely, I do not look at him, certain all my resolve to distance myself from him will crumble. "If I decide to leave, you can't stop me."

"Try me, baby. You're coming up to my apartment."

I whirl on him. "I don't want—"

"I do," he vows, and before I know his intent, his fingers twine into my hair and he pulls me into his arms, against his hard, warm body.

"Let go," I hiss, my hand flattening on his chest. I intend to push him away, but the heat of his body seeps through my palm, radiating up my arm. My elbow softens, and I am instantly closer but not close enough.

"Not a chance," he promises, his mouth closing on mine, firm with demand. His tongue licks into my mouth with one brutal, commanding swipe followed by another, and I have no resistance left. I'm weak, so very weak, for this man. As always with Chris, he demands my response and I helplessly respond. I am instantly wet and wanting, my nipples tight points of aching need.

I try to resist the lure that is Chris, but the taste of him, familiar and almost brutally male, mixes with his anger and mine, and the effect is explosively passionate. I want to shout at him, push him away, pull him close, strip away his clothes, and punish him for what he is doing to me, what he takes from me. What he makes me need.

When his lips part from mine, too soon and not soon enough, I barely fight the urge to pull him back. "Was that for the cameras, Chris?" I pant at him, furious at myself for such weakness.

"That was because you scared the shit out of me when you didn't answer your phone. I don't give a damn about the cameras." His mouth comes down on mine again, and his hand slides under my jacket, over my backside, pulling me flush against his thick erection.

I whimper, impossibly aroused, and my hands slip beneath the thick leather of his jacket, wrapping his waist. His hand caresses up my back, molding me tighter to him, branding me with heat and fire and sizzling passion that threaten to steal all the reason I possess. No man has ever made me forget where I am, forget why I should care.

"That," he says roughly, when he pulls back again, "was for the past twelve hours that I should have been thinking about business. Instead, I was incessantly thinking about pink paddles, butterfly nipple clamps, and all the places I'm going to lick, kiss, and now, you can bet, punish you when we get home."

I almost moan again from his words and have no idea how I manage enough coherent thought to issue a warning, but somehow I do. "If you think sex is going to make this argument go away, you're wrong."

"You couldn't be more right, but it's a good place to start and end the enlightening conversation you can bet your sweet little ass we're going to have." He sets me back from him and away from the door enough to open it. "Let's go home where I can fuck what you've made me feel out of my system and you can do the same."

Staring up at him, a million things I might say or do are wiped out by the word *home* replaying in my head. He keeps using that word, and it affects me when he does; it affects me in a deep, painfully real way that leaves me raw and vulnerable. *He* leaves me raw and vulnerable.

When I don't move, he pulls me close again, caresses my

hair, and gives me a quick kiss on the lips. "Get in the car, Sara," he orders softly, and as always—though I'm fairly certain he'd disagree—I do as he tells me.

When I pull up to Chris's building ten minutes later, I'm still practically panting from his hot assault, but I've managed small pieces of reasonable thought. I am calmer and the understanding that Chris was truly, sincerely worried about me is as much an aphrodisiac as the taste of him lingering on my lips and tongue. There is no question that I gave Jacob reason to worry about me. Add the storage unit incident to my failure to answer calls, and Chris had every reason to be concerned. I can accept that. But Chris is a control freak in every possible way, and while I've found that in private giving him that control has almost become a physical burn, outside the bedroom I need my freedom. And I'm not sure Chris is capable of giving me that.

The doorman opens the door to the 911, and the last remnant of my anger flees into the chill of the night. I need Chris. I need to be in his arms. I need to feel him close. I need and need and need with this man and it's impossible to escape.

I step outside the car, and my hungry gaze seeks Chris, finding him dismounting the Harley, and holy hell, he *is* sex on a Harley. If Mark is power, Chris is absolute dominance, and he knows it. I see it in his casual grace, which manages to be alpha roughness at the same time. He doesn't need people to call him by a certain name, nor intimidate them into drinking cold coffee like Mark once did to me. When he needs power, he has it. When he wants it, he claims it. When he wants me, he claims me, and my stomach clenches with dread at the idea that one day he won't.

He hands his helmet and keys to a second doorman before his attention shifts fully to me. Pure, white hot lust pours off Chris and over me, and I can't move from the impact. He saunters toward me, all loose-legged swagger, and when Rich hands me my briefcase, Chris takes it instead and slides the strap over my shoulder. His fingers caress my arm and my jacket is no defense for the electricity his touch ignites inside me.

"Let's go inside and . . . talk," he murmurs and I swallow hard.

"Yes. Let's go talk."

We've made it all of two steps when I hear the doorman call out, "Don't forget this." He appears in front of me and hands me the journal.

My breath lodges in my throat as my eyes go to Chris, and his gaze lands on the red leather I now hold. Eternal seconds tick by in which I know I should explain, but some part of me must secretly want to be punished, because I wait for his reaction. Finally, his gaze lifts to mine, and there are accusations and doubt in his eyes that shred my heart. I confessed my slip about the journal entry and instead of my honesty winning me his trust, it's earned me the opposite. It is all I can do not to explode right here in this moment, with eyes on us, and I draw a deep breath and clamp down on my reaction. Making a scene isn't my style and it won't give me more than momentary satisfaction.

I call out to Rich and turn to catch him. "I need my car," I tell him.

"No," Chris says, his voice low and lethal, his hand shackling my upper arm. "She doesn't."

I blast him with a look meant to flatten him but find myself captured by his sharp, commanding stare. "I promise you, Sara," he says, his voice low and intense, "I'll carry you upstairs over my shoulder if I have to."

Momentarily, I'm disarmed by the thrill that shoots through me at the threat. I am wet and hot and aching to be over his shoulder and in his apartment, naked and at his mercy. His distrust cuts me deeply, yet I'm thrilled at the barbaric statement that proves I am without defenses where he is concerned.

I hold his stare, and I don't doubt he means his words. "I'll go up, but I'm not staying."

He doesn't blink or respond immediately; he's studying me, sizing me up, and I wonder if he can see my reaction to his threat in my face, if I am as transparent as the window he'd once fucked me against.

Without a word, he releases me and I start for the door. He falls into step with me. My fingers curl around the journal and I remind myself of his distrust and my stomach knots at the idea that, even if not about this, I deserve what he feels. I'm getting a tiny taste of what it will feel like if and when he knows the real lie I've told, and I don't like it. I feel an eruption building inside me, emotions boiling in a wild mixture, hot and dangerous, that I can barely contain.

We enter the building and Jacob is at the front desk. I manage a nod and a small greeting. Chris and I step into the elevator side by side, and face forward, only inches separating us. The air is thick with unspoken words, the tension certain to snap any second.

Without making a conscious decision to act, that second comes for me when the doors slide closed. I whirl on Chris and shove the journal at his chest. "Mark gave this to me today.

It's Rebecca's business notes. I told you I locked up the damn journals, and I *did*."

He shackles my wrist and pulls me close. The journal lodges between us. "Do you know how much I don't want to hear Mark's name right now? He shouldn't have let you go to Alvarez's alone."

His words are tight, laced with the anger he'd confessed back at Alvarez's house, and I now realize he's been carefully controlling his fury. I feel it in the tightness of his body against mine, see it in the hard glint in his eyes. Everything about Chris is wrapped around control and I forget too easily.

"He's my boss." My bottom lip trembles with the words. "He's not my keeper, and for that matter neither are you."

His green eyes glint with amber blades of pure steel. "I told you, Sara. I will keep you safe."

There is a possessive absoluteness to his words that both arouses and infuriates me. I am once again struck by how little I seem to know about myself and why I respond to this side of Chris. "The line between protecting me and controlling me, Chris, is my job."

"Ask me if I care about the lines right now, Sara. Ask me if I have any intention of ever living the hell I lived tonight when you wouldn't answer the phone."

I am taken aback by the deep, vehement reply that is laced with a threat I do not understand. "What does that mean?"

His fingers twine into my hair and he pulls my mouth just beyond his, so close I can almost taste the control he holds so easily. "It means," he rasps, "that tonight, Sara, I'm not pink paddles and fluff, and neither are you."

Thirteen

The elevator door dings open, and Chris grabs my hand and pulls me into his apartment. Before I can blink, I'm facing the entry room wall, one hand clutching the journal, the other flat on the surface in front of me. Chris steps behind me, framing my body with his bigger one, and I feel the hardness of his body as intensely as I feel the hardness of his mood.

His hand settles on the center of my back, branding me, controlling me, and he pulls my bag and purse from my shoulder and dumps it on the floor. I feel him shrug away his jacket and he reaches for mine. It catches on the journal and his hand closes around it.

The air seems to thicken and for several seconds we hold the journal, both our fingers gripping the red leather. Erotic images created by Rebecca's words play in my mind and I remember reading one of the entries with Chris. I wonder if he is thinking about that day, too, or something completely different. About

Rebecca perhaps? I want to ask, but there is this sharp pinch in my chest that holds me back.

Chris takes the journal from me and I have no idea where he puts it. It is gone and my jacket follows. He steps behind me, and I forget everything but him. His hands settle possessively on my hips, and his mouth, that delicious, sometimes brutal mouth, brushes my ear. "You want pain and darkness, baby, you got it."

Shock slides through me at the unexpected promise and I think of us holding the journal, and of the dark entries inside that terrify and intrigue me. "What happened to me not being able to handle this part of you, Chris?" I ask, and my voice trembles with the question.

"Tonight happened," he replies and there is nothing unsure about his voice, just hard steel and more anger. "And I damn sure want to give you a reason to think twice before it repeats."

Conflicting emotions overcome me. I crave and resist the possessiveness I sense in him. I'm jerked out of this thought when Chris yanks my dress up my hips, exposing my backside. I hear the silk of my panties tear before I feel the bite of the material ripping from my body. His hands caress my backside, and the edgy tension in him is like a wave crashing into me.

He leans in, his lips brushing my ear, hot breath fanning my skin, promising delicious, forbidden fantasies only Chris can fulfill. "I'm going to spank you before this night is over, Sara."

His words are a velvety seduction and taut threat and I cannot catch my breath, let alone form a coherent reply. Chris turns me to face him, shoving my hands over my head and shackling them with one of his. "But first, I'm going to take you to the edge of bliss and pull you back so many times, you'll think you're going insane, just like I was when you didn't answer your phone." He tugs down the front zipper of my dress to my waist, unhooks my bra, and begins to tease one of my nipples. "Any objections?"

"Would they matter?" I whisper, waves of pleasure washing over my body.

"Not unless you tell me to stop what I'm doing." He leans in and nips my lip as he had the night before, laving the bite with his tongue. "But if you say stop, Sara, make damn sure you mean it because I will stop. Understand?"

"Chris—"

"Answer, Sara." His fingers slide between my thighs, spreading the slick heat of my sensitive flesh, and leaving my nipples aching for more. I have the distinct impression he's reminding me why *stop* is a bad word.

"Yes," I pant. "Yes, I understand."

His thumb strokes my clit and he slips two fingers inside me, filling me, stretching me. I pant with the pleasure, imagining the moment he is inside me. "Come before I tell you to, and I'll spank you right now."

"What?" I gasp. "I can't—"

"You can and you will."

His words are as powerful as his touch, and I feel the bittersweet build of release. "Why do I get the idea you'd enjoy my failure?"

"Because I want to spank you." His lips brush mine, his fingers stroking me with slow, sultry precision that is driving me wild. "And you want me to."

I do and I have no clue why but the certainty that he will is so intensely erotic that my sex tightens around his fingers. The beginning of an orgasm is almost as alluring as his hand on my backside.

His fingers are suddenly gone, denying my pleasure, and I growl my frustration. "Damn you, Chris."

"Damn me all you want but you still won't come until I say you come." He strokes my nipple and flicks it back and forth. "I'm going to release your wrists and you will not move them. Understand?"

No, I do not understand! But I nod my agreement, certain that doing as he says is my only path to satisfaction.

His hand teasing my nipple falls away and he studies me, seeming to assess my willpower, or maybe just torturing me with the absence of his hands on my body. I'm ready to scream with the injustice of it when he sinks to one knee in front of me and his hands settle on my hips.

His gaze lifts and snags mine and I want to order his mouth to the most intimate part of my body. Slowly, his mouth lowers, not to the spot I crave him to be, but to my stomach. The soft, seductive touch of his lips, followed by the gentle stroke of his tongue, sends a shiver through me and my belly quivers beneath his mouth. The contrast of how tender he is in one moment and how hard and demanding he can be in the next fills me with anticipation and is as arousing as anything I've ever experienced.

Slowly, he trails his lips over the tender skin, his tongue dipping into my navel, tracing my hip bone, and finally traveling to just above the V of my legs.

I am breathing hard with the restraint I use to stop myself from reaching for him, and the muscles of my sex clench so tightly it hurts. "Chris," I plead when I can take no more.

He rewards my urgency by licking my clit. Yes, please, more, I think, but do not dare say out loud, for fear he will do the opposite. I moan and another lick follows and it's nothing shy of sweet bliss when his mouth closes down around me. He suckles my swollen nub, drawing deeply on my sensitive flesh and using his tongue at just the right moments until I am going insane. Sensations ripple through me and I have no willpower, no control. I tumble into orgasm and he immediately pulls his mouth from me, denying me full satisfaction, leaving my muscles clenching in partial release.

My knees buckle but he is on his feet, wrapping his arm around my waist, and holding me up. He lifts me into his arms and starts walking toward his bedroom. His words replay in my head. *Come before I tell you to, and I'll spank you right now.* Chris doesn't say anything he doesn't mean, and my heart races at the certainty of my punishment.

Fourteen

Chris carries me into his bedroom and I find I am far more aroused than fearful of the spanking. I am too lost in my desire to crawl inside the deep, dark secrets that are Chris Merit, to care. This look inside his psyche is what I have craved, what I thought would take much longer to discover. I'm fully aware that his anger, and his possessive need to protect me, have opened a door to his darker side, and I revel in my ability to create such things in him. I'm not beyond seeing how our responses to each other reflect how damaged and messed up we both are, but I choose not to care right now.

Chris sets me down in the center of the room with the side of the bed to my back and the bathroom directly in front of me. I catch a glimpse of myself in the mirror. My dress is gaping at the top and the bottom is at my waist, leaving me exposed and looking ridiculously not sexy.

Attempting to tug it down, Chris comes to my aid, shoving

the straps to my dress and bra down my shoulders and over my hips. The material pools at my feet, leaving me in nothing but thigh-highs and high heels.

I step out of my clothes and Chris catches me around the waist, his strong arms encasing me, and I melt into the hard lines of his body. He lifts me, kicks my clothes away, and slowly eases me back to the ground without releasing me.

Our eyes meet and hold, and there is no mistaking the predatory gleam in his, or the anticipation charging the air between us. "I told you not to come until you had permission," he murmurs, his voice husky, affected.

I scrape my bottom lip nervously. "I've never been good at following rules."

His eyes glint with amber flecks. "I'm quite aware of that. And I might just enjoy it more than if you did."

My fingers curl around his shirt. "Because you want to spank me?" I ask, cutting my gaze, embarrassed by my own question.

His finger slides under my chin, forcing me to look at him. "And you want me to."

"I . . . I don't know what I want."

He turns me to face the bed, his hand settling possessively on my stomach, and the thick ridge of his erection nuzzles my backside. "Then it's time you find out." His voice is a seductive purr and his lips brush my shoulder, sending a shiver down my spine. "Don't turn around."

My panic is instant. "But—"

"You'll know before it happens," he promises, and his hands travel a path from my waist to my bare backside, where he caresses and lightly smacks one cheek.

I yelp at the unexpected sensation and I hear the soft rumble of his deep, sexy laughter vibrate through me from behind. He is no longer angry, no longer driven by the emotion I thought was dictating his actions, and yet he still intends to spank me. I don't know how to process this and I'm too distracted and nervous to try. I hear the rustle of clothing as he undresses and I try to predict everything he is doing, for fear of being surprised. Yes, he's told me he'll warn me before he spanks me, but for all I know, it will be three seconds before it happens. He seems to be taking forever, or perhaps time is ticking by in slow motion. I can't take it anymore. I start to turn and he catches me around the waist, the thick pulse of his erection pressing against my hip.

"We really do have to work on the following-orders thing," he murmurs, lifting me without warning, and setting me on top of the podium supporting the bed. "You're going to climb onto the center of the bed on your hands and knees, Sara. Once you're there, I'm going to spank you only six times, fast and hard, and then fuck you until we both come. Count the blows and you'll know when it's about to end. Understand?"

My reason for welcoming this spanking finds me in this moment. I've sensed from the beginning not only that is Chris able to understand me, but that he alone, because of the connection I feel for him, can help me deal with the "me" I have left floundering deep in some secret compartment of my mind. He's forcing me to face that me, yet he's also my escape when it becomes too much. Tonight that escape is going to a new level. He is taking me to a place where the pain of my past becomes pain that is here and now and somehow morphs into pleasure. I hope.

"Say no and we stop," Chris murmurs gently by my ear.

"Yes." My voice is hoarse and I repeat my reply in a stronger voice. "Yes. I understand what's going to happen."

"Say it so I know you're sure."

I wet my lips. "I'm going to get on the bed on my hands and knees. You'll spank me and then we fuck. I'm supposed to count to six."

"Climb on the bed, Sara," he says after a pause, and there is a tenderness to his voice that hasn't been present this night until now.

Slowly, I step toward the bed and the mattress shifts behind me as he follows me. His hands are on my backside, caressing, touching, teasing me with what will come next. Once I'm in the center of the bed, adrenaline surges through me, the anticipation of when he will spank me almost too much to bear. I glance over my shoulder, seeking that answer, and find him on his knees behind me.

"Face the front," he orders, and I jerk my head away, but panic expands inside me. Chris's hands caress up my waist and over my backside. Again and again, he caresses me and I can't take not knowing when gentleness will become something very different. I have to stop this now. I have to—

His hand comes down on my backside, a sharp blow that stings, and I want to cry out but the next blow is already there, and the next. Somehow I remember to count. Three. Four. Five lands and this one is harder, deeper. I arch my back against the sensation and six lands with even more force. I barely process that the spanking is over and Chris is pushing inside me, his thick cock stretching me. He thrusts hard, burying himself deeply, wasting no time. Immediately, he begins to pump his hips, his cock pounding into me and stroking out of me, and he repeats it over and over again.

I feel each thrust in every part of my body, as if my nerve endings are alive in a way they have never been. Pleasure overcomes all else, and I push back against him, until I am moaning and panting and that sweet release I'd been denied previously is right there within reach, right there where I can grab hold and take it.

I hear myself cry out but I don't recognize the sound as mine. I would never be so vocal, but yet I am, and I ache with the need for completion. Every muscle in my body feels as if it's on fire a moment before my sex clenches around Chris and begins to spasm. My body jerks, and pleasure spirals deep in my womb and spreads through my body. A low guttural sound escapes Chris's lips as he buries himself deep inside me. I feel the warm, wet heat of his release and the tension in my limbs begins to ease. My arms are suddenly weak and I sink to my elbows only to have Chris roll to his side and spoon me, my back to his chest.

His leg twines with mine and he wraps his arms around me. I feel protected, cared about, and, to my utter shock, immensely emotional. My eyes prickle and there is a storm brewing inside me that I cannot seem to control. Tears spill from my eyes and a sob slips from my throat. Then I am bawling uncontrollably, my body quaking along with my emotions.

Embarrassed, I try to get up, but Chris holds me to him, burying his face in my neck. "Just let it happen, baby."

And I do, because I really have no choice. How long I cry, I do not know, but when it ends, I bury my face in my hands, ashamed by my lack of control. Chris strokes my hair in that gentle way I'm coming to love, and hands me a tissue. I swipe at my eyes, wishing my nose didn't feel like it had a clothespin on it.

Still I don't look at him. "I don't know what happened."

He turns me to face him and captures my let with his. "It's the adrenaline rush," he explains, then slides a pillow underneath both our heads. "It happens to a lot of people."

"I thought the idea was *pleasure* through pain, not a melt-down."

"You have to find your hot spots and your limits." He brushes my hair behind my ear. "I knew from our pink paddle conversation that you wanted to try this, or I wouldn't have gone where we did tonight."

I remember the moment I thought Chris wasn't angry any-more, yet he still spanked me. "So you've changed your mind about exploring darker interests with me?"

"I was never unwilling to explore with you, Sara. But I have hard limits that won't change."

"What does that mean?"

"No clubs. No collars. No canes and whips. No Master and Submissive roles." His eyes twinkle with mischief. "As long as you understand I'm in charge, that is."

I laugh and I know he's keeping things lighthearted and somewhat avoiding my question, but I decide to let him slide on everything but the control issue. "During sex only."

He wiggles a brow. "We'll see about that."

"No. We won't."

"Then maybe I should tie you to the bed," he suggests and pulls me close, and I'm not sure he's entirely joking.

"I guess I should be glad you didn't think of that while you were still angry. You were pretty intense."

His mood does the one-eighty shift I've come to expect from him and his voice becomes somber. "I'm still pissed as hell at you, Sara, but you need to know that I'd never touch you if I had anything but your pleasure as my motivation. That doesn't mean I didn't enjoy driving you insane like you did me tonight. I did. You shouldn't have gone to Alvarez's alone."

My defenses bristle. "Chris—"

He leans in and kisses me. "It's your job. I get that. But if you think I'm going to let that stop me from protecting you, you're wrong. Don't leave your phone in your coat next time."

I purse my lips. "Don't assume the worst of me next time."

"You mean the journal."

"Yes," I say in agreement. "It hurt that you thought I would lie to you."

"I'm sorry. I would never hurt you on purpose."

None of the many dominant males I've known in my life would apologize so easily. To me, this speaks of confidence, not weakness.

"My reaction wasn't about trust," he continues. "It was about how crazy it makes me to think you might judge me by other people's actions." Then tenderness lightens his eyes. "I don't have to leave until late tomorrow. I know what your first reaction is going to be, but hear me out. I'd like it if you could work it out to fly back with me."

I open my mouth to object and he kisses me, his tongue stroking mine in a slow, sensuous caress. "Hear me out," he repeats.

"You convinced me."

"To come with me?"

I smile. "To hear you out."

"There are a number of big names involved in the activities over the next few days who I know Mark would salivate to get as clients. Your going is an investment for him."

"Like who?"

"Maria Mendez. She's never shown her work with Allure. I think she can be convinced to donate a painting and use Riptide to manage the sale. Nicolas Matthews, the New York Jets star quarterback, will also be there. While he's not an artist, I believe getting a Riptide donation would be as easy as handing him a football and pen to sign it."

The possibility of going on this trip with Chris excites me. "You think it's enough to get Mark to support me going?"

"I know it is."

"Because you know Mark?"

"I know Mark far more than I wish I did." He rolls off the bed before I can dig for more information, and walks in all his bare naked beauty across the room to snatch up his pants. He holds up his cell and tosses it to me.

I grab the phone. "I don't have his number memorized."

"Auto-dial number four."

"You have Mark on auto-dial?"

"The price of doing business with him is that I can never get rid of him, and since he donates to my charity I don't want to." He saunters toward me, all male grace and confidence, and joins me on the bed again. "In case you need further incentive to take off work, I'm meeting with the PI tomorrow and you can come with me if you're free."

I punch the auto-dial. "Merit," Mark says tightly when he answers the line.

"Actually, it's me," I say.

"Ms. McMillan. I guess I know why I haven't received my phone call after your meeting with Alvarez. You've been occupied."

Oh crap. "I left my phone in my coat, but anyway, it didn't go well. He says there's a reason you're aware of, and that's why he won't do business with you."

"Then why did he see you?"

"To try to recruit me away from you."

Chris arches a surprised brow and I nod to confirm it really happened. He scrubs his jaw, and I can tell he's not pleased.

Mark's silence tells me the same of him and it seems to stretch eternally. "And what did you tell him?"

"I told him I am loyal to Allure. Speaking of Allure, I have another opportunity." Nerves get the best of me, and I begin a long spill about the event and the guests and Riptide. "And you see—"

"Enough, Ms. McMillan. Tell Chris he's done a good job of arming you with reasons for me to agree, but make sure you bring me back clients." He hangs up without saying good-bye and I hold out the phone and stare at it.

Chris laughs and takes it from me. "Stop looking like it will bite." He pulls me beneath him. "I believe I owe you an orgasm or two."

"Six," I correct. "One for every time you spanked me."

His eyes twinkle. "Five. You had one already."

He leans in to kiss me and I press my fingers to his mouth. "If you make good on this, you can spank me again."

"I've always enjoyed a good challenge." His mouth covers mine and I am quite certain that no matter what the final number is, this is a challenge I can't lose.

Three orgasms later, I am naked when Chris carries me to his bathroom and sets me on the edge of the sink. Chris heads to the towel closet and I study the dragon tattoo, thinking about the wounded, lost teen he'd been when he'd gotten it. How young was he when he entered the BDSM world, and what is he keeping from me?

"Have you ever had a reaction to the adrenaline rush like I did tonight?" I ask, hoping to get him talking.

He freezes as he's about to toss the towels over the top of the shower, and it's clear I've hit a nerve. "No," he says, completing his task, and glancing at me before opening the shower. "I told you. I'm always in control. I take people for the ride. I don't go on it myself." He turns on the water.

"But how do you do that and have someone inflict . . . pain? Isn't that what you said you need?"

"Needed," he corrects, walking over to me and lifting me off the counter. "And sex is never involved."

"You just have someone beat you?" I choke out, appalled.

"It's past history," he says, pulling me toward the shower and inside, the warm water enveloping us. He molds me to him and stares down at me. "If I need to get lost, I'll get lost in you." His mouth comes down on mine, and the kiss is laced with the torment and pain he never lets me see. He is so much more damaged than I've imagined, and I wonder what I have yet to discover about my talented, beautiful artist. I wonder if I will ever truly reach him, if I will ever truly be enough to stop the pain inside him. If I dare love him for fear I won't be . . . but then, it's too late. I already do love him and I yearn to tell him so, to have him feel the same way. But there are other things I must confess first—things sure to bring me more pain than the whip he's vowed to never use on me.

Fifteen

I do not like public floggings, but I don't have a say in the matter. He is my Master, and I've agreed to do as he bids. It's better than when he shares me, though. I hate it when he shares me and I don't care that he says it's to please me. It pleases him, not me, as do the many watchful eyes I endured tonight. The flogging went on endlessly, with me tied to a post while he circled me, paying equal attention to every part of my body. When it was over, my nipples were sore, my back raw, and my backside red. I was upset. I do not know why tonight was different than any other night, but it was, and I was. And then . . . he was.

I am not sorry it happened. It pleased him, and after the flogging he seduced me as perfectly as he'd punished me. And as I sit here writing this, I love him more than I ever have, but I can't help but wonder what price I will pay for such an emotion. He's made it clear there is no room for such things in his life, and mine too, for that matter. He believes claims of love complicate life and make people react irrationally. He says there is no such thing as love, only different shades of lust.

I blink awake with Rebecca's journal entry in my head, and the soft glow of light in the room drags me from the hauntingly provocative entry. The dream fades, and my lips curve as I realize that Chris is holding me. His body is curved around mine, one of his gifted, artistic hands on my hip, and for once I'm not thinking of his talent on a canvas, but his skill at pleasing me. A girl could get used to falling asleep after being thoroughly sated and waking up with a big hunk of hot man wrapped around her.

"I like you in my bed. I think I'll keep you here."

My smile widens and I turn around to face him, finding his hair a sexy, rumpled mess partially because of my fingers. "It'll be hard to catch our flight from bed."

"I mean ever. Move in with me, Sara."

I blanch. "What?"

He caresses my cheek. "You heard me. Move in with me."

"You've only known me a few weeks."

"I know enough."

But he doesn't. "You didn't even invite women to your bed before me and you want me to live with you?"

"They weren't you."

I am warmed by his words, tempted to dive into a deep blue sea of risk with Chris, and I would, if not for my secret. "Chris—"

"Don't answer now. Think about it over the weekend." His cell phone rings and he rolls over to grab it from the nightstand. "Morning, Katie."

I sit up against the headboard at the mention of his god-mother and watch as he hits the remote control to open the electronic blinds over the window. Slowly, the gorgeous glow of the San Francisco skyline comes into view but I can't appreciate it. I am reeling from the knowledge that I am out of time. I have to tell him everything and I am not ready.

"Yes, she's here," Chris replies to Katie.

My gaze goes to Chris. "Katie says hello," he informs me.

"Hi Katie," I call out, touched by her asking about me, and doing my best to seem cheerful when I'm holding it together as well as shattered glass.

"I'll have to see what Sara's schedule is and see when we can come out," Chris continues to his godmother. I'm thrilled at his assumption that I'll be by his side, until he adds, "I won't head back to Paris without stopping out to see you."

Paris. I wouldn't believe I could be more shaken this morning than I already am, but that one word does the job of a jackhammer. All my assumptions that this invitation meant something are crushed. The journal entry I woke to screams in my head. *He says there is no such thing as love, only different shades of lust.* I can't help but wonder if Chris feels this way, too. How can he ask me to move in, to change my entire life, when he's going back to Paris soon? All for what? A few weeks of hot sex? It's enough to shred my heart.

Tossing aside the blanket, I climb out of the bed, snatching Chris's shirt I'd worn during a late-night kitchen raid, and the earthy, male scent of him sizzles through me when I pull it on. But then, why wouldn't it? Hot sex is his expertise.

I rush across the room and I can feel Chris's eyes following me, and I pray he doesn't pick up on my frazzled mood. Seconds before I escape, his hand comes down on my arm, and I squeeze my eyes shut as I hear, "Let me call you back, Katie."

Chris turns me to face him and I'm at the disadvantage of him being breathtakingly naked. "I have to go back for the holidays and my charity commitments," he explains, as if I've asked a question. "I want you to go with me."

I shake my head, knowing this will lead to certain pain. "I—"

"Have a job," he completes for me. "I know. Do you have your birth certificate?"

"At my apartment, but—"

"Good. We'll run by there and grab it so you can apply for your passport today."

"I can't just leave."

"There are amazing opportunities in Paris and I can help open those doors for you."

"My entire life has been about what someone else got for me. I don't want to repeat that scenario. I won't."

"You're afraid to count on me."

"I'm afraid of not being able to count on me."

There is a hint of emotion in his stare before his expression becomes unreadable. He drops his hand from my arm. "I understand," he states, his voice monotone, his expression impassive.

I think I've hurt him, and reality slaps me in the face. I've let myself think of him as some kind of demon, to avoid the real demons of my past.

In two small steps I am in front of him, wrapping my arms around him, and pressing my cheek to his chest. "I don't think you realize how much I care about you, or how easily and badly you could hurt me." I lift my head and let him see the truth in my face. "So yes, I'm scared to count on you."

Tension eases from his body, his expression softening. He runs his hand over my hair and there is gentleness in his touch. "Then we'll be scared together."

"*You're* scared?" I ask, surprised by such a confession.

"You're the best adrenaline rush of my life, baby. Far better than the pain you replaced."

For the first time, I think that maybe, just maybe, I am all Chris needs.

An hour later, I'm standing at the kitchen sink, sipping coffee, while Chris talks to one of the charity organizers on the phone in the other room. I am still reeling from his invitation to move in with him, my mind tossing around one worry after another. How will I keep my job and identity? Do I need my job to have my identity if I delve into new opportunities? Will any of this matter when Chris finds out I've lied to him? Will he understand why I did? Why I'm so ashamed of the truth? If anyone could, I believe it's Chris.

"Ready to head out?"

Chris saunters into the room and my lips curve at the sight of him. He is wearing jeans and a brown Allure Gallery tee to match the pink one I have on, both compliments of a special delivery from Mark. "I still can't believe you actually wore the shirt."

He stops in front of me and that earthy, deliciously Chris scent of his teases my nostrils and tingles through me. "I have my disagreements with Mark but he's been supportive of the hospital."

I open my mouth to ask exactly what the disagreements were, but he takes my cup and finishes off the contents. This isn't the first time we've shared a cup but there is this new intimacy between us and I feel it in every part of me. Our eyes meet and I am instantly wet, squeezing my thighs together.

Chris reaches around me and sets the mug in the sink, bringing his hand to the back of my head, and leaning in to brush his mouth over mine. I shiver and his lips hint at a smile that tells me he notices. "You taste like coffee and temptation," he murmurs. "If we don't go now, we won't." He straightens, and I approve of the new brown tee that molds every rippling muscle of his torso.

As we head to the living room, I freeze when I see the stack of journals on the coffee table. "What are they doing there?"

Chris grabs a leather bag and begins loading them inside. "The PI wants to see them."

"We can't just let him have them."

"Jacob's copying them and then locking them up for us."

"You trust Jacob?"

"Completely. I had him checked out before I hired him for some private work for the charity."

"But what about Rebecca's privacy?"

"If we end up going to the police, the journals are as good as public record. Better to let the PI check things out completely."

"Does the PI think we need to go to the police?"

"All I know is he needs more to go on, and he's hoping the journals and your insight from basically living Rebecca's life will help."

My eyes go wide. Am I living Rebecca's life? The idea sends

a wave of nausea through me. I'm trying to find myself again, to create the life I always wanted. Have I simply lost myself in Rebecca's?

I think of the man who'd stolen her identity and I stare at Chris, thinking about how he's consumed me, and I reject the comparison of him to the Master in the journal. Chris has helped me face myself. He's forcing me to face the past.

After I apply for my passport, Chris pulls the 911 up in front of several big-name retail stores only a few blocks from the gallery and parks at a meter. I frown. "Where's your bank?" I ask, since he's told me that's where we're headed.

"Around the corner. I thought we'd shop first."

"For what?"

"You need a dress for Saturday night."

"I have something at home." A pathetic dress, but a dress.

His fingers slide into my hair and he pulls my mouth to his, caressing my lips with his. "I'm buying you a dress. You can pick it or I will."

"I don't need—"

He kisses me and his tongue is a delicate whisper gone too soon. "You do and so do I." He lets me go and gets out of the car, and I don't think he's talking about the dress.

By the time I shove open my door, Chris is beside me, offering me his hand. The instant my palm touches his, a sharp pang of awareness rushes through me. "You know," I start to say as I stand directly in front of him, "I don't like—"

"Spending my money," he finishes. "But I like it enough for both of us."

"You don't have to spend money on me. I love—" I stop, astounded at how easily it had slid to the tip of my tongue.

His gaze sharpens and he steps closer, his arm wrapping my waist. "You love what, Sara?" he prods softly.

I am on the verge of a confession better made in private. "I love . . ." I pause, torn about what comes next. "Being with you."

His eyes dance with mischief and his lips curve. "I love . . ." He pauses as I had. "Being with you."

My eyes go wide. Have we just confessed our love? Surely not. "You love . . . being with me?"

"Very much," he assures me, and slides his fingers between mine. "And Saturday night I'm going to love peeling off the dress you're about to buy. I'm imagining it will get me through the torture of my monkey suit."

I laugh. "I can't wait to see you in your monkey suit."

My mood is light and spirits high as we walk into the Chanel store that I adore but have avoided since becoming a struggling teacher. Chris releases my hand and I start wandering the store. A long, slim-cut, emerald dress catches my eye and I walk toward it; the color reminds me of Chris's eyes when he's in that dark, dangerous place I've come to crave.

I stop in front of it, admiring the silk material, and I can't help reaching for the price tag. Chris's hand slides around mine. "Don't even think of looking at that." I tilt my head back to look at him over my shoulder. "Try it on," he orders.

"Yes, Master."

He laughs. "Like you'd ever allow that." I gape at the implication that he would, and he smiles wickedly, then lowers his voice. "I don't want to be your Master, Sara. I just want you to do what I say."

I snort and pick up the dress. "Good luck." He glances at it and back at me, and I glower. "I like it. I'm not trying it on because you told me to."

"Of course."

Strolling away, I grab several more dresses before heading to the dressing room, only to find Ava standing at a rack near the entry, looking gorgeous in a pale blue dress with a belted waist.

"Sara!" she exclaims and hugs me. "What a small world." She gives Chris a nod. "I see you know how to take good care of a woman."

My face heats and Chris's hand slides to my back, silently soothing the burn of the comment. "Hello, Ava," he offers in a taut greeting.

Ava runs her hand down the green dress. "Oh, this one is going to look gorgeous on you. I have some time. I can't wait to see you in it."

Chris turns to me. "Why don't I leave you to shop and I'll run to the bank. I'll leave a credit on the account. Buy whatever you want. We have a good hour before we have to leave for our appointment. The restaurant we're meeting at is a few blocks away."

I can feel Ava watching us and it's uncomfortable. "I'll be ready when you get back."

He leans in and whispers in my ear. "I'm always ready."

I bite my lip to keep from laughing. "Yes. I know."

His hand glides down my hair, and while his expression is unreadable as he says good-bye to Ava, I have the distinct impression he is not pleased she is here.

A few minutes later I walk out of a room into the open area where Ava is lounging with a glass of champagne. "It's spectacular on you," Ava exclaims of the emerald dress.

"I like it," I agree, moving to a three-way mirror. "I usually don't like something as much on me as I do on the hanger, but I do this one."

"Well then, this is reason to celebrate." She calls the attendant. "A glass for Sara. We are celebrating a perfect dress." She pats the blue velvet bench she is sitting on. "Join me. I'm dying to hear about you and Chris."

There's simply no escaping her curiosity. I sigh inwardly and claim the spot she's indicated. "We're going to a gala in L.A. and I needed a dress."

"Interesting," she comments, her lips pursing in a smirk that on her is still beautiful. On me it would just be twisted.

"What does that mean?"

"In all the years that man has been around my coffee shop, not once have I seen him with a woman. I figured he had some hottie back in Paris."

I instantly think of the tattoo artist, and she might as well have punched me in the chest.

"Oh honey," Ava purrs, grabbing my leg. "I upset you. I didn't mean I think he has another woman. I was just telling you what I assumed because a man like that has to have women lined up."

Lined up? Lots of women?

"Sara!" Ava exclaims. "He doesn't have lots of women. You have it bad for Chris, don't you?"

"I . . ." I nod. "Yes. I guess I do."

She smiles. "He's a catch, honey. Be happy, not paranoid. The man looks at you like you're the biggest treasure on the island."

"I thought you said he looks at me like he wants to gobble me up?" I ask, reminding her of the day Chris and I had both been in her coffee shop.

"That, too. That, too." Her cell rings and she grimaces. "My ex. Grrrr. I can't stand the man but I have to take it or he'll call twenty times." She stands up and walks to the other side of the lounge.

The attendant appears with a glass of champagne. "This is for you," she states, handing me a note.

I frown and open it to find Chris's writing. *I put five thousand on my store account. Spend it or I will.*

"Should I bring you some items to try on?" the woman asks, and the eagerness of her tone tells me she works on commission. I'm also certain Chris is quite serious and that we have to have a chat about money.

"Yes, please," I concede for now, and I give her a laundry list, distracted from the money issue by the Paris issue, and what, or rather who, might await Chris when he returns. He asked you to go with him, I remind myself.

"You are the biggest prick I've ever known," I hear Ava hiss a moment before she ends the call.

"Everything okay?" I query as she returns.

"He's trying to get half the coffee shop."

"Oh—are you going through a divorce now? I thought you meant your ex as in already divorced."

"We've been separated two years. He's dodged signing the papers and last year he started running around with some model to make me jealous. It didn't work. Not only is he a jerk, but he has the sexual expertise of a Gummi Bear."

I choke on a sip of champagne. "Gummi Bear?"

She smiles. "I prefer my men far more commanding than he will ever be."

"Well, you have a prime prospect in Mark."

Ava downs her champagne and cuts her gaze away, and I am quite sure I've hit a nerve. "Yes, well, Mark is the kind of man who tries you on for size and then moves to the next one."

"You and he—"

"Fucked our brains out? Yes, but I knew the score. He's an all-night kind of man, not an all-your-lifetime kind."

"So . . . were you involved in his club?"

Her lips curve, more disdainful than amused. "You know about the club."

"Yes. I know."

"And are you a member?"

"No. That's not for me."

"No?"

"Not even close," I say firmly.

"I guess that explains why Chris hasn't been around."

Has she seen Chris at the club? Yes, of course. She all but said that. Have they been together? I shove aside that ridiculous idea. No. Absolutely not. Chris would have told me. And the way Ava runs her mouth, I think she'd probably speak up as well.

The attendant appears with an armful of clothes, and I rush to the dressing room and quickly close the door. Ava starts talking about some lingerie store I should go to, but I don't hear half of it. I think back to her commenting about wanting to try out Chris, or some similar remark. I'm not jealous, but the remark continues to grate my nerves for reasons I can't put my finger on. It's not logical; she's raved on and on about how Chris is so into me. Something about Ava is just not sitting right with me, though.

By the time I'm trying on my final items, a pair of dark blue jeans and a bright orange shimmering tank, I've managed to make small talk and Ava is so complimentary about my style, I really don't understand why I'm so edgy with her.

I open the dressing room door to discover Chris has returned. Ava is sitting with her skirt hiked up her gorgeous crossed legs, facing him. Chris's jacket is gone, his arms crossed and his tattoo stretched over impressive biceps. He's staring at me but I can't look him in the face. I feel awkward about this new knowledge that they are both members of a club I will never make part of my world. A club that Chris has made part of his.

"Oh, I love that tank!" Ava exclaims, hopping to her feet to inspect me, her expression animated, wiped of the admiration for Chris I suspect had been there moments before. "You have to get that one."

Somehow, I manage a stiff nod. "Yes. I like it." My gaze flicks to Chris. "I'll just change so we can go." I back into the dressing room and shut the door. Flattening myself against it, I squeeze my eyes shut and will my stomach to calm, forcing my mind away from weaving what-ifs into the worst possible conclusions. I must walk out of here with my composure intact.

I yelp as the door behind me jerks and pushes me forward. "This room is taken!"

"Sure is." Chris pushes into the room and shuts the door. "By us."

"Are you crazy? This is a women's dressing room."

"My woman's dressing room." He presses me against the wall and one of his hands rests by my head, the other at my waist. Those too-perceptive eyes of his pin me in a stare, and I can't help being affected by both him and his claim of me being his woman.

"Talk to me," he orders, his expression implacable.

Plain and simple, I am cornered.

Sixteen

I shove at Chris's chest but he is a solid wall of stubborn, sexy man. "Why do you do this?" I growl, exasperated.

"Do what?"

"Push me to talk when I don't want to talk."

"Because I care."

"Do you?" I challenge before I can stop myself.

"I asked you to move in with me, Sara. That should answer that question." He slides a lock of hair behind my ear, and I barely suppress a shiver. I've lost count of the times I've thought he had too much power over me. Times like now, when I feel insecure, and—

"What's wrong?" he prods firmly.

"I can't talk about this here. Someone might hear."

"I sent them all away."

I gape. "Just like that? You sent them all away."

"Yes," he states flatly.

Trapped. I'm not getting out of here without having this conversation. I drop my gaze, curling my hands on his chest, and damn it, it's a stellar chest, and he smells good. I wonder if Ava knows how good.

"Sara."

I jerk my gaze back to his and blurt, "I wish you would've told me Ava was a member of Mark's club. It was awkward hearing it from her."

"I would have if I'd known."

"You didn't know?"

"I never say anything I don't mean."

He's right; he doesn't. I like that about him, and I especially like it when I want answers. "She knew that you're a member."

His brows dip. "What? That makes no sense. The membership is guarded and I stayed out of the public forums."

I shake my head, confused and not at all comforted by his answer. "Then how would she know?"

"Good question, and one I want answered. Members who want privacy pay well to receive it."

"She wasn't one of the women you—"

"Absolutely not. I chose from the club files and with great caution."

Is this what I've sensed in Ava? What is bothering me? "You wore masks, right? Couldn't she—"

"Sara. I wasn't with Ava."

"So you knew the names of the women you chose?" His jaw flexes and I read my answer on his face. My stomach takes another roller-coaster ride all on its own. "You might have—"

"No." The word is firm, absolute. "I told you. I wasn't with Ava."

I reach out and trace his brightly colored tats. "Your ink is hard to miss or forget."

He wraps my hand in his and pins me in a look. "I'd know, Sara. I'd sense it when I'm around her."

My chest tightens, another part of my conversation with Ava bothering me now. "When I said I wasn't a member of the club and didn't want to be, she implied you gave it up for me."

"And you're already worried I'm going to need that world again. I won't, Sara. I don't. And I'd like to know what her agenda was, to make you think that."

"I don't think it was an agenda. I think she thought it showed you care about me, that you would leave it for me. She had no idea that was a hot spot for me. I overreacted. I'm sorry."

"I'd rather you overreact than not tell me, Sara." Chris curves his hand over the swell of my backside and molds me close. "You're the hot spot for me." Dipping low, he nuzzles my neck, his warm breath fanning my neck. "You know that, right?"

"Hmmm," I murmur, helpless to fight the desire his teasing seduction arouses in me. "You can remind me as often as you like."

His tongue flicks over my earlobe, and he whispers, "How about now? Have you ever had an orgasm in a dressing room?"

"What?" I gasp. "No." His face is filled with wicked determination. "And no, we can't."

He tugs my top shirt up and over my head so fast that I have no hope of stopping him. The instant I'm free, I try to slow him down. "Chris—"

His mouth comes down over mine, a hot, fiery claiming

he uses as a distraction to unhook my bra. When he molds his palms to my breasts as he pinches my nipples, I barely contain a whimper sure to draw attention.

Chris reaches for the button on my jeans and I manage a weak "Stop. You said you'd stop if I said stop."

His deep, sexy laugh ripples through me and my body clenches. "That was last night. New day. New rules."

"But—"

He kisses me again, a slice of his seductive tongue, before proclaiming, "You will not leave this dressing room until you have a smile on your face." He goes down on one knee and presses his mouth to my stomach as he had the night before and the effect is just as sizzling. I know where that mouth is headed, and while my mind sees the problem with the location we're in, my body likes the location he's at.

That deliciously skilled tongue of his dips into my navel, and I shiver. He smiles against my skin, casting me a heated look. "I've noticed you like that."

"I've noticed you can be overwhelming." And playful and dark, and for that matter a mix of all things contrary that makes me insanely aroused.

Unsnapping my jeans, Chris tugs the zipper down. "I plan to be that and more before we leave." His fingers slip into the waistband and he slides the jeans downward.

I reach for them but it's too late to keep them up. "We don't have time for this."

"Which is why you need to undress quickly. Step." He orders me out of my pants, and I do as he says, because having them at my ankles feels ridiculous.

"We don't have time—"

His fingers stroke my panties aside, trailing the sensitive skin beneath.

"Chris, no—"

"Chris, yes," he counters, lifting my leg to his shoulder.

"Chris—"

His mouth comes down over me.

"Oh," I gasp, and my head falls back against the wall as he begins to lick and explore. He is merciless in his exploration, flicking my clit with his thumb while his tongue is delving in and out, over and around. Fingers stretch me, pressing inside me and traveling the sensitive passage. My breath rasps from my dry throat, my hand goes to his head, and he actually lets me touch him for once. This pleases me, and is as erotic as his fingers and tongue working magic together, stroking me, driving me wild.

Blood roars in my ears and I forget everything but the sweet spot he's touching, and the next. Every place he touches is a sweet spot. Time ceases to exist and the room fades away. A tight, hard clenching begins to form in my stomach and swiftly travels lower. Remotely, I hear my own panting, the soft moans slipping from my throat that I can't contain and I don't remember why I should. Chris flicks my clit in just the right place and my fingers tighten in his hair. This spot, yes. Stay in this spot. Heat radiates from that pressure point, spreading like wildfire through my limbs. I arch against him and I pump my hips against his hand, all but crying out for that place just out of reach. My body clenches and my heart seems to still. My vision goes black and the first spasm jerks my body. Pleasure surges through me so deep that I feel it in my bones.

I am limp when Chris sets my leg down and slides up my body. He kisses me, the salty taste of his kiss flavoring my tongue. "Taste you on me. That says you belong to me. Don't forget it."

Fifteen minutes later, with too many bags in hand for my comfort, Chris and I exit the store. Ava wasn't there when we exited the dressing room and for that I'm thankful. Regardless of the throb of my clit to remind me that Chris is as skilled with his tongue as he is with a paintbrush, my discomfort over Ava is still quite intense.

By the time we pull up at the restaurant, I haven't figured out why. It's not about distrusting Chris. But there is a gray area in my mind I can't muddle my way through, and it's bugging me.

Inside the chain restaurant, a "something for everyone" kind of place, I force myself to forget Ava. Rebecca is who matters and just thinking about what we might find out from the PI has me balling my hands by my side.

The hostess motions us forward and Chris reaches over and pries my fingers apart and slides his through mine. "Relax, baby."

It's amazing how well he reads me. "I just want to find out that she is okay and I'm paranoid to think otherwise."

"I know," he agrees. "Me, too."

Two men greet us at the table we're shown to and I am in testosterone overload. Good-looking, fit, and dressed in jeans and Walker Security T-shirts, they both stand to greet us.

"Blake Walker," one of them says, offering me his hand. He has long black hair tied at his nape, and intelligent brown eyes that have a been-through-hell depth to them.

"Kelvin Jackson," the other one, with sandy brown hair that

curls at his brow, and bright blue eyes, announces. "I'm the head of the San Francisco office."

Blake snorts. "Once we *have* offices. He's working from home until the building gets the construction done, thus the lunch meeting. I'll be glad to get back to New York and out of his living room."

My brow furrows. I'm concerned that they're not more established here, and Chris seems to read my thoughts as we all sit down. "Walker Security is not only one of the best in the business, but Kelvin is a former FBI agent out of the San Francisco office."

"I was ATF," Blake adds. "My brother Luke is a former SEAL. My brother Royce is former FBI. The list goes on." He cuts Chris a quick look. "Your man got us the journals, by the way."

I'm impressed and relieved. Chris leans back and drapes his arm over my chair. "Jacob's a good man."

"I noticed," Kelvin comments. "I need a man like him."

"Stay away," Chris warns. "I like my building more with him on the job."

Kelvin looks encouraged. "That he's impressed you only makes me want him more."

"Have you found out anything about Rebecca?" I interject, eager to find out what they have to share.

The waitress appears and kills my chance for immediate answers. Chris opens his menu. "We'd better order. We're going to be cutting it close for our flight."

With effort I focus on the menu and order my first choice everywhere: pasta. The men all order burgers.

After the waitress leaves Blake picks up the conversation

again. "About Rebecca. We tracked down the mysterious new boyfriend in New York. He said they took a trip to the Caribbean and they were going to travel to Greece next but she had a change of heart and wanted to come home early. We checked out his story. She flew out with him and came back alone."

An icy chill slides down my spine. "She came back here?"

Kelvin gives a decisive nod. "Six weeks ago."

I am sick to my stomach all over again. "She never got her things out of storage. She never came back to work. So where *is* she?"

"We don't know," Kelvin confirms, "and there's no record of her leaving by any means of public transportation."

"We also checked car rentals and found no record," Blake adds, buttering some bread. "And she didn't own a car for us to track down."

Guilt twists me in knots. I sensed Rebecca was in trouble. I should have trusted my instincts and pushed harder for answers sooner. "Where does that leave us?" I ask, and I can't keep the urgency from my voice. "The police?"

Blake sighs heavily. "This is tricky. We have enough to support a missing person's report, but she's an adult who has the right to come and go as she pleases."

"And she told everyone she was leaving town," I say.

Blake nods. "Exactly. It's hard to get attention to these types of cases."

Kelvin slides his silverware out of his way and sets a folder on the table. "We also don't want the police asking questions that could trigger someone to hide evidence we might find otherwise."

Evidence? I straighten. They are clearly are thinking crime, too.

Kelvin continues, "At least right now, we think a missing person's report is a bad move."

"You can trust these guys, baby," Chris assures me, his finger lightly caressing my shoulder. "They know what they are doing."

"I do," I assure him and the entire table, "and I understand the view on the missing person's report. I just don't like the direction this seems to be headed or the things it's making me think might have happened to Rebecca."

Blake's lips tighten. "Believe me, none of us do."

"Which brings me to Sara's involvement," Chris says. "Anything new on the storage unit incident?"

Kelvin flips open the folder. "We lucked out and got our hands on some interesting footage from a camera at a nearby business." He pulls out a photograph, setting it in the center of the table. "This guy entered the building after Sara and exited about ten minutes after she left."

I suck in a breath. "That's the creepy attendant I met."

"He's not an employee of the storage facility," Kelvin informs me. "He's a lowlife PI named Greg Garrison. He was hired by someone to find the journals."

"Who?" Chris asks sharply.

"He says he doesn't know," Blake supplies. "Blind cash by wire and e-mailed instructions from an untraceable location."

I hug myself and shiver. I was right. I wasn't alone in the darkness.

Chris takes my hand and squeezes. "You okay?"

"I am," I reply bleakly. "I'm not so sure about Rebecca,

though." My attention flicks between Kelvin and Blake. "There are no names in the journals. I've read them all."

"Yet someone wants them badly enough to hire Greg," Blake said. "That means we need to dig for why, and use their resources to look for things we might all miss."

"Exactly," Kelvin agrees. "And keep in mind that there could be more journals. We'd like to dig around in the storage unit."

"We'll give you the combination before we leave," Chris says.

My worst fears about Rebecca are taking root. I want these men to do whatever is necessary to find her.

Kelvin slips the picture back inside the folder. "I know how Greg works. If he killed the lights, I'm guessing it was to get the opportunity to replace your lock with one that only he can open. Have you been back since?"

As I shake my head, our food arrives. Once the waitress is gone again, I ask, "What if he did?"

"If that's the case we'll cut it off and replace it again," Kelvin answers, popping a fry in his mouth.

Chris ignores his food, looking as concerned as I feel. "How worried should I be about Sara's safety?"

I've completely lost my appetite. There is no way I'm eating now. I didn't really want to in the first place.

Blake sighs, and I can tell from his tense expression I am not going to like his answer. "I wouldn't get paranoid, but on the other hand, someone is desperate enough to hire Greg to find the journals. Add that to Rebecca being MIA . . . I would be cautious."

"Don't ask questions about Rebecca," Kelvin adds. "Let us do it."

Chris cuts me a look. "You hear that? Let them do it."

"I'm in a position to find out things they can't," I object, remembering my talk with Ralph. "One of the sales reps hates Rebecca."

This leads into us discussing the entire staff as we finish our meal. By the time we leave the restaurant, I'm eager to get out of the city, where I won't have to look over my shoulder for a few days.

Seventeen

Chris and I stop back at his apartment and pack a few final things, including my dress. Jacob had already returned the journals and I convinced Chris we should take them. If he reads them maybe he'll pick up on some clue I have missed.

With both our bags, the 911 is too small, so we call for a car service. Once we're inside it the freshness of what we've learned about Rebecca has me worried about Ella all over again, and I try to call her. After several fruitless attempts to reach her, I give up.

"She's fine," Chris assures me, squeezing my leg. "She's on her honeymoon in Paris."

I manage a tight smile. "I know."

"You don't know. I see it in your face." He snatches his cell phone from his belt and punches a button. "Blake. Yeah man, you got an extra guy you can have check something else out for me?"

I am beyond touched by Chris doing this for me. I remember the first time, at the wine tasting, when he told me he was protecting me, and I said that I didn't need protection. I tell myself now I don't, but it feels good to have a protector in my life. Maybe too good considering how uncertain I feel about our relationship.

"Sara's friend left on her honeymoon and her phone hasn't been working," Chris continues to Blake. "This Rebecca thing has her thinking the worst. Can you check the airlines and make sure she left and see when the ticket says she will return?" He moves the phone from his mouth. "What's her last name and when did she leave."

After checking the calendar on my phone, I relay the details he's requested. He relays them and hangs up. "We'll have good news by the time we land."

A small bit of the tension eases from my body. "Thank you, Chris."

He kisses me. "Anything to keep you from worrying."

I relax into his arms, and for the short drive I allow myself to let him be my Dark Prince, without worry of what the future holds.

Almost two hours after our lunch meeting, Chris and I finally board the plane. We stop beside the first-class seats that Chris has purchased for us and I cannot help but think of all the money he's spent on me today.

He motions for me to claim the window seat. "I've had more than my share of good views. You haven't traveled much."

I slide into the seat and he follows. Once we've buckled up,

I turn to him, and I can't help but stroke a wayward strand of his hair. "Thank you."

He closes his hand around mine and settles it on the arm on the seat beneath his. "For what?"

"The clothes. First class. Helping with Rebecca and Ella. All of this costs money."

"Money doesn't matter to me." His tone is nonchalant, dismissive.

"What about the teen you once were who wanted money and power?"

"He grew into a man."

"With money and power."

He gives me a wry smile. "I'll rephrase. I don't mind spending my money because I have plenty of it. I'm not about to give it up. It's control. I like control."

"No kidding," I tease.

He runs his thumb over my bottom lip and follows with his mouth. "You like it when I'm in control."

"Sometimes," I agree.

"I'm working on all the time."

"Don't hold your breath, or the world will lose a brilliant artist."

"I'll have to make you pay for that one," he taunts as the flight attendant begins standard announcements.

A dart of heat races up my spine. I don't know where Chris might take me next, but I have no doubt it will be deliciously unforgettable. He leans closer and whispers, "You know, I know a club we could join together."

I stiffen and his low rumble of laughter fans my neck with seductive promise, before he adds, "The mile-high club."

I jerk around to face him. "Forget it, and that's nonnegotiable no matter what you do. There are people everywhere."

"What if I rent a private plane for our return?"

He can't be serious. "You'd do that just for us to, ah, get membership?"

His lips curve devilishly. "Without hesitation. In fact, since this trip is one of many I'd like to take you on, I think that might be the way to fly." A puzzled look slides over his face. "How is it again that you grew up with money and never traveled?"

As if hit by a bullet, I stiffen before I can stop myself. "Busy with childhood and teen activities, I guess." The plane is taxiing and, afraid he'll read my panic, I quickly turn to the window and feign interest. Silently, I kick myself for missing an opportunity to begin to share my past with Chris. I just have this unyielding sense that once I open Pandora's box and let one demon out, even if it's one of the smaller ones, the bigger, darker ones will escape before I am ready.

Chris's hand falls away from mine, and I feel his withdrawal reach well beyond a small physical connection. It is all I can do not to drag his hand to my lap. "It looks like it's going to storm," I murmur, noting the dark heaviness of the clouds above burdened by a downpour yet to happen, much like the weight of my secret.

"You aren't afraid, are you?"

I wonder if he's talking about flying in the storm. With Chris, there is often a double meaning. With effort, I school my features and turn to him and meet his penetrating stare. He knows I was dodging his question; I see it in his eyes.

"I don't know what to expect. This is new to me," I say.

"Because your travel has been limited to almost never."

It's not a question and this time I'm certain we aren't talking about the weather. I blink into his unfathomable expression, but there is expectancy in the air. The answer to why I never traveled is on the tip of my tongue, lingering there, but I cannot seem to push it out. "Right. Because I almost never traveled."

We lift off and the bumps are instantaneous. My fingers curl around the armrest again, but this time with white-knuckle intensity. Chris's hand comes down on mine as it had before and I sigh inside with the return of his touch. "Just a little turbulence," he assures me. "It'll even out when we get to a higher altitude above the clouds."

As if in defiance of his claim, the plane jerks and we seem to drop. I stiffen and my breath lodges in my throat. "You're sure this is normal?"

"Very."

"Okay." I breathe out. "I'm trusting you on this."

"But not on everything."

There is a coolness to his eyes, and I wonder how soon his walls will slam down in front of mine. I'm backed into another corner. If I tell Chris everything I may lose him. If I keep him shut out, he may shut me out, again. It's time to at least start down a path that leads to my hell.

The plane jolts again and my heart drops to my stomach.

I tug my hand from underneath his and lift the armrest, and hopefully the proverbial wall separating us as well. "We were my father's pets," I say, angling in his direction. "He left us at home and ran off to his many mistresses."

Understanding seeps into his expression and he shifts to face me. "When did you find out about the other women?"

"Once I moved away for college. That's when my mother's rose-colored glasses came off me."

"She knew." It's not a question.

"Oh yes," I confirm. "She knew." I can't tame the bitterness seeping into my tone. "If we were his pets, she was his lapdog. She was so in love with him that she'd accept anything she could get from him, which wasn't much."

His expression is thoughtful, concerned. "How active was he in your life?"

"He was my idol who was never home. I worshiped the ground he walked on, just like my mother. I had no idea we were his token family to look good for business or whatever his reason was for keeping us around. I think it was about power. Or because he could. Or because he didn't want my mother to get all his money. I have no clue. I stopped trying to figure it out years ago. There had to be a reason that made sense to him."

"Do you think your mother knew why?"

"I think she convinced herself he loved her. She was blinded by love."

"Don't take this wrong," he warns gently, "but was it love, or the money?"

I hate the question I've asked myself, and rejected, too many times to count. "I don't know really what was in her head. The mother I thought I knew wasn't the one I discovered after I took those glasses off." I shake my head. "But no. I never felt like she was about the money." My mind travels the past. "She gave up

everything she loved but painting. She'd hide her work and supplies when he was home."

"You said she created your love of art."

I nod. "Yes. Very much so." I let out a heavy sigh, trying to
escape the tight sensation strangling my airways. "Looking back,
it was an abusive relationship, almost like Stockholm syndrome,
where the captive adores her captor."

The plane jumps again and I grab his hand. As his strength
and encouragement seep into me, I'm glad I told him.

"Do you have any of her artwork?" he asks after a few moments.

"No. After I left for college she gave it up completely. My
father wanted her time spent doing high-profile charity events
that made him look good. She was coming home from one of
the events organized by the network when she died. He wasn't
even in the country at the time, of course."

"That's why you blame him for her death."

My gaze drops to my hand that has somehow settled on his
leg. I relive a searingly vivid memory of the moment I heard my
mother was dead. Chris caresses my cheek. "You okay?"

"I just . . . I'm remembering the day she died." I have to
mentally shake myself to continue. "I don't blame him for her
death. I blame him for her miserable life. Though she made her
own choices, that doesn't make his abuse of her acceptable." An
acid burn slides through me just thinking about what I'm about
to reveal. "He didn't even cry at her funeral, Chris. Not a single
tear. Not one."

His hand goes to the back of my head and he rests his

forehead on mine. He opens his mouth to speak and I quickly warn him, "Don't say you're sorry. You know that doesn't help."

"No, it doesn't."

Slowly we sink back against our seats and I settle onto his shoulder. He doesn't say anything else, but he doesn't have to. He's here for me yet again, and it's bittersweet because I know the next few demons will be more than mine. They'll become his.

Once we're in L.A. and in the back of a private car to the hotel, Chris checks his messages. "Blake found Ella's flight out. It was one-way. Do you think she planned on staying in Paris and didn't want to tell you?"

"She left everything she owns and she said she'd be back in a month." I shake my head. "No. She didn't intend on staying. She was going to Italy, too."

He punches in a text to Blake with that information and gets an instant reply. "Blake says he checked any outgoing destination from Paris for Ella. There is no record of her leaving for Italy. He wants to know if you're sure she didn't resign her job?"

My brow furrows and I'm already dialing. "I hadn't thought of that." I have to leave a message for the right person. "I hope they call back quickly."

"Find out about her status at the school, and if she hasn't resigned I'll have Blake's team dig around some more."

I nod and prepare myself mentally for the school's returned call. Not only do I need to hear that Ella is safe, but it's time I officially resign. It's a bit daunting despite my new dream career.

The car pulls up to the hotel and we rush in to drop off our things in our room and head to the hospital. We arrive just in time for an event Chris is holding for a group of twenty kids all battling cancer, along with many of their parents. After Chris and I receive excited welcomes from everyone, and pose for pictures I didn't expect to be included in but am, I finally meet Dylan, the young boy with leukemia. It's clear that Dylan is deeply attached to Chris, and Chris to him. He's an extremely likable kid, both friendly and smart. My heart twists at the dark circles under his eyes, his bald scalp that tells of his cancer treatments, and the frailness of his thin body, which makes him look younger than his thirteen years.

Chris takes a seat at an easel at the front of the room, and I sit beside him with Dylan. Together, Dylan and I watch as Chris draws special pictures by request. Spellbound by Chris's interactions with the crowd, my heart is truly in my throat more than in my chest as he brings smiles to many a haunted face.

An hour into the event, I head to the cafeteria to grab Chris a drink and a candy bar since he hasn't eaten since lunch and it's now seven o'clock. Dylan's mom, Brandy, a pretty thirty-something blonde, catches me in the hallway and falls into step with me. "Do you mind if I join you?"

"Not at all," I assure her. "Dylan's a great kid. I see why Chris is attached to him."

"Thank you, and yes, they have a special bond. Chris has been a godsend on so many levels." The elevator door opens and we step inside as she continues: "Did you know he calls Dylan every day, and on top of that, he calls either me or my husband, Sam, to check on us?"

"No, but I'm not surprised. He talks about you guys often."

The elevator door opens again and we head to the cafeteria. "He's paid what our insurance hasn't, and that isn't a small figure." There's a mix of appreciation and sadness in her voice.

"He'd pay whatever it costs to save Dylan," I say simply.

She stops walking. "No money will save him." The words tremble from her lips and fade to a whisper. Unshed tears gather like raindrops in her eyes. "He's going to die." She grabs my arm, her fingers biting into my arm, her urgency obvious. "And you do know that Chris is going to blame himself, don't you?"

My throat restricts. "Yes. I know."

"Don't let him."

"I don't think I can stop him, but I will be there for him." I say softly, "And for you, too, if you need me. Please put my number in your cell. Call me anytime, Brandy. Ask me for anything."

Her grip slowly loosens on my arm and we exchange cell numbers. We silently head to the cafeteria, and after a somber silence, remarkably we manage to shift to random chitchat and it's not long before Brandy and I are in the back of the room watching Chris and Dylan in animated conversation while they scarf down chocolate.

"The doctors don't like him to have candy," Brandy whispers, "but how can I deny him the things he enjoys?"

"I wouldn't deny him anything he wants, either," I say, my eyes falling on the young boy and shifting to Chris. He's good with the kids, and I wonder if he's thought about having his own. I've never thought about kids, but after today, I'm not sure I want to be a mother. How can you love this much and have that child stripped away from you? Losing my mother was hard enough. If I lose Chris—

"You love him," Brandy says softly. "I see it in your face when you look at him."

My gaze lingers on Chris. "Yes. Yes I do."

"Good," she says approvingly as I shift my attention to her. "Sam and I see the pain that man carries around. He needs someone to hold some of it for him."

This analysis punches me in the chest. Chris has held everything life has burdened him with all on his own since he was a teen. That Brandy sees what he hides beneath his affable exterior speaks volumes about the kind of people she and her husband are. They are living in excruciating pain, but they still see beyond it to worry about Chris. I think about how upset he was on the phone two nights before, and it's crystal clear to me that he needs me to carry some of his load this weekend. This isn't the time to share my inner demons with him, and not because I want to put off the dreaded event. Because now is a time for me to be here for him, to show him I love him, even if I don't dare tell him until I make sure he knows who I really am.

Brandy points to the front of the room. "We're being summoned."

I glance up to find Chris and Dylan waving us forward and a few minutes later I have caved to the impossible. I've agreed to watch *Friday the 13th* with Chris and Dylan while Brandy and Sam have agreed to go home and get some much-needed rest.

Three hours later, Chris and I have curled onto the hospital lounge chair by Dylan's bed, with Chris's painting of Freddy and Jason propped on a roller table, when our horror flick finally ends. Dylan hasn't stopped laughing at my yelps and complaints, and his pleasure is music to my ears. He is such an amazing kid. He deserves to live.

Chris picks up the remote to the DVD player, turns it off, and checks the clock. "It's eleven o'clock. You better go to sleep, Dylan."

I grimace. "Sleep for both us, Dylan. I sure won't be getting any myself."

Dylan laughs and snuggles down into the bed. "Will you stay until I fall asleep?"

Chris and I share a look and I nod my agreement. "We're right here, buddy," Chris assures him and he lowers the lounge chair downward like a bed. I curl up with my back to his front and his arm wraps around me.

Dylan dims the lights with the button on his bed and I close my eyes. I'm exhausted. It's been an insanely crazy day, full of jagged edges and twists and turns.

"I'm glad you're here," Chris whispers in my ear, sending a shiver down my spine.

"Me, too," Dylan whispers, clearly having overheard.

"Me, too," I reply to them both. It's been a day full of jagged edges, twist and turns, and bittersweet discovery.

Eighteen

*He is everything I am, and everything I am not. I do not remem-
ber where I begin and he ends, or where he ends and I begin. He
is my Master. I am his slave. I'm struggling to remember who I
was before he was. It's terrifying to think that I could give myself
to him this completely when I know he has not done the same
for me. What will I be when he is gone? Do I dare stay and find
out the answer is nothing? And what will he do if I tell him I'm
leaving?*

I jerk awake with one of the final chilling entries in one of
Rebecca's journals spinning in my mind. Sunlight beams into
the hospital room, which is empty but for me, and I realize Dylan
and Chris are gone.

A piece of paper crinkles under my hand and I lift it to
find Chris's handwriting. *Snuck Dylan out for secret meeting with
kitchen and a stack of chocolate chip pancakes. We have to get to the*

hotel and shower by ten. The nurse left you an overnight kit in the bathroom.

I glance at the clock and it's 8 a.m. I can't believe Chris and I both knocked out this hard and long on a lounge chair. I stand up and stretch and head to the bathroom, taking my phone with me in case Chris calls. On the sink, under the small bag of toiletries, is a folded newspaper I'm clearly meant to see. I pick it up and blink at a photo of me with Chris and Dylan, and Chris has scribbled, *Mark should be happy.* I frown a moment until the light bulb goes off. Oh yes, Mark will be happy. Chris and I have on our Allure shirts and they are clearly visible. I snap a picture of the paper and text it to Mark. I've barely opened my new toothbrush before Mark replies. The shirt looks better on you than Chris. I stare at the message and let out a short laugh. Huh. This is one of those off-the-wall replies Mark gives me in e-mails, and apparently text messages, where he seems more man than Master. There's more to him than his stiff "Ms. McMillan this, Ms. McMillan that," and I wonder if he really is the man in the journals. Somehow, I can't see the Master Rebecca has written about making jokes like this one or ending an e-mail quoting *The Hunger Games* with "may the odds be forever in your favor," as he once did to me. I type a reply and delete it two times and then snatch my toothbrush. Why am I fretting over a text to Mark?

A few minutes later I've combed my tangled mess of hair into order, and my equally brown eyes seem to make my pale skin two shades paler, which is pretty darn pale. But it doesn't matter as it might have just twenty-four hours ago. Watching these kids and their families fight for their very lives has given me perspective on my own insecurities. It also makes me think about how important living in the now is, how easily life can be ripped away, as it was for my mother, and for Chris's. No matter how terrifying the ultimate decision is, I have to resign from my teaching job on Monday.

I leave the bathroom and walk back into Dylan's room, thinking I will share this decision with Chris, to find I'm still alone. The sound of voices draw my gaze to the half-opened door where I glimpse Brandy in deep conversation with a man in scrubs and a white coat, and she doesn't look happy. The man I assume to be the doctor squeezes her shoulder and walks away. Brandy drops her face in her hands.

I'm across the room and out the door in a quick dash. "Brandy?" Her hands fall away from her face and I see the tears streaming down her cheeks. "Oh honey, what's wrong?" I wrap her in a hug and she clings to me.

"His cancer is progressing faster than expected."

I feel as if I've just had my insides carved out, and Dylan isn't even my child. How must she feel and how can I possibly console her?

After several moments, she steps back. "I need to see my son. I need to call Sam. He's at work."

"I'll call him," I offer. "You go freshen up and be with Dylan."

She gives me Sam's number and hugs me again, her body shaking. I look up and my heart lurches as Chris steps off the elevator with Dylan by his side. I wave him off and he quickly backs into the car and pulls Dylan with him. A silent breath of relief escapes my lips at what could have been an emotional meltdown between mother and son. Somehow, I have to help

Brandy gather her composure and be strong for her son, when I know she's dying inside with him. And somehow I have to get Chris through this. Deep down, I am certain this is going to wrench open deep wounds in my already damaged man, and I hurt just thinking about it.

When finally I have Brandy somewhat composed, I text Chris that he and Dylan can join us. A few minutes later, Dylan ambles into the room, grinning and singing the song from *Nightmare on Elm Street,* "One, two, Freddy's coming for you. Three, four, you better lock your door. Five, six, grab your crucifix."

Chris follows behind him, a one-day dark blond shadow on his jaw, his hair rumpled and sexy, and his eyes as haunted as Brandy's. He's not heard the news about the cancer progressing but he's smart enough to assume bad news is coming.

Dylan continues to sing as he plops onto the bed. "Seven, eight, you better stay up late."

"Enough," I exclaim, but I am smiling at his attempt to tease me.

"Yes, enough," Brandy agrees, laughing. "I get creeped out from that song, too."

"You two can't be scared just by hearing the song," Dylan argues.

I shiver just thinking about that movie. "There's plenty of reasons why I agreed to watch *Friday the 13th* instead of *Nightmare on Elm Street,* and that song is the top of the list."

"We'll make her watch it next time," Chris promises, sitting down next to him.

Dylan pumps his fist. "Yes!" he says and laughs.

It hits me as I watch the two of them say their good-byes for the day before we depart that Dylan and Chris both replace one horror with another. Dylan uses fictional movies and monsters to combat cancer, and Chris uses pain to combat pain. No wonder these two are bonded so tightly.

"Well?" Chris asks as we step in the elevator.

It takes effort to get myself to tell him what I know will hurt him. "His cancer is progressing faster than expected."

His head drops back, face lifting to the ceiling, and the torment in him claws at me. I wrap my arms around his waist and press my cheek to his racing heart. "I'm sorry."

He buries his head in my hair and inhales as if it gives him relief. "I've been through this before, but this kid, he's special."

My chin lifts, my gaze finding his troubled one. "I know. I can see the bond you've formed with him."

The elevator opens and he laces his fingers with mine. It's not long before we are in the much-warmer-than-home L.A. weather, trying to flag down a cab, which turns out to be a struggle Chris doesn't need right now. Finally, we're on the way to the hotel and I bring up the difficult topic of Dylan's father. "I told Brandy I'd call her husband. I think she knew talking to him would make her melt down again. Do you want to talk to him or should I?"

Chris grabs his cell off his belt. "I will."

I watch Chris as he explains to Dylan's father, Sam, what has happened. Chris wears an emotionless mask throughout the conversation, but he's gripping his leg so tightly that the muscles knot beneath his dragon tattoo.

When we pull up to the hotel Chris is still on the phone, and he tosses a hundred-dollar bill for a ten dollar-trip at the driver and waves him on. He finally hangs up with Sam when we are exiting to our floor, and the edginess of his mood is downright palpable. He doesn't look at me, either, and I struggle with what to say or do, standing in silence as he swipes the card in the door and pushes it open.

I'm surprised when he enters ahead of me when he would normally follow me inside. I shut the door behind us in time to see him pound the wall and then press his fists against the surface. His head drops between his shoulders and I can see the long, lithe muscles rippling through his body.

I close the distance between us and reach for him. "Don't," he commands sharply, stilling my hand in action, his voice gravelly, rough. "I'm not in a good place."

"Be there with *me*, Chris. Let me help."

The depth of despair in his eyes seems to tunnel straight into hell. "This part of me is why I warned you away."

"It didn't work then and it's not working now."

He grabs me and puts me between the wall and him. "This is when I'd—"

"I know," I interrupt. "This is one of those times you need pain to replace pain. I understand it, after what I saw these past twenty-four hours. But if we're going to make it, Chris, you have to find a way to go there with me."

'There's nothing gentle in me while I'm like this. You don't want who I am right now."

"I want every part of you, Chris."

For several seconds, he stares at me, and then suddenly his fingers twine into my hair and he's kissing me. His anger and pain bleed into my mouth, searing me in their intensity. My hands go to his chest and he shackles them with one of his. "Don't touch me. Not until I'm past this."

"Okay." Somehow I manage to sound strong when I'm shaken by just how out of himself he truly is.

"Undress," he orders. "I don't trust myself to do it."

I have no idea what he means by that, but he steps back from me and tugs his shirt over his head. I pull my own tee off, along with my bra, and I reach for my pants but struggle as my hand is trembling uncontrollably.

Chris is in front of me in an instant, holding my wrist. "Damn it, I knew this was a mistake. I'm scaring you."

"You don't scare me, Chris. You hurt, so I hurt."

A thunderstorm of emotions crosses his face and he drops his forehead to mine like he did on the plane. His breathing is ragged and he's obviously battling to rein in whatever he's feeling.

It is nearly impossible to resist the powerful urge to touch him. "Stop trying to control it, Chris. Just let it out. I can handle it."

"I can't."

He steps back from me and shocks me by walking toward the bathroom. I blink after him. He can't? What does that even mean? I hear the shower come on and I try to stay where I am because he obviously wants space, but *I can't*. I ignore the fact that my nudity isn't the best confrontational attire, but then he's not exactly dressed himself.

I charge to the open bathroom door and enter as he steps inside the see-through glass-encased shower. I keep walking and I open the shower. "You can't?" I challenge. "What does that even mean? You can't be with me? Do you want me to leave?"

He leans out of the shower and kisses me. "It means I can't, and won't, do anything I think will make you want to leave." He strokes a wet thumb over my cheek. "And right now, I will."

But the edge of his mood has shifted in that rocket-swift way it does. He is not who he was just a few minutes ago. I dare to step into the shower and hug him, the spray of warm water enveloping me, and to my relief his arms do as well. I feel the hard length of his cock expanding, thickening, and I am further encouraged until I blink up at him and see the barely banked storm. He's not as okay as I thought. Not even close. He says sex isn't a part of how he deals with his pain, but he's aroused, and I can't hurt him. I *won't* hurt him. I have only pleasure to offer him.

I press him against the wall, out of the beating force of the water, and he lets me. Taking that as a good sign, I slowly slide down his body and drop to my knees. His soft intake of breath is further encouragement I welcome. I brush wet hair from my mouth and wrap my hand around his pulsing shaft. I don't tease him. He needs hard and fast, a release, relief. I think. I hope. I suckle the soft skin of his taut erection into my mouth and the salty taste of his arousal teases my tongue. Without lingering, I take all of him I can and his hand comes down on my head.

"Harder," he orders, his voice a gruff command, his hips arching into the suckle of my mouth, and I can feel him throbbing against my tongue.

My gaze lifts, and I watch him watching me, the grit of his teeth, the tightness of his jaw, the lust and fury, in his hot stare. It's arousing to have this powerful, sexy man respond to me, want me, need me. And he does. I have never been as sure of this as I am now.

My fingers tighten around him and I draw on him with more force, taking him deeper. He pumps against me, driving to the back of my throat, fucking my mouth, and his desire is a living, breathing thing that possesses me. I can't get enough of it, of him. My tongue slides down the pulsing underside of his cock, and he moans, deep and guttural. His head falls back against the tiles and I feel him slip into mindless oblivion.

My body burns from the taste of him, the feel of him against my tongue, with the power I have to take him away from his pain. I wrap my hand around his thigh for leverage, the tension there telling me how close he is to release.

"Good, baby," he murmurs, his voice low, husky. Sexy. "So good." His hand tightens on my head and urgency surges through him into me. He begins to pump harder, pushing his cock deeper into my throat and I take him, I take him, hungering for the moment that arrives with a hoarse moan sliding from his lips. His shaft spasms in my mouth and I taste his salty release seeping into my taste buds, where his anger had bled not long before. I drag my tongue and lips up and down him, slowly easing him to completion.

His chin lowers and Chris gasps and stares down at me. I push to my feet and he drags me against him. "Tell me I helped," I say, and it's a demand. I need to know I can be what he needs, that we can get through the darkness together.

"You do more than help. You're the reason I take my next breath." The hoarse declaration whispers against my lips a moment before he kisses me, the tenderness in the touch of his tongue caressing mine telling me more than his words.

The kiss ends and we don't speak. We lather each other up,

lost in each other, and it has nothing to do with sex, and everything to do with the deepening bond between us. When the moment comes that he presses me against the wall, and slides inside me, our eyes connect the way our bodies have, and what passes between us fills me in a way I have never been filled. He needs me and I need him. I've never doubted that to be true. I've always known we were two puzzle pieces that fit together in a hollow that is our pain. There was a time when I was certain we were too damaged not to destroy each other. Now I think we are saving each other.

Nineteen

My hope that the turbulence in Chris has passed is quickly dashed not long after we arrive at a charity luncheon. We sit at one of twenty-five tables and listen as a man tells potential donors the story of his child dying of cancer. I cannot help but think of Dylan and my gaze leaves the speaker to study Chris. He's in profile to me, his expression impassive, his spine stiff. I know he knows I'm looking at him but he just stares forward, the muscle in his jaw flexing back and forth. I reach down and take his hand and he slowly turns to me, and for just a moment, he lets me see the pain splintering in amber flecks through his green eyes. I trace his cheek, silently telling him I understand, and he squeezes my hand, his attention slowly returning to the front of the room.

Once again, a stark certainty fills me. Chris *is* darkness and pain, and no matter how much he says he has that part of him under control, he doesn't. I'm not sure he truly wants to have it under control. I want to heal him, to be there for him, but I wonder if I really can be. I'm not sure he will let me.

This thought lingers with me through the rest of the speakers, and I am relieved when the luncheon comes to a close, but there is no fast escape from the event. Chris and I mingle with the guests and I'm amazed at how well he maintains a façade of lightheartedness, tossing out just the right comments at the right times, to bring smiles to many faces.

An hour later, we are at the hospital visiting some of the kids, and Chris crafts sketches of funny animals and cartoon characters. Amazingly, no one but me seems to notice how troubled he is. I watch him, seeing beyond my gorgeous, sexy man to the man who, despite his own pain, gives so much to these families, and I fall even more in love with him.

Once we've finished our visits, Chris and I are heading down the hall toward Dylan's room, which we plan to make our final destination, when Chris stops walking and glances down at a text message.

The grim look on his face has me worried. "What?" I demand.

He punches in a message before replying. "Blake says the lock on the storage unit wasn't changed but the unit looked rifled through. He wanted to know if things were thrown everywhere when we were last there."

"No. Tell him no."

"I already did." He reads another message, starting to relay information as he does. "He thinks that lowlife PI changed the locks while the power was off and the combination was popped open."

I see where this is going and fill in the blanks. "We didn't seal the unit with my lock. We popped his into place so he could return when he was ready."

"Right. I'm sure he was looking for that opportunity the night you met him. We can assume he replaced the original lock that was yours when he got what he wanted out of the unit."

My head begins to throb. "How bad was it rummaged through?"

"Sounds like her things are tossed all over the place."

A frustrated sound slips from my lips. "Can we call the police?"

"Blake says we'll never prove someone else was inside the unit and we still shouldn't involve the police when we've decided to hold off."

Reluctantly, I accept the helplessness of the situation. "If there were any more journals, they're lost forever." And with them the potential answer to where she is, and who is responsible for her disappearance.

"Blake and the entire team at Walker Security are the best. If anyone can find Rebecca, they will."

"If they're as good as you say, and it hasn't been easy to find her, Chris, I'm more concerned than ever."

Chris's mouth tightens. "Unfortunately, I agree."

I try to shake off my somber mood before we enter Dylan's room, but it's an effort lost once we arrive. The energetic boy I'd met the day before is nowhere to be found. He's in bed, bent over a pan, throwing up, while his mother is beside herself trying to soothe him. The only thing that keeps my feet on the ground is the absolute need for me to keep everyone else's feet there.

Brandy's hand shakes every time she moves, and Chris's energy ratchets up a notch. He's like a wild animal pacing a cage he cannot escape.

Somehow, though, he reins it in and discovers Brandy hasn't eaten or slept. He forces her to go take a break while we sit with Dylan. Chris sits on the edge of Dylan's bed and caves to a plea for him to draw another Freddy Krueger picture. Miraculously, Dylan perks up when Chris starts to sketch on the pad he's been carrying with him.

At four o'clock Chris has to leave for a donor meeting, and I stay behind with Dylan and Brandy with plans to meet him at the hotel at five thirty. At five forty-five, I'm still standing in front of the hospital after waiting for half an hour on a cab. I've texted Chris but he hasn't replied.

Finally he calls. "I just got out of my meeting. Did you get one?"

"No," I answer frantically. "There's two big conventions in town and a movie premiere."

"Tell the cab company there's a hundred-dollar tip in it for them and I'll meet you at the front of the hotel to pay them. If that doesn't work I'll send a private car."

Fifteen minutes later, Chris greets me at the front of the hotel in jeans and a plain white T-shirt, with his hair lying in damp tendrils around his face. He yanks open my door and leans inside the front passenger window and pays the driver. In a rush to shower and dress, I step out of the cab, and Chris settles his hands on my shoulders and kisses me solidly on the lips. "I missed you."

Though Chris is inherently private, right now he's oblivious to the people all around us. I blink up at him and glimpse that rare vulnerability in his expression that always roots its way deep inside me and turns me inside out. I stroke a damp strand of his hair and a waterfall of emotions crashes down on me. "Chris, I—" A horn honks and Chris pulls me forward as a cabbie guns by me. I step onto the curb and silently finish my sentence . . . *love you*.

"Crazy cabdriver," he grumbles, twining his fingers with mine.

We start walking toward the hotel entrance, but my spontaneous confession has been sideswiped by a yellow cab. I tell myself that's a good thing. I was crazy to do this now. It's the wrong time and place, but I can't seem to rid myself of the feeling that I've lost a moment I will regret.

I rush through my shower and slip into the hotel-provided robe to do my makeup and hair. I've just finished flat-ironing my hair into a sleek straight style when Chris appears in the doorway, wearing his tuxedo. I set the brush down and turn to him, soaking in the way he defines his clothes. Perfectly fitted and pressed, the pants and jacket hug his lithe, muscular frame with delicious results. And while he's conformed to the expected "monkey suit," as he's called it previously, he is unshaven, a light brown shadow dusting his jaw, and his blond hair is rumpled and a bit wild, the contrast declaring him both the man I know and love and a rebel with a cause.

"You are the sexiest man alive," I declare.

Chris smiles, and for the first time all day it reaches his eyes. "I'll let you prove you mean that when we get back tonight." He pulls a black velvet box from behind his back. "This is for you." His lips curve. "And me."

My breath catches as I read AdamandEve.com on top of the box. It's the sexy online store I'd told Chris about on the phone two evenings before. "I'm guessing that isn't a pink fluffy paddle."

"Don't look disappointed," he teases. "I'll order one to be delivered when we get home." He flips open the lid and lying on black silk are three pieces of jewelry. Two matching silver hoops, each having a long strand of dangling rubies. The third has a silver hoop and a teardrop laced with the same rubies.

"To wear under your dress," he announces.

Unbidden, I hear one of Rebecca's entries replay in my head, as if she is speaking to me. *He turned me around, tugged my dress and bra down, and clamped my nipples, ordering me to endure the pain.* I cross my arms in front of my chest and shake my head. "No. I can't wear those to the party."

Chris sets the box on the vanity and advances on me. I step backward, but he's already in front of me, framing my face with his hands. "They aren't clamps, if that's what you think. I wouldn't ask you to wear clamps for an extended period of time. This is jewelry. Nothing more than delicious friction for you, and a tempting distraction for me, which, believe me, I need tonight."

"Oh."

"Oh," he repeats, his lips curving. He reaches for the thick tie on the robe, his stare holding mine. "Let me show you."

The panic of moments before transforms into a simmering warmth low in my belly. I don't look away from his penetrating gaze. I drop my arms and the robe gapes open, the cool air teasing my bare skin. Approval slides over his face and his fingers lightly brush my nipples. I attempt to swallow a whimper and fail. Chris shifts our position, settling my backside against the vanity, his hips molded to mine, the thick pulse of his erection settling against my stomach.

Lazily he tweaks the rosy tips until they are hard knots, and sweet, delicious sensations ripple through me. I grab his wrists. "Stop. We have to leave. I have to get dressed."

"Just making sure you're ready."

"I am ready. That's the problem."

He cups my breasts and pushes them together, leaning down to lave both of my nipples at once. My lashes flutter and my hand goes to his head. I don't have it in me to tell him to stop. I'll just have to dress faster. I don't notice when he reaches for one of the nipple rings. He's just suddenly slipping it over one of the swollen, aroused tips.

I bite my lip and stare down at the dangling jewels. "Hurt?" he asks, flicking it with his finger and sending darts of pleasure straight to my sex.

"No," I breathe out. "It doesn't hurt."

Satisfaction slides over his handsome face and he dips his head low again, rasping my bare nipple with his tongue. This time, as I watch him place the second ring into place, I'm aroused by more than the sight of the jewelry on my body; it's also the idea that Chris will be thinking about this all night.

He lifts me to the counter and spreads my legs, his palms traveling up my thighs, stopping at the slick swollen flesh of my sex, where his thumbs stroke and tease. "Are you thinking about fucking me, Sara?"

"No. I'm thinking of *you* fucking *me*."

He laughs, a deep, sexy sound that turns me to soft, melting honey. I feel myself grow wetter beneath his touch, and so does he. I see it in the darkening of his gaze, the amber heat dancing in the depth of his green eyes.

"As much as I'd like to fuck you, baby, it'll be all the better for the wait." He holds up the clit ring and proceeds to close it around the swollen, sensitive bud. He presses my legs apart wider still. "Don't move. I want to look at you." He takes a step backward.

I yank the robe shut and scoot off the vanity, positioning myself in front of him without touching him. My chin lifts. "You teased me. You can wait until later to see me." I sidestep him and put distance between us, before whirling around to face him. "Now out, and let me put my dress on."

"No bra and panties." It's an order, the alpha Chris I know and find so damn arousing, in all his glory.

"We'll see."

He's closed the distance between us and pulled me hard against him in an instant. "No bra. No panties. Understand?"

His heart thunders beneath my palm. He is not unaffected by this exchange. He does not have all the power, but his need for it permeates the air, as alive as I am when he is touching me.

I press to my toes and kiss him. "Yes. I understand."

For a moment he's stiff and unyielding. The next his hand is melded on my back beneath the gaping robe. His lips brush mine, then his tongue, a whisper of a touch before it's gone. "How is it that you always do exactly what I don't expect you to do?" he asks in a gravelly voice. He sets me away from him and exits the bathroom, pulling the door shut behind him.

I stare after him for several seconds, wondering if doing the opposite of what he expects is a good or a bad thing. But the truth is, I don't try to be someone else with Chris, as I have with other men in my life. I'm rediscovering myself, or perhaps finding myself for the first time ever.

With an inner shake, I spur myself into action, sliding on my black thigh-highs, black high heels, and finally, the emerald green dress. No bra. No panties. Already, the rubies are teasing me unmercifully just as Chris had with his mouth and fingers. I inspect my reflection in the mirror, loving the dress even more than I did in the store. The vibrant green complements my pale skin, and the dress hugs my body without being overtly sexy. And thankfully the fitted bodice provides enough coverage to hide the ruby-covered rings on my nipples.

Reaching for the bathroom door, I pause a moment as adrenaline pours through me at the idea of Chris waiting beyond. I step into the bedroom to find Chris leaning against the front door, one leg crossed over the other, his arms over his chest. He watches me expectantly, silently willing me to walk to him, and I am powerless to defy him, aroused by nothing more than the way he consumes the room, and me, with it. He tracks my every step, touching me without touching me, seducing me with the promise of the pleasure he's proven that he, and he alone, can give me.

I stop in front of him and still he doesn't move, doesn't reach for me. "Turn around."

Doing as he says is automatic. He's right. I crave these moments where he's in control and anticipation simmers low in my belly to discover what he intends next. With him I can let go, when I don't dare do so elsewhere or with anyone else.

A cool sensation slides around my neck and I become aware of the necklace he's hooking at my nape. Surprised, my hand goes to the jewel at my throat, and he leans down and whispers. "Go look in the mirror."

Curious, I rush to the bathroom to stare into the mirror at the round emerald pendant with diamonds glistening like stars around the edges, where it dips into the V of my neckline. Chris appears behind me, his eyes meeting mine in the mirror, and the connection delivers the now-familiar punch of awareness he creates in me that never gets old. There is a stark hunger in his expression that runs far deeper than the ripe physical need between us. This gift matters to him. It's special, nothing like the tokens my father gave to my mother, and my liking it is important to him.

"It couldn't be more perfect," I say softly. "Thank you."

His hand splays possessively on my stomach, and he buries his face in my hair, his mouth pressing to my ear. "You're perfect." His voice is rough.

Everything Chris does is as raw and real as the pain he struggles to bury in some deep, dark cavern of his soul. And I dread the moment he discovers just how *not* perfect I am.

Twenty

After leaving our hotel room, Chris and I step into the packed elevator. Chris leans against the wall, settling me under the crook of his arm, and his touch is like a hot, welcome branding too intimate for the public setting. The rubies dangle between my legs, a teasing friction against my clit that, while not painful, is inescapable—as is the thick ridge of Chris's arousal against my backside. Chris nuzzles my neck, and I shiver. I can almost taste his pleasure at my reaction, and his hands travel up and down my rib cage, tugging the silk of my dress and the jewels on my nipples. My hands go to his, holding them steady in a silent reprimand, and his soft, sexy rumble of laughter touches my ear.

My lips curve at his playfulness, and the contrast of this moment to another occasion when I wore no bra and panties, at the winery, strikes me. I'd scolded myself for daring to see romance in what was a sexy adventure. Even meeting his godparents that warm August night still left me wondering where Chris and I were headed. I could easily spin doubts and get tangled up in all that could go wrong tonight if I let myself. The list of worries is long. Chris's return to Paris. My impending career decisions. My secret. My gut clenches and the elevator opens.

I step off the car and mentally leave my concerns inside. Tonight Chris needs me to be clear and present. My Dark Prince is teetering on the edge of darkness over Dylan, and I have to be the rope he clings to for a lifeline.

Once in the corridor, Chris twines his fingers with mine, and this small, intimate act makes my heart squeeze, warming me far more than the gentle sway of the jewels between my thighs while I walk. I cut him a sideways glance to find him doing the same to me, and it is as if I'm experiencing a summer breeze. He floats inside me and completes me, and for the first time in my life I have a sense of being in a relationship, rather than being alone or possessed. Ironic, I think, considering this is the same man whom I've all but begged to claim me and possess me. He is dark passion and wicked heat and I can't get enough of him.

We exit the hotel into the warm, cloudless night, dozens of stars shining brightly above, and I slip my small sparkling black purse over the thin emerald strap on my shoulder. The private car Chris ordered for us is waiting, but we turn when we overhear an elderly couple, also attending the gala, struggling to find a cab.

Chris and I share a look of understanding before he addresses the couple: "You can join us. We're headed to the same place."

A sleek 911 halts beside a doorman, and I have a momentary flashback to the night of the wine tasting at the gallery. I'd walked out of the gallery to find Chris leaning on the 911, my father's car of choice. I'd compared the two men who are incomparable, and the smiles Chris has just put on the elderly couple's faces drives home that point.

Inside the back of the car, sitting in the middle, I begin chatting with the woman beside me. Chris settles his hand on my knee, his thumb absently caressing my silk stocking, heat seeping through to my skin. Darts of pleasure shoot up my leg and straight to my swollen, overly sensitive clit.

It's becoming impossible to focus on my conversation, and when I can take no more, I grab his hand and hold it still, shooting him a warning look.

Chris arches a brow. "Something wrong?"

I cut him a look and spoke softly. "You know exactly what you're doing."

"Yes," he agrees and his lips twitch. "I do."

"Of course you do," and the fact that he does is enticingly erotic rather than enticingly frightening. It's also the reason I hold his hand for the duration of the ten-minute drive.

We exit the car at the Children's Museum, where the gala is being held, and cameras begin to flash. Chris's discomfort is palpable as we walk the red carpet laid out on the stairway to the entry, and I'm not surprised when he declines visiting the press room. His dislike for the spotlight and his willingness to put himself there for his charity speaks volumes about how much this cause means to him.

Once inside the building, we pause under a massive archway that is the entry to the main triangle-shaped event room, where about one hundred guests mingle in the open area between us and the band performing on the opposite side of the room. Music echoes upward, spiraling into the massive dome covering us, and I am in awe of the artwork painted on its interior.

Reminded of another wall closer to home, I cannot help but say, "This reminds me of Mark's office. You painted his wall, didn't you?"

There is a slight tightening around his mouth. "Yes."

"Yes? Just yes?"

He shrugs. "He swore he'd sell one of my paintings at Riptide for a ridiculous figure and I agreed to paint the wall if he did."

"And you donated the money to the hospital."

I watch the emotion flash across his face and his expression becomes all hard lines and ridges. "It paid for Dylan's treatments and set up a trust fund for his family they don't know exists yet."

I feel his words like the punch in the chest I know they are to him. "You and Mark seem to do a lot of good together, but you have a strange relationship."

"We have a business relationship."

"But you were once friends."

"*Friends* is a word used too loosely by too many people," he comments dryly, and clearly he has had enough talk of Mark. He motions to a table of food. "Are you hungry?"

"I'm starving," I say, but I'm bothered by the way he avoids the topic of Mark.

Chris's hand slides around my waist, discreetly molding us hip to hip, thigh to thigh, and all thoughts of Mark are gone when he softly murmurs, "I'm starving, too—and not for food." And he looks like he wants to gobble me up right here and now.

My body reacts, and my lack of panties makes the damp heat between my thighs more than a little evident.

I blush, and I don't know why. Less than an hour before, the man licked my nipples and attached rubies to them, but there are just these moments when Chris is such a powerful male that I melt for him.

And he knows it. I see it in his face, in the wicked heat burning in the depths of his green eyes. I don't care, either. I don't fear him knowing how I react to him as I once might have. I watch as a slow, sensual smile slides onto his lips, and with it I am relieved to see the dark lines and ridges of moments before fade away. "Ah now," he says softly, seductively, "there is my sweet little blushing schoolteacher. Seems I haven't corrupted her completely just yet." He pauses. "But I'm working on it."

"You accused me of corrupting you."

"You did, but in all the right ways, baby."

My brows furrow. "What does that mean?"

"If you don't know yet, you will."

He sweeps me into the crush of the crowd, leaving me guessing his meaning, which shouldn't surprise me. He is all about coded double meanings, and hidden messages I understand later, if at all.

We survey several tables of food and stop at one filled with a variety of finger foods. We fill small plates and do our best to eat between chats with the many people who want to talk to Chris. I'm finishing a bite of a finger sandwich when out of nowhere, it seems, Gina Ray, a rather famous actress, who according to a Google search once dated Chris, appears by his side.

Her hair is brown silk, her dress red and cut to display her ample cleavage, which she presses against Chris's arm as she hugs him. "Chris!" she exclaims. "So good to see you." Her voice is a rich, lovely mix of wild vixen and Hollywood bombshell, just as she is.

The only thing ample about me is my insecurity I swore I left in the hospital, but apparently it's hitched a ride to the gala. Compared to her, I feel awkward and unladylike, and absolutely not star- or Chris-worthy. I feel like the sweet little schoolteacher who has no business being here at this party with a man like Chris. I set my plate down and fight the urge to dart away, though I have no clue to where.

Chris seems to sense my reaction and dislodges himself from Gina's embrace, wrapping his arm around my waist. "Sara, this is Gina Ray. Gina's been a huge supporter of our charity for several years now, and"—he glances down at me meaningfully— "contrary to the paparazzi who chase her around like starving animals, I have never dated her. Gina, this is Sara McMillan, whom I *am* dating, and who is someone I hope you'll be seeing by my side often."

His announcement delivers relief and a sweet, warm spot in my chest. I melt into Chris and his fingers flex on my hip.

Gina rolls her eyes playfully. "I've apologized with my checkbook for that dating scandal, Chris. Stop guilting me for putting you through that." She fixes her attention on me, and her pale blue eyes, so unlike my deep, dark chocolate ones, remind me of diamonds in the moonlight. "And very nice to meet you, Sara." She extends her hand and I accept it. A camera flashes and still holding my hand, she casts Chris a quelling look. "It's not my fault if tomorrow's news is Gina Ray has run-in with ex-lover's new girlfriend. Not. My. Fault." Someone calls Gina's name and she releases me. "I'll catch up with you two in a bit."

"You read the gossip about me dating her," Chris accuses the instant we are alone again.

"Why do you say that?" I ask guiltily.

"You almost choked on your sandwich when she hugged me."

I shrug. "She's a movie star. I was starstruck."

His lips quirk. "Is that so?"

"Okay. I might have googled you at some point."

"Anything else you discovered I need to explain?"

"No. Nothing." And I mean it. I believe he still has secrets of his own, but none of them will be found on Google. They'll be found in the midst of his pain, which I hope he allows me to fully understand one day. My voice softens. "I know everything I need to know."

A hint of the torment I seem to excel in creating in him flashes in his green eyes.

"Sara—" He is cut off when we are suddenly surrounded by a group of people who all want to speak to Chris and meet me, leaving me wondering what he'd been about to say. We fade into the conversation but our eyes lock and hold, unspoken words twining between us, burning to be heard.

Over the next hour, Chris and I mingle with the lively crowd, and I'm relieved when we relax into a light, fun evening. I revel in how he touches me often, each brush of his hand adding warmth to my soul, where he has found a place and taken root. And when our eyes meet, awareness sizzles through me that that has nothing to do with the never-ending friction created by the rubies, and everything to do with our deepening bond. I am happy, and that isn't something I remember being much in my adult life. Happy never lasts but I plan to fight for it this time.

I spot the waitstaff preparing a table filled with a variety of coffee and chocolate concoctions with whipped cream, and while I am dragging Chris in that direction, he is accosted by an excited, sixty-something fan. Seems she has a paintbrush he'd autographed at another event and she wants another for her son.

"I'll be at the chocolate," I tell him. I kiss his cheek, whispering, "Next to you, it's my favorite temptation."

He whispers something in French and I have no doubt it's naughty. I bite my lip at just how sexy it sounds.

I'm still smiling inside over the exchange when I am handed a mocha with whipped cream on top. I move to a small round standing table and scoop up a spoonful. It's delicious, like my flirtation with Chris. I'm amazed at how comfortably me I am with him.

"Hello, Sara."

I freeze with a second spoonful of sweet cream in my mouth, and my eyes are locked on the tuxedo directly in front of me, on the familiar hand now resting on the white tablecloth. On the familiar voice that might as well be acid burning a path down my spine. It can't be. He can't be here. It's been two years of silence, since I threatened a restraining order. Two years I thought would be forever.

Slowly, I set down my spoon on the saucer and curse the tremble of my hand I know he will see. He is a manipulator, a user. A bastard I never wanted to see again but I am not the girl I was five years ago or even two years ago. I will not cower.

Steeling myself for the impact, I lift my gaze, but I do not see the man whom most see as personifying tall, dark, and handsome. Nor do I feel the striking impact of his crystal blue stare the way others do, the way I once did. I see nothing but the monster I discovered the last time we saw each other.

"Michael." I hate how his name rasps out of my mouth, how my throat tightens uncomfortably. How I am letting him have an impact on me. I feel a moment of panic, a sense of the ground falling out from under my feet. No. This isn't when or how Chris was supposed to learn about my past. He has too much on his shoulders this weekend to carry my load, too. Which is why I cannot crumble. I won't. I will be strong.

My fingers curl into my palms. "What are you doing here?"

"I saw your picture in the paper, and needed to take a trip to our research facility in Silicon Valley anyway. Your father and I thought it was a perfect opportunity to contribute to a good cause and catch up with you at the same time."

My father—who has not made one single attempt, with all the resources he possesses, to contact me in five years. Who wasn't even at the event to honor my mother, and where I last saw Michael. I hate how much his actions still twist me into knots. I hate how much I ridiculously yearn for a parent who never gave a damn about me, who never gave a damn about my mother, who loved him with all of her heart.

My lips tighten. "We both know my father didn't send you here."

"Actually, he did. See, we keep tabs on you, Sara. We always have. That means we keep tabs on the people you include in your life. Which brings me to the here and now and your recent choice in companions."

Heat floods my face and my heart races wildly. "What does that mean?"

"It means that Chris Merit has some *interesting* diversions, don't you think?"

My heart explodes in my chest. Chris. He's using Chris against me. He knows about the club. That has to be what he means. This can't be happening. It can't be happening.

He continues, "We'd hoped you'd realize his destructive nature and walk away, but now that you're going public with him, getting your picture snapped and slapped in the newspapers, we can't stay out of what could be damaging to you and us."

"Us?" I demand. "You're not a part of any 'us' I am a part of."

"Wrong again. See, as your father's new VP, what hurts him hurts me, and vice versa. And I'm quite certain a children's charity would be more than a little disturbed by Chris's *interests*. Don't you think?"

He's obsessed and sick. "You just want me so I can inherit and you can take my money."

He leans closer and it's all I can do not to jerk back, to show weakness. "I just want the woman I love to come home, Sara." There is no love in his voice, only possessiveness, ownership. "I'm at the Marriott airport hotel. I expect to see you soon." He steps around me and he is gone, leaving me in the quicksand of his threats.

I stand there frozen, eroding inside. The room falls away and there is nothing but what happened two years before, and the black hole of my torment. And the certainty that I brought this on myself and Chris, with my actions, my foolishness. My weakness. I'd just been so damn alone, so lost, and Michael had been the one connection I had to my mother, and the father who seemed to want nothing to do with me. And he'd seemed different. Or maybe I just wanted him to be different. Deep down, I'd craved an excuse to go home, to have a home. Michael had been warm and charming, and I'd felt like I was meeting him all over again, that I'd judged him harshly in the past. But I'd been wrong, so very wrong.

I can feel myself spiraling down into the hell of that night. I'm starting to crumble and I know I have to get somewhere private and pull myself together, to think and find a way out of this. My gaze lifts, seeking an escape route, and collides with Chris's from across the room. I see the worry in his face, feel it from a distance. That's how powerful our connection is, and the vise around my chest tightens. Oh, God. I love this man, and I'm about to destroy him. I turn away from him and weave through the crowd. I cannot face him until I pull myself together, to get through tonight without a public meltdown.

Darting away, I weave through the crowd, worried Chris will catch up to me before I gain my composure, before I figure out how to fix this mess, but I have no idea where I'm going. I'm just walking, weaving, blindingly seeking escape.

I grab a passing waiter. "Ladies' room?"

He points to a sign and I rush away, turning a corner, close to escape, when I bump right into Gina. "Sorry. I'm sorry."

She grabs my arms to steady me and casts me a concerned look. "Are you okay?"

"Yes. Yes. I ate something that didn't sit well. I need a bathroom." It's a horrible excuse but it's all I have.

"Okay." She steps aside and calls, "Do you want me to get Chris?"

"No!" I exclaim, whirling around. "Please no. I don't want him to see me like this." I push open the door and walk past the woman at the sink, and I don't dare look at her. I head inside the handicapped stall directly in front of me and lock the door. On wobbly legs, I fall against the wall opposite the toilet. This is what everything in my life has collided together and become. Me, staring at a toilet, trying not to fall apart. Somehow it's perfectly appropriate.

A flashback of two years ago overtakes me. Of Michael driving me back to my hotel and walking me to my door. Of how gentle and sweet he'd seemed. I'd invited him in to talk. Just talk, I'd told him.

The instant the door had shut, everything had changed. He'd been angry, damning me for leaving, for making him look bad. I can almost feel the moment he slammed me against the wall and his body covered mine. And his hands were everywhere, all over me. I start to shake again. I can't stop shaking. I hug myself and will away the memories. My eyes prickle and I will away the tears. I will not give Michael the satisfaction of making me cry. I have to go back to the party and look presentable. I have to smile. I have to get through this night without ruining it for Chris.

"Sara!"

It's Chris's voice, and I can't believe he's in the bathroom. He never does what I expect or what is normally considered acceptable. And he is always there at my worst moments. Always. The only person who ever has been.

"She's in the back stall," the woman at the sink instructs.

"Can you give us a minute?" he asks.

"I'll watch the door," she tells him, clearly knowing him.

Great. Already someone to tell the world about some incident Chris's date had tonight.

"Sara." His voice is a soft caress, a promise he is here for me, maybe for the last time.

"You can't be in here, Chris." And damn it, my voice cracks.

"Open the door, baby. I need to see you."

"I can't. I can't open the door."

"Why?"

"Because if I do I'll cry and mess up my makeup."

"Let me in, Sara." His voice is gentle but insistent.

"Please, Chris. I'll be out in a minute and I'll be fine." But I don't sound fine. My voice is strained, barely recognizable.

"You know me. I'm not going to leave without you opening up."

You know me. I do know him and I know how much trust and privacy means to him. Not only did I lie to him, but he let me inside his world, and Michael is about to make it public.

"Sara." There is a push to the way he says my name, a gentle command, but still a command.

He isn't going away. He's too ridiculously stubborn. I unlock the door and step back to the wall, telling myself to make up yet another lie to get him past this evening, to protect him. Once we are back at the hotel, then I'll tell him everything. That's my plan but I fail miserably. The instant I see Chris, my brilliant, damaged, amazing artist who's let me into his life, and who I am about to lose, *I* lose it. My legs give out and I sink to the floor, tears bursting from some deep hidden place I've never visited but I knew existed.

Chris squats down in front of me and his hands are on my

shoulders, strong and sure, and I cry harder. I can't stop the waterfall. He shifts to lean against the wall and pulls me against him. "This isn't how this is supposed to happen."

"This isn't how what was supposed to happen?" he asks, stroking my hair and urging me to look at him with a finger under my chin. "This is about the man I saw you talking to, isn't it?"

"Michael." My stomach knots just saying his name. "That was Michael. I . . ." I draw a deep breath of courage and rush into my confession. "There are things I haven't told you. I meant to. I wanted to. I knew I had to but I just . . . I just wanted to forget and . . ." I bury my hands in my face. I can't look at him. I can't. My body shakes and I will away the tears I can't seem to escape.

Chris slides his hands to my head and forces my gaze back to his, his green eyes searching mine, and he sees too much, he sees what I don't want him to, what I can't hide from. He sees the demons I'm battling and how easily they have owned me.

"We all have things we want to forget. No one knows that better than me, but you can tell me anything. You have to know that by now."

"You're going to hate me, Chris."

"I can't hate you, baby." His thumbs stroke away my tears and his eyes soften, warm. "I love you way too much for that."

I feel as if a clamp has just slammed down around my heart. He loves me. Chris loves me, and while it's exactly what I've burned to hear, I can't accept it now. He doesn't know me well enough to love me. I shake my head. "No. No, don't say that until I know you mean it."

"I already mean it."

"I lied to you, Chris," I blurt out. "I didn't want you to know something about me so I just . . . I lied. I . . . told you I hadn't had sex in five years but that wasn't true." His hands go to my knees, and I feel him withdrawing already, preparing for whatever I'm about to say. I press my fingers to my temples and they tremble. "Two years ago—no—that's not true, either. Nineteen months and four days ago, I flew back to Vegas for a charity event honoring my mother. My father was a no-show and that hurt. It hurt so damn bad. Michael was there and I was alone and vulnerable and he acted like he cared, and I—"

"Wait," Chris says, his voice sharp, biting. He rotates me to press me against the wall, his hands on my arms. "You know exactly how many days it is since you fucked him last?"

I flinch. "No. I mean yes. But it wasn't like that, it was—"

"Do you still love him? Is that what this is about?"

"No—God, no! I love you, not him. I never loved Michael. He . . . he came to my room and I made the mistake of letting him in." Memories rip through me, and I tilt my head down. I can barely breathe with another flashback of Michael touching me, his hand on my breast. "I let him in." I force my gaze to Chris's and whisper, "I let him in, Chris."

Chris's hands go to my face, his gaze searching mine. "Are you telling me he raped you?"

"I just . . . I did what he wanted."

"Did you want him to touch you, Sara?"

"No," I whisper, and the tears have faded. The cold seeps into my limbs, slithering down my spine and settling deep in my soul, settling into the space where it's lived for two years.

"Did you tell him no?"

"Yes. Over and over I told him, but he didn't listen." My voice is calmer now, but strained. I still don't sound like me but then, who the hell am I? I don't know anymore. "And then, I don't know what happened. I just . . . gave up."

"Then he raped you."

"I gave up, Chris. He told me to do things and I did them. I *did them*. I was pathetic and weak, and I gave up. I don't know why I didn't just tell you it had been two years. I just . . . If I don't block it out, I unravel. We'd just met and I didn't think you were . . . that we were . . ."

He strokes my cheek. "I know, baby."

"You don't know," I say vehemently as I push to my feet.

Chris is there in an instant, his hand on the wall by my head, and he repeats what I'd said to him earlier in the evening. "I know all I need to know, Sara."

I shake my head again. "No. You don't see how bad it was. I woke up with that man in my bed and I have no one to blame but me. I let him put a ring back on my finger and order me back to Vegas."

"But you didn't go."

"No." My skin crawls just thinking about that morning, how Michael was touching me, acting like he owned me.

"Tell me," he prods. "What happened?"

I drop my gaze to his chest and draw a breath, trying to calm down, but it seems to lodge in my throat, and I barely get it out.

Chris's fingers slide under my chin. "What happened next, Sara?"

"I convinced him I was returning to California to pack.

Then I waited until I landed in San Francisco, and I called him and threatened him with a restraining order."

"And?"

"He laughed and told me I'd practically begged him to fuck me, and that's what he'd tell the cops. I told him I'd go public and he said he'd paint me as the disinherited daughter looking for revenge."

"And you said?"

"Bring it on. I didn't care about my reputation, but he did his."

"And he stayed away."

"Until tonight."

Chris frames my face with his hands and he kisses me, just lips to lips, but it's not just a kiss. It is fire and ice, and passion and heat, and love. There is love in this kiss and I lean into him, my hands going to his wrist, and I don't want this moment to end. His lips linger against mine, and just for these few moments there is nothing else but us, no Michael, no past, no future to worry over.

"Sara," he whispers, stroking my hair and searching my face. "It's a testament to how much that man fucked with your head that you'd think I'd hate you over this."

"*I* hate me for that night, Chris. I hate how weak and pathetic I was. I hate how—"

He cuts me off with a kiss, then strokes his thumb over my lip. "You are the furthest thing from weak. You were very brave and smart about how you handled what happened. And he will never touch you again. You have my word."

"Chris," I whisper, my hand going to his wrist. "Chris, there's more. Tonight—"

"Later. Tell me later. Right now, you stay here. I'll come back and get you."

He starts to move away and panic overcomes me. I grab his arm. "No. Stop. What are you doing?"

"I'm going to deal with Michael myself."

"No!" I say quickly. "That's what I have to tell you. I think he knows about the club, and he threatened to ruin you with the charity. He'll do it. He's that much of a monster."

Chris cups my cheek. "If you think that prick is going to destroy me, you don't know me as well as you will one day." He leans in and kisses me again hard on the mouth. "He will not touch you again." He's gone before I can stop him.

I touch my lips where the taste of him still lingers, this man who swept into my life and awakened *me* again. What have I done by telling him about Michael now? I shove through the door and head for the exit. I have to stop Chris from doing something he'll regret.

Twenty-one

I make it halfway to the exit of the bathroom when Gina rushes inside, blocking my path. "Oh, no." She holds up her hand. "You aren't going out there looking like you do. The press will butcher you and Chris. They're vicious."

"Move, Gina," I order. I have never wanted to physically hurt another person before, but I do now. I want her out of the way. "I have to stop Chris from doing something he'll regret."

She fixes me with a determined stare. "You'll thank me for this later. Chris called security to have whoever gave you trouble taken to their booth in the back of the museum. We'll fix your makeup and then you can meet him there."

"No, I—"

"Look in the mirror, Sara." Her command borders on a bark. "Think about the kind of attention you will get for Chris and you."

I draw several heavy breaths and do as she says. And she's

right. My mascara is streaked down my cheeks, impossible to miss. I am a front-page nightmare.

She holds up a bag. "My miracle bag. Let me do my magic."

My fingers trail the puffy skin under my eyes. "No amount of makeup is going to fix this."

"I have a miracle gel for that in my bag," she assures me. "Let's get to work."

I hesitate. I don't have time for this. I don't want to do it with her. I don't even want her involved.

"Let me help. You have time." She moves to the sink and sets her bag down. "It'll take security several minutes to find whoever Chris wants found and escort him to security with any level of discretion."

Slowly, my shoulders slump and I join Gina at the sink. "Please hurry."

"Speedy is my middle name when it comes to outsmarting bad press." She removes a towelette from her supplies and gently starts wiping my cheeks. "And don't worry about Chris. He never does anything he isn't sure about."

My gut clenches at the hint of intimacy between them. "You seem to know him very well."

Gina applies the cooling gel to my eyes. "Don't start imagining something that isn't there. We never dated, and we'd be a horrible couple. I adore the spotlight and that man acts like it's poison." She swallows hard, her delicate neck bobbing with the action. "I . . . my sister died of cancer."

Taken aback, I barely manage to spare her the "I'm sorry" that I know will make her cringe. "How old was she?"

"Sixteen." She starts to apply foundation to my face with a

roller brush. "She had all the medical care available to her but she worried that others didn't." Her voice cracks. "She volunteered until she was too sick to keep it up. That's how we met Chris."

Her words wreak havoc on my calm. Chris will lose everything he's created with the charity if Michael paints him as some kind of freak. I can't let that happen. No matter what that means, or what I have to do.

"I have to go," I say, and dart around Gina before she can stop me.

"Sara!"

I ignore her shout and I'm past the other woman guarding the door before she even knows I'm gone. I dart into the main events room and head toward the back of the museum, where Gina said I'd find security. "I'm supposed to meet someone at security," I tell the first waiter I find. "Where is it?"

He points to an archway and a set of steps, and I rush toward them and take the stairs too quickly for my high heels, righting myself from a near trip. Finally, I see the sign indicating the security offices, and any hope I had of catching Chris before he talks to Michael evaporates when I hear his voice.

"I'll take that number now," I hear Chris say.

"Dream on, asshole," Michael responds. "You aren't getting shit from me."

"Have it your way. I can get the number myself."

Michael snorts. "Good luck with that. Even Sara doesn't have it."

I hear the phone go to speakerphone and a number being dialed before Chris is speaking again. "Yeah, Blake. I need a

personal cell number for a Thomas McMillan, and yes, I'm talking about the CEO of the cable company. He's Sara's father."

He's calling my father? Why is he calling my father? I reach
for the door to stop him, then I hesitate. I know how vicious
Michael is. He'll say horrible things to me in front of Chris, and
Chris will flatten him regardless of later consequences. I bite my
lip and lean against the wall, squeezing my eyes shut and waiting
for what will happen next.

"Give me about, oh, sixty seconds," Blake replies, and I can
hear him typing through the speaker. He'll never be able to get
it. It's unlisted. I don't even have the damn number. Blake proves
me wrong in less than sixty seconds. It's more like thirty seconds
when he calls out the number "702-222-1215. Anything else?"

"Not at the moment," Chris replies. "I'll be in touch." The
line goes dead and Chris snorts, imitating Michael. "I guess I'm
lucky."

Michael barks out a laugh. "Call him. He'll bury you and
your perverted self under a rock you'll never climb out from
under."

"Will he now?" Chris asks. "I'm predicting you'll be the one
buried under a rock." There is a pause when I assume the phone
is ringing and I hold my breath, waiting to see if my father will
answer. "Thomas McMillan, this is Chris Merit. That's right. The
artist who is dating Sara." There is a silence and Chris makes an
amused sound. "Really. That rich. That's really not all that rich.
Right." Another pause. "I'm not one to throw around wallet sizes
but you just won't stop going there so I'll go with you. Add a
'filthy' to the front of that rich, and that's how rich I am. In other
words, your threats to crush me don't scare me."

As impossible as it seems, I find myself smiling at the reference to me asking him if he was filthy rich, but it fades and burns quickly. This is my father Chris is talking to. My father, who some part of me wanted to believe isn't a part of this with Michael but is. It's clear that he is.

"We're still comparing wallets? Okay, then. Yes, that's right. I make a few million a year for my art, which you make sound like nothing. Fortunately, the charities I donate it to don't take it for granted the way you apparently do. You should have had your boy Michael here find out more than my personal habits when he was digging around before you decided to threaten me. My banker is Rob Moore at Chase Bank in San Francisco. Call him and he'll confirm just how much money I have to blow. And there is nothing I'd like to blow it on more than ruining you and your pal Michael here, who seems to think 'no' means 'yes' when it comes to putting his hands on Sara." There is a silence when, I assume, my father is talking, then Chris adds, "I really don't care what you believe happened or didn't happen. If Michael ever comes near Sara again, I *will* ruin him and you with him. I'm sending Michael back to you now. And Mr. McMillan, I didn't understand until tonight why Sara would walk away from her life. Now I do. She doesn't need you or your money. She has me, and I'll take far better care of her than you ever did."

Frozen against the wall, I hug myself, bleeding and healing at the same time. My father . . . Chris . . . my father . . . I remember being a little girl eager to see him, hoping he'd come home. But he was never home with us. *Home.* That word still haunts me.

"Are we done here?" Michael asks.

"You were done before you ever got here," Chris replies.

"Sorry, sir, but you can't leave until we finish our paper-work," I hear an unfamiliar voice say from inside the room, and I'm surprised Chris has allowed someone else in the room.

"This is ridiculous," Michael growls. "I did nothing wrong."

"It's protocol, sir. All security action must be properly docu-mented."

My stomach twists in knots just hearing Michael's voice and I fight the memories threatening to take shape. Why can't they just go back in the hole where I buried them? That place where two years ago didn't exist.

Footsteps sound on the opposite side of the door, and I turn as it opens and Chris appears, his blond hair rumpled, as if he's been running his hands through it. His green eyes fall on me and the hard glint in their depths softens instantly. He pulls the door shut behind him and drags me against him, murmuring softly, "I understand why you left. I understand everything."

I cling to him, holding on for what feels like dear life. "I should have told you."

"You would have." He pulls back to look at me. "When you were ready. We all have to deal with our inner demons in our own way, in our own time."

My fingers trail over the stubble on his jaw, and I understand too well what he's telling me. He hasn't told me everything, either, and I can't bear the idea that there is still something else, some dark secret that could potentially tear us apart when I'm not sure we'll survive what is already before us.

"Your car's ready at the back door, sir." Chris and I turn to the uniformed guard who has appeared beside us. "The press has been cleared."

Chris shakes the man's hand and it's clear this isn't their first meeting. "Thanks, Max. You're a good man."

We exit to a parking lot and slide into the car. I settle under Chris's arm, seeking the warmth of his body, the protection I've sworn I don't need, too many times to count. But I need it tonight. I need it and him, in ways I've never needed another human being. It's both comforting and terrifying to realize that the very thing I've feared would happen has happened. I don't know who I am without Chris anymore. I don't know where he begins and where I end. He says he's mine. He says I'm his, but no matter what Chris says, he isn't really mine at all. He's still a prisoner of his own inner demons and now, I worry, of mine, too.

We don't speak on the short drive back to the hotel, both of us lost in thought. The cold reality of what has just happened seeps into my mind and crawls through my body. Despite it being eighty degrees outside, I shiver, and Chris runs his hand up my arm. I turn into him, settling my ear on his chest, listening to his heartbeat, trying to lose myself in the steady rhythm. But my thoughts find a way inside the rhythm. My father finds a way inside my head. I should be beyond his reach, incapable of feeling anything where he is concerned, but I am not. My mother is dead. My father couldn't care less if I'm dead. Michael is the son my father wanted and he would justify anything Michael did as necessary, even forcing himself on me.

By the time we are walking through the hotel lobby, I am one big ball of explosive emotion. I am clawing my way out of my own head but there seems to be no escape, and this damnable, pinching pain in my chest won't go away.

We step inside the elevator and Chris wraps me in his embrace, settling my hips against his, his hand at my back. I run my fingers through his blond hair, searching his face, and I find exactly what I fear. He is worried about me, about us, concerned that my past, my weakness with Michael, means I'm too fragile to be a part of his life. It wasn't hate I'd worried about from Chris. The hate was mine. I own it. I've lived it. No. What I feared from Chris was this: pity. Him looking at me like I'm a wounded animal. I push away from him and try to step out of his reach. His fingers snag mine and he pulls me back. I see the question in his face and I plan to answer it, just not here.

The elevator doors open and I rush forward, seeking privacy before I explode. The instant we are in the room, I whirl on him. "Don't look at me like I'm some helpless pup that has to be coddled, Chris. That's not what I need now. I need what you needed today. I need an escape. I need to know . . ." So much. Too much. "I need . . ." I have no more words. I just need.

Stretching behind me, I unzip my dress and shove it down my body, leaving myself in my thigh-highs and heels, and the dangling rubies. I'm desperate to push Chris over the edge, to make him take me the way he always does—passionately, completely.

Chris pulls me hard against his body, and he is hard where I am soft, strong where I am still weak. *Yes.* This is what I need. "Fuck me, Chris. Take me to that place you go and don't be gentle."

He runs his hand down my hair. "Not tonight, Sara. Not after you just told me that bastard forced himself on you."

"It was two years ago, Chris."

"Which you had to relive tonight."

"Don't do this. Don't treat me like I'm breakable, or Michael wins."

"I'm not treating you like you're breakable."

"You are, and if you do it now, you always will. It'll change us."

"No. One night is not a lifetime."

"This isn't just one night. It's this night. It's the night that—" The pain in my chest cuts off my words and I shove it away. "Pain that is pleasure. Pain that is an escape. I need just what you need tonight."

"No, baby. I'm not going there with you tonight."

"You mean you're not going there with me ever!" I charge. "You're afraid to take me there now. This isn't going to work. He's already ruined us." I shake my head. "I need out of here. I need to go home." I tug on my arms, but he holds me easily. "Let go. Damn it, let go!"

"Sara—"

My hands close around the sleeves of his jacket. "I *knew* this would happen. I knew if I told you, you'd be afraid to be you." My cheeks are wet with tears. I don't know why the hell I keep crying. "Just let me go, so I can get all the hell over with in one night, Chris. Let me go find my way of dealing with this again. My way without you."

He backs me against the desk, his hands on my hips, his expression unreadable. He's still so damn in control. I'm naked inside and out, and he's no closer to letting down the wall this night has erected, than when I was fully dressed.

"Just let me go now, Chris." My voice is a barely audible. I am defeated and beaten. "Please."

His expression softens and he wipes my tears away. "Sara, baby, you aren't alone. And I'm not going to shut you out."

"You will. You are. You tried to shut me out today before you even knew about this. How can I believe you can go those places you need to go with me when you didn't even believe you could earlier today?" My fingers close around his lapels, and the absolute torment I'm feeling is like gravel in my throat, and I barely find my voice. "And what if I need to go there now? I need to escape. I need to feel something other than what I'm feeling right now, Chris."

He stares down at me, and I see the shadows in his eyes, I see the turbulence, a deep sea of emotions I don't understand, and I fear we are both drowning. It's too much. Everything feels like too much. "Chris," I whisper, and it's a plea for him to make this ache inside me go away. A plea for him to take me away like only he can do.

Suddenly, he's picking me up and carrying me toward the bed. We go down on the mattress and he quickly shrugs out of his jacket and tosses it away. And then he's on top of me. The weight of him, the sweet wonderful weight of him, is all that keeps me from completely losing my mind.

He raises up on his elbows and our eyes meet, and I am lost in the fiery depths of passion this man stirs in me. "Sara." He whispers my name and the air around us shifts and I feel Chris everywhere, in places he isn't touching me. A shudder runs through me and I pull his mouth to mine, drinking him in, burning for him.

Then his lips leave mine, and I physically ache with the loss of the connection. This man can hurt me so deeply. He could hurt me in a way I'm not sure I'd recover from, and it's too late to stop it from happening.

As he starts to undress, I sit up to watch him. His gaze sweeps the jewels dangling on my nipples, bringing a welcome heat in contrast to the icy pit in my stomach. And I think that tonight just might be a new beginning for us, instead of our final destination.

Twenty-two

All sinewy muscle and masculine perfection, Chris presses me back down onto the mattress, his hands covering my breasts, fingers flicking the rubies. Little darts of pleasure rush from my nipples to the V of my body, where the thick ridge of his erection settles.

My hand curves on his face. "I need what you needed earlier today." My voice is raspy, urgent, etched with the weight that today has been, and all it has revealed. I barely recognize it as my own. "Take me there, Chris. Please."

"Where I needed to go was where I ended up. I was shutting you out, like I shut everything out, and you pulled me back. You made me see what was important. What's real. You made me see you." His lips brush mine. "See me now, Sara."

"I do see you."

"No. You don't. You see what happened tonight and what you've decided that means for us. See me now, Sara, like you made me see you." He kisses the corner of my mouth and his lips travel down my jaw. "Really see me."

"I'm trying." My hands slide to his hair. "But, I—"

He kisses me, a soft caress of tongue against tongue. "No buts. Either you see me or you don't. Either you let me in or you don't." His mouth touches mine again, a feather-light, barely there brush. "Let me in, Sara."

Confusion ripples through my mind. Am *I* shutting *him* out? Isn't it he who has shut me out? No. Yes. I don't know. His fingers caress my nipple, and his mouth travels my jaw to the delicate curve of my neck, and I can barely think. His breath fans hot against my ear, and his voice is a low, deep, sensual promise. "I'm right here." His words whisper in my ear and travel down my neck, over my skin, and settle in that deep hole inside me that only he can fill.

My hand slides to his face and I pull his mouth back to mine. "Part of you isn't enough, Chris. You can't hold back because of what you found out tonight. You can't."

He strokes his tongue against mine, and it is sweet velvet seducing me. "Taste that. That's me. That's us." His tongue strokes mine. "Us, Sara. Forget everything else." His mouth comes down on mine again, and I fight the passion consuming me. I fight because he didn't tell me he wouldn't hold back. He didn't say what I needed to hear and I know why. Because he never says what he doesn't mean. But it's a worthless battle I cannot win. Not when his hands are on my breasts and his mouth is caressing a path down my neck.

The last of my will to question who we are together and where we are going is lost when his tongue flicks the ruby strand. He suckles my nipple, tugging on the attached ring, and oh God, his other hand slides between my legs, applying pressure to the jewels attached to my clit. I moan and my hands slide into his hair, and he lets me. Some part of my mind registers this as abnormal, as him allowing me control I don't normally have, but I can't seem to process. Not when his mouth is doing the most amazing things to my nipple and his fingers are pressing inside me. His thumb strokes my clit, and he seems to have found the exact right spot to send sensations spiraling through me. I gasp at how quickly I am on the edge and he swallows it, kissing me. I shatter at the touch of his tongue against mine, pleasure trembling through me in a long wave of sensations.

"Sometimes pleasure is just pleasure," he promises against my mouth.

"And that's enough for you?"

"We aren't even close to the place I call enough."

And with that promise he slides down my body, and spreads my legs to lick my swollen clit.

I gasp. "No. I can't. I'm too sensitive. It's too much." Everything is too much tonight.

"I'll tell you when it's too much." He licks me again and I feel him tug away the jewel, replacing it with his mouth. I shudder with a mix of pain and pleasure. No, it's all pleasure. It's pleasure and I am lost to the way he licks and strokes and teases me until I am impossibly on the edge again. So close, and yet I'm not there. I need to be there. I'm desperate to get there again. And *this* is pain. It's pain and pleasure and it's Chris, pushing me, taking me there. Always taking me someplace I don't know I can go.

He is not so far out of reach, and neither is my release. My sex clenches and spasms, empty and needy, and I whimper. Chris answers my cry, covering my body with his, but he doesn't enter me. He strokes his shaft over the sensitive V of my body and I whimper again, my lashes fluttering.

His hand slides to my face. "Look at me when I enter you." His voice is rough, intense. "See me, Sara."

"I do."

He presses inside me and thrusts, burying himself deeply, completely. "Feel me."

"Yes."

He lowers his mouth a breath from mine. "But do you feel us?"

My hands slide around him, holding on to him. "Yes."

"I'm not sure you do." He brushes his mouth over mine. "But before tonight is over, you will."

The sound of the phone ringing on the nightstand permeates the sweet, sated state of my slumber. I'm immediately aware of the sunlight glimmering through the hotel window and the wonderful weight of Chris's leg draped over mine, his hard body curved around me.

Chris reaches over me and grabs the phone. "I need the car at nine fifteen. Right."

I roll to my back while he listens to whatever he's being told. I stroke my hand over the shadow on Chris's jaw, letting it rasp along my fingers before tugging a strand of his sexy, rumpled blond hair, which is all the sexier because I know my fingers helped create the disarray. Memories of the night assail me in a mix of hot and cold, ice and fire. The lovemaking had been nothing shy of amazing, but there is so much more to Chris, and to me, that I need to know still exists.

Chris reaches over me again and hangs up the phone. "Morning," he says, pulling my back to his front, his arm wrapped around me as he nuzzles my neck.

"Morning," I whisper. "What time is it?"

"Eight. And since we need to swing by the hospital on the way to the airport, that leaves us only about thirty minutes for a good-morning fuck." He nuzzles my neck and his stubble is deliciously rough on my skin, the way he can be when he wants to be. The way I want him to be now.

I feel a pinch in my chest, a hint of the ice returning. "I thought you might think I'm too delicate for such things."

His hand slides over my breasts, caressing my nipple, and a sound of pleasure slides from my lips. How is it possible that I never get enough of Chris?

"Why don't we find out?" he asks, and he nips my ear, settling the thickness of his erection against my backside before pressing between my thighs.

"Yes." I reach between my legs and stroke him, challenging him. Pushing him the way I burn to have him push me. "If you dare."

He covers my hand on his shaft and leads it to the silky wet heat of my sex. "If *you* dare. Because, baby, just because I protect you doesn't mean I'm not going to fuck you. I'm still me and I'm still going to fuck you in all kinds of ways you haven't imagined." He squeezes my breast and pinches my nipple and I hold his hand there, not wanting him to stop. His voice is as rough as his touch, both like sweet cognac that burns going down and leaves me wanting more. "I'm going to tie you up the way I painted you, Sara. Does that scare you?"

"No. Nothing with you scares me."

"No?" His hand curves my backside.

I remember his palm on my backside, the erotic sting. The moment his thick cock pumped into me, the pleasure. "No."

"You should be."

His finger slides down the cleft of my backside and I gasp at the intimate intrusion, and then pant. "Are we back to this again? You warning me away?"

He explores me from the front and the back. "Last night earned you one last warning. One chance to run while you still can." His lips press to my shoulder, teeth scraping, nipping. "But know this, Sara." His fingers slide deeper, between my cheeks, while his other hand teases my clit, flickering it with delicate fingers that contrast the near hard command of his voice. "I'm going to own you, body and soul. I *will* bind you. I will fuck your ass. Your mouth. I will do what I want. And none of this even comes close to where I've been and where I will never take you."

My body reacts to the primal erotic promises, and I am hot and wet, and more aroused than I have ever been in my life. I fight the haze of arousal, the deep ache in my sex, threatening to become an orgasm. He's testing me, trying to scare me, and it twists me in knots to know it's because last night made him doubt me and us.

"This is who I am, Sara. I will protect you from everything and everyone else, but I can't protect you from who I am or who we will be if you stay with me."

"I know who you are," I whisper, and I am more clear of mind than I have been in a very long time. I need him. I've needed him from the moment I first met him. Even then, that first night, I felt free to let go with him, to be me, when I didn't even recognize me. "But you need to know this, Chris. I know who I am now, too. I know what I need to stay with you. If you own my body, I own yours." I've walked away from too much to be willing to settle for less than everything now.

His body stiffens, tension rippling through his muscles. Anger and hurt spike in my chest and I try to turn. He holds me, his arm a vise around mine. "You own as much of me as I have to give," he says, his voice hoarse.

"No, I don't. Not until you take me to those places you say you never will. I need to know that one day you will."

Suddenly he is gone, no longer touching me, and I roll over to find him sitting at the edge of the bed, the muscles in his impressive shoulders bunching.

I scramble to my knees and reach for his arm. "Chris—"

The instant I touch him, he pulls me around into his lap. "I love you, Sara." He strokes the hair from my face. "But there are parts of me that I hate. We don't go there. We won't ever go there. Understand?"

No, I don't. But I do understand the self-hate. I understand the emotion. "I love you, too." I cup his cheek and he leans into it, his lashes lowering, his jaw softening. "And there is nothing you can do that will change how I feel."

His jaw flexes and his eyes dilate. "Yes. There is, and I should walk away before it happens, for both our sakes." He rests his forehead against mine. "But I can't."

My fingers tunnel into his hair. What is so horrific that it haunts him this completely?

He picks me up and carries me toward the bathroom. We shower together, but we don't make love and we don't even just plain fuck this out of his system. We just hold each other. Where I was once lost, he's found me. But I know now that I have only begun to truly discover Chris. He's still lost.

I stand at the bathroom sink next to Chris, and it's an odd, wonderful, intimate moment to be finishing my hair while he brushes his teeth. I'm dressed in jeans and a green V-neck T-shirt to show off the emerald necklace I don't want to take off, and I can't stop peeking at Chris, who even with a toothbrush in hand looks anything but domestic. I can already tell I'm going to spend the day deliciously distracted by my intimate knowledge of the sinewy muscle and hard perfection beneath his brown Harley T-shirt, faded jeans, and boots.

I unplug my flatiron and wrap it up while he closes his travel bag, and I stare at our reflections in the mirror. I am a good foot shorter than him and my dark hair contrasts with his light chin-length hair, which is damp and wavy by his ears. There is a confidence about him, a power I find addictive. He is masculine and hard in all the right ways and he makes me feel feminine and soft, and strong.

His gaze lifts and our eyes connect in the mirror. Awareness tingles over my chest and shoulders and spreads like liquid fire through my body. "Keep looking at me like that," he warns, "and you won't make it back to work tomorrow because we'll miss our flight."

My lips curve. "Very tempting."

A knock sounds on the door and he gives me a nod. "Room service or me at your service?"

I bite my lip in utter consternation and reluctantly sigh. "Considering Dylan's waiting, I guess I have to settle for my second choice. Room service."

He reaches for me and gives me a fast, hot kiss with a burning swipe of his tongue and heads for the door. "Hmmm," I call behind him, biting my lip. "Minty fresh."

The phone starts ringing. "Grab that, will you, Sara?"

I rush into the bedroom and snatch up the bedside phone to hear, "One, two, Freddy's coming for you."

"And we're coming for you, Dylan," I promise, laughing. "We'll be there in about half an hour."

"Can you bring me a chocolate bar?" he whispers conspiratorially.

"Yes," I promise. "I'll bring you a chocolate bar. I'll see you soon." I hang up as Chris tips the waiter and we sit down on the bed to eat.

"How'd he sound?" Chris asks.

"He answered singing me the Freddy song."

He arches a brow and a glimmer of hope fills his eyes. "Really? I guess the treatment aftereffects have passed."

"Yes," I agree cautiously. I'm worried about how far Chris is going to fall over Dylan. "One big positive for sure." I lift the lid on my food and inspect the eggs.

We're just digging into our omelets when Chris's cell phone rings. Chris glances down at it. "Blake," he answers.

I listen hopefully and Chris's gaze goes to mine as he replies to something Blake has said: "Mark is the Master in the journal. I know there are no names, but yes, I'm sure. They had a relationship. I have no idea who the second man in the journal is."

"Ryan Kilmer," I offer, and receive an arched brow from Chris, prodding me to add, "The real estate guy—"

He holds the phone from his mouth. "I know who he is. How do you know who he is?"

His scowl tells me he is not happy. "I'm doing a job for him. I think it's him in the journal."

"Why?"

"It's a gut feeling. A strong gut feeling."

"Based on what?"

"He seems to be a good friend of Mark's, and"—I hesitate, certain Chris isn't going to approve of my observations—"he isn't as dominant. I don't think Mark could share with someone too like himself." *Like you,* I add silently.

Chris stares at me, unmoving, stone that can't be chipped away, and I hear a murmur on the other end of the line that Chris responds to. "Yeah. I'm here. There's a guy named Ryan Kilmer. He's a member of the club Mark owns. They're friends. Sara thinks it's him." He listens a minute and then ends the call. He sets his phone on the nightstand beside me and pulls me to my feet, his hand sliding around my back. "I do not like how well you know Mark Compton."

The possessiveness of his touch, and in his expression, shouldn't please me. It doesn't, and yet it does. "What I know is from the journals."

"Then stop reading the damn things."

"I brought them for you to read."

"I don't want to read them, Sara. It just makes me think about what Mark wants to do to you, and I'm trying to be understanding about your job. The journals won't help me do that. We lock them back up when we get back to San Francisco unless Blake needs us to read something specific."

"Yes, Master," I tease, trying to bring his tension down a notch.

His scowl is instant. "Don't call me that. I'm not your master. You aren't my submissive. And you damn sure won't ever be Mark's."

Okay, so that joke went over much better the last time I told it. I push to my toes and press my lips to his. "No. I won't, because I love you, Chris."

His hand closes down on my neck and he kisses me, and it's not gentle. It's a hot, possessive, turbulent claiming that sends a swell of desire through me so intense I tremble. "What are you doing to me, woman?" he growls against my mouth. "Besides making me crazy. Do you know how badly I want to take you to Paris and away from that man? But I know right now you won't go. You want this job and I'm trying to understand." He sets me away from him and runs a hand through his hair, walking in a circle and facing me again. "I don't like Ryan suddenly hiring the gallery. It's just a little too reminiscent of the journals."

Unbidden, a shiver runs down my spine and I hug myself. There is a lot in my life a little too reminiscent of the journals but I'm trying to fix that. "You said Mark wasn't capable of hurting Rebecca."

"I don't think he could or would, but he brought her into

his world where she didn't belong, and he's responsible for where that might have led her. I know nothing about Ryan or anyone else he might have put her in contact with. I don't like this, Sara. I don't like that he's trying to pull you into his world. And he is. He absolutely fucking is."

His torment over this is palpable, a ball of fire burning away at him. I go to him and hug him, settling my chin on his chest. "He can't. As long as you're in my life, sharing it with me, there's nothing but us, Chris."

The tension fades away as we finish breakfast and then head to the hospital, where we find Dylan and Brandy in contagious good spirits. By the time we're on the plane back to San Francisco we are relaxed and laughing, and I am more comfortable with Chris than I have ever been.

We settle into our seats and Chris pulls out his iPad. "I have a cure for your nervous flying—a movie. We can start it here and finish it at home."

"Home," I repeat softly.

He cups my face. "Yes. Our home. You belong with me now."

Mark's words come back to me: *Don't let Chris convince you there's an in between.* If I want it all with Chris, I can't stand on the line; there can't be an in between. The details will work out. "Yes. I do."

He rewards me with one of his breathtaking smiles and kisses me. "Yes. You do."

It is nearly seven by the time we land in San Francisco and finish the drive home. The doorman greets us and offers to bring our bags up for us. "I'll let you tonight," Chris says, and glances at me. "Finishing our movie over pizza okay with you?"

"Perfect," I agree eagerly.

Chris slips the doorman some cash. "How about ordering us a couple of pizzas while you're at it?"

"You got it, Mr. Merit."

Chris draws my hand into his and we are laughing over a scene in *Bridesmaids,* which had been my choice of movie, as payment for watching *Halloween,* when we find Jacob in our path.

"Good evening, Mr. Merit, Ms. McMillan." Jacob greets us with a little bow of his head.

Chris wraps his arm over my shoulder. "Did Blake stop by?"

The reminder that Rebecca is missing and that it looks like foul play takes me for a hard, quick ride.

"He did," Jacob confirms. "We beefed up security here at the building. Anything else you need, I'm available."

My nerves are officially frazzled and when we step into the elevator, I say, "Blake was worried enough to stop by and help with security?"

Chris frames my face with his hands. "We're just being cautious."

"Because you think Rebecca's dead?"

"Because I want you safe. Just be careful and tell us where you're going for a few days, while we get more information."

Fighting my unease, I nod. "Okay."

The elevator opens and he motions me inside. "Let's finish that movie. The rest will be waiting on us in the morning. Tonight, let's just enjoy being home together."

Home together. I like how this sounds. I give him a small smile and nod. "I'd like that."

We step off the elevator and Chris catches my hand and embraces me. "I'm not giving you time to change your mind. I'm arranging movers for your apartment."

I have a fleeting moment of uncertainty but shove aside the millions of things that could go wrong. I've spent a lifetime sinking into the quicksand of life, and Chris is the only person who has ever set me on solid ground. I wrap my arms around his neck and take a leap of faith. "All right."

He kisses me and leads me to the living room. *Our* living room.

Half an hour later, Chris and I have kicked off our shoes, and we're watching the rest of the movie on the big screen over the fireplace, trying to eat pizza through our laughter. When the movie is over and our stomachs are stuffed, Chris replays a particular scene and we laugh all over again. I wipe tears from my eyes and he pulls me down to the couch beneath him.

As I stare up at him, I feel the low burn in my belly he creates so easily. And I realize that though I've had a hellish weekend, I'm laughing. I'm happy. Happiness is unfamiliar to me, but I feel it now.

Because of Chris.

Twenty-three

I walk into the gallery on Monday morning in a pale peach dress and black heels and with a smile on my face. How can I not be smiling? I woke up to a sexy, brilliant artist in my bed and now I'm going to work at my dream job. So what if said sexy, brilliant artist was worried enough about my safety to drive me to work? I choose not to dwell on that part or I'll make myself sick with nerves.

"Morning, Amanda," I say, and Amanda studies me with a keen eye.

"Morning. You look amazing today."

"Well, thank you."

I enter the back office and stop dead in my tracks when I come face-to-face with Mark. The man is so damn disarming. Like fire scorching ice, he melts a girl right in her high heels. "Morning," I manage, and I wonder if he ever has a hair out of place, or a suit that isn't as perfectly fitted as his choice today of a pale gray that makes his eyes all the more compelling.

His gaze sweeps my body and lifts. "Amanda was right. You look quite amazing today, Ms. McMillan."

"Thank you."

He steps aside and lets me pass. I have this moment of frozen, deer-in-the-headlights helplessness when I realize he's going to watch me walk to my office. Damn this man and his power trips. I don't like this or how he has suddenly made my mind go to Michael and my father, and my fears that they still might cause Chris trouble. What does it say, that Mark reminds me of Michael?

I draw a small breath and take a step, trying not to wobble on my heels and blow the whole looking-good thing I've just been praised for. Not that I need Mark's praise. I don't.

But as I settle at my desk and put my things away, I bitterly acknowledge that I *do* need his praise. Why is this still who I am? I don't want Mark; he's too dominant. "No in between, all right," I murmur.

"Something wrong, Ms. McMillan?"

Mark leans against my door frame, and my gaze flickers to the delicate roses of the O'Nay painting on the wall—the one he put here for Rebecca. What is wrong is that Rebecca is missing. He is the Master in the journal, and he *has* to know more about where she has gone.

I open my mouth to say that, then close it, remembering the warning to be cautious. I don't want evidence being tucked away, any more than I want to be in danger myself.

"I'm nervous," I tell him. "I'm going to resign from the school today."

One blond brow lifts. "Are you, now?"

"Yes."

Approval gleams in his eyes and it pleases me to think he values my presence here enough to be pleased. "Well, then. Let me leave you to it."

He disappears and I slump in my chair. I swear that man winds me up and leaves me exhausted from every encounter. My gaze goes back to the picture on the wall, my thoughts to Rebecca. *I'm not taking your job. Come back. Be okay. And that goes for you, too, Ella.* Just thinking of Ella sets me into motion. I sit up and dial the school. I have to leave a message. Great. More fretting.

Ryan calls and e-mails me staging pictures of the property I'm to help decorate, and I get to work looking for possible art purchases for the project. By midmorning I have a lag in my work, and I pull out Rebecca's work journal and begin scouring it for helpful sales tips. My brows dip at a page of random notes. *Riptide auction piece. Legit? Find expert.* I inhale sharply. Rebecca was looking into a counterfeit piece that was listed at Riptide? Could that have gotten her into trouble? Surely, Mark knows, though. He had the journal. He had to have read it. Unless . . . Mark was involved. No. He'd never have given me the journal. Is this why he gave it to me? He wants me to know? I'm dumbfounded about what this could mean.

I glance up just in time to catch a glimpse of Ricco walking by my door. Panic assails me. Is he here to complain about Chris showing up at his house? I push to my feet and rush to the hall and watch Ricco disappear inside Mark's office. I seek out Ralph, as my resident knowledge keeper, for a possible explanation that does not involve me, but he isn't at his desk.

The kitchen is my next stop, and it's a mistake. I walk right into the lion's mouth. Mary turns as I enter, cup in hand.

"How'd it go with Ricco?" she asks.

Doing my best to appear unfrazzled, I walk to the coffeepot and fill my cup. "Not good. He pretty much sent me packing."

"Really? And yet he's here?"

I add cream to my coffee. "I have no idea why."

She stares at me. "You must have done something to piss him off."

The evil gleam in her eyes tells me she intended to upset me, and it works. Could she be any colder and meaner?

"Right. Thanks for the words of encouragement." I start to turn.

"Honey, you don't get any more encouragement than the boss wanting up your skirt."

How has my happy morning turned to total crap? I'm about to quit my teaching job yet I'm clearly not the only person who has worries that I have this job because Mark wants "up my skirt." What am I thinking? I walk back to my office and shut the door and I call Chris.

The instant he answers, I say, "You once told me I don't belong in this world. You didn't mean in the art business, right?"

"No, baby. You know what I was talking about."

"I can't resign my job if Mark only gave me this one because he wants to turn me into Rebecca. Would he do that? Would he hire me for strictly personal reasons?" He's silent too long and I can't take it. "Chris."

"I'd like to say anything to get you out of that place, but no.

He wouldn't. He sees your talent, Sara. And so will anyone who gets any quality time with you."

Amanda buzzes in with my call from the school. "Have him hold," I tell her.

"You're not a schoolteacher, Sara," Chris says. "No in between, baby."

"Right. No in between. I have to go."

"You're going to be glad you did this. Call me after."

"I will."

Ten minutes later, I am no longer employed by the school. But Ella is still scheduled for teaching and I'm not sure what to think. If she'd resigned, I'd feel hurt she'd cut me out of her life, but I'd know she'd gone silent by choice. I text Chris to tell him and he congratulates me and promises to check more into Ella's location.

I have just put my phone back in my purse when a knock sounds on my door and it opens. Ricco appears, looking oh so Antonio Banderas–esque, with his dark good looks, dressed in black slacks and a black button-down shirt with several of those buttons loose at his neck. "Let's go next door for coffee, Bella."

An order. "Of course." I stand and slip on my jacket. "I hope your visit means you've reconsidered working with us?"

"We'll talk next door," he replies, his expression impassive.

Inwardly, I sigh and grab my purse. Every man who walks into this place seems to get injected with an intense need for control and doing things on their terms.

When we get to the coffee shop, Ricco opens the door for me and I step inside. I feel Chris's presence immediately, as if another part of me is coming to life. Oh, no—knowing how he feels about Ricco, this is an explosion waiting to happen. Ricco offers to take my jacket and I decline. I'll hang on to my armor, real or imagined.

I take a few steps into the shop and catch a glimpse of Chris at the back table. Ava calls my name and smiles brightly, announcing my presence to Chris if he hasn't already seen me. I manage a smile at her. I think.

"You sit with your things," Ricco commands. "I'll order. What would you like?"

"White mocha, please."

As Ricco turns to the counter, I walk toward the tables and right into the beam of Chris's sharp gaze. I quickly lower my lashes, unable to look at him. Not and still manage this meeting.

Still, I scoot into a wooden booth that puts me facing Chris, because even though I'm afraid of what I might find in his face, I can't stand not being able to see him, either. Oh, yes. I am one big mess.

Setting my purse beside me, I slip out of my jacket just to have something to do. The intense pull willing me to look at him overwhelms me, and before I can stop myself my lashes lift and our eyes lock. The familiar jolt of awareness he creates in me spreads through my body and becomes the crackle of our mutual bad moods.

Ricco sits down across from me and slides my coffee in my direction. He then glances over his shoulder at Chris before turning back to me. His lips quirk and it's clear he is aware Chris was at his house. He opens his mouth to speak and I hold my breath, preparing for a confrontation.

"Have you reconsidered my offer?"

Relieved to be on the hot seat with a topic I have a clear answer for, I say, "I'm committed to the gallery."

"Honorable," he comments dryly. "I told Mark he doesn't deserve you, any more than he did Rebecca."

My eyes go wide. "Oh. I . . . Ricco, I—"

A low rumble of laughter escapes his lips. "Don't worry, Bella. It's no reflection on you. Besides, I plan to give you job security today. I have an auction piece I have given to Crystal, which I'm sure you know is Riptide's biggest competing auction house. I'm considering pulling it and giving it to Riptide"—he pauses for obvious effect—"in your care, of course."

My scalp prickles with warning. "Why, and on what condition?"

"I want you to find a way for me to reach Rebecca."

I blanch, shocked at this turn of events. "But I don't know her. I have no idea how to reach her, Ricco."

"I'm aware of that, but you can tell me if she has contact with the gallery. You might even be able to access Mark's personal files."

Is Ricco the other man in the journal? Is he the man Rebecca used to make Mark jealous? "No." My voice is firm, certain. "I won't touch Mark's personal files."

He scrubs his jaw and casts a glare at the ceiling I suspect is meant for me. "Acceptable," he states tightly, returning his now unreadable gaze to mine. "All I ask is you do what you can within your comfort zone."

His insistence is both compelling and frightening. If he loved Rebecca, I cannot imagine the pain he must feel at her absence, but there is another, more insidious possibility. He hurt her and he's trying to stay in tune with what is being discovered about her absence.

"I want your business, Ricco. I'd hoped you'd give it to me because you have confidence in my skill."

He leans in closer, his hand sliding over mine on the table, his torment over Rebecca clear. "Just tell me you will try, Bella," he presses. "That is all I ask."

Imagining Chris seeking me out if I suddenly disappeared drives me to promise, "I'll try."

The tension in his body eases considerably. "Excellent. We have a deal, then." He pushes to his feet and I follow him. He takes my hand and kisses it and I feel the weight of Chris's crushing stare. "I have fifteen days to pull my painting from Crystal before I'm contractually incapable of doing so. I expect I'll hear from you by then." He turns away, sauntering toward the door.

I gape after him. Have I just been blackmailed?

Twenty-four

I'm just gathering my things to leave when I hear Mark's voice in the reception area. I step out of my office and catch his attention. "Can I speak to you a moment?"

He motions me back into my office and follows me inside. He leaves the door open. "Can you shut it?" I ask, and I regret the request almost instantly. Suddenly we are in a tiny office facing each other, and there is a simmering awareness of that fact between us, and I want to run from it. "I saw you met with Alvarez today."

He leans on the door and crosses his arms over his chest. "We completed some final business matters."

He's intentionally making me pull teeth to get what I want. "Nothing about my meeting with him?"

His lips twist wryly. "He told me not to corrupt you as I did Rebecca."

I am speechless for a moment. "And you told him what?"

"I told him you are quite capable of deciding who corrupts you on your own."

I think this is a compliment. Or not. I really am clueless with Mark. "He asked me to have coffee with him."

"And did he get what he wanted from you during this coffee meeting?"

"I don't know what he wants from me." I sound as exasperated as I am. "You both talk in coded messages."

"Well, then, let me decode for you, Ms. McMillan, because frankly I'm tired of playing Ricco's games. He wants Rebecca. He can't have her. He blames me. I'd thought perhaps you could help him separate business and personal. After talking with him today, I don't believe that is possible."

His blunt answer disarms me. "No. I don't think it is."

"Then we won't do business with him. Some things, Ms. McMillan, are just better left alone." I immediately think of Rebecca, but he's quick to keep me off that topic, asking, "Did you resign from the school today?"

"Yes."

"Excellent. Then you're all mine now." His eyes glint and I know he's chosen the words fully aware of the double meaning. "Good night, Ms. McMillan."

He starts to turn and I don't know what comes over me but I blurt, "Did you?"

He freezes in place and then turns, fixing me with his steely gray stare. "Did I what, Ms. McMillan?"

"Did you corrupt Rebecca?"

"Yes."

"And?" I ask because nothing else will come to my mind.

"And clearly it was a mistake or she'd still be here."

I'm speechless yet again. I just can't find words. Mark uses the empty space to sideswipe me with another unexpected question. "You do know Chris is thoroughly fucked-up, don't you?"

My reply is instant, defensive. Protective. "Aren't we all?"

"Not like Chris."

I don't ask how he knows. It could be the club. Maybe a friendship that once was and is now lost. It doesn't matter. "It's his imperfections that make him perfect," I reply, and there is conviction in my voice.

His gaze is fiercely penetrating. "I just don't want to see you get hurt."

There is a slight break in his voice that I've never heard in him before, and I believe him. "Like you hurt Rebecca?"

Some emotion flickers in his eyes and is gone as quickly as it appears. Guilt? Pain? "Yes." His voice is soft, missing the unwavering command that is his norm. "Like I hurt Rebecca."

"Is that why she left?"

"Yes."

I am more confused about this man and his actions than ever before. "Then why attempt to take me down that path?"

"You aren't Rebecca, any more than I'm Chris."

He leaves my office and I stare after him.

I exit the gallery's front door and spot the 911 parked at the curb. The relief that Chris is here does little to eliminate my apprehension; I know he'll be upset about seeing me with Ricco.

The door pops open and just seeing him threatens to consume me. This is one time I do not want to be consumed by all

that is Chris. Not with my unsteadiness about where this weekend has led us.

I lean into the car to maneuver my bags into the backseat
and Chris takes them from me. For an instant he freezes, and I
wonder if he too feels the charge darting through me. He sets
my things behind us and I slide into the passenger seat, shutting
myself inside the small space with him. I burn for his touch, for
him to touch me.

Tense seconds tick by, where neither of us moves or speaks.
With an irritatingly shaky hand, I reach for the seat belt and it
slips out of my grasp. Chris reaches over me to help, his arm
brushing my breast, the heat of his body pouring into me. His
hair tickles my cheek and he lingers, his mouth close to mine.
It's all I can do not to reach up and pull it to mine, but then he's
gone and I let out a trembling breath. He pops the buckle into
place by my seat and settles into his. Still he doesn't look at me.
He eases the gear into drive and maneuvers onto the road.

My fingers ball on my lap, and I'm about to explode by the
time Chris pulls into a random parking spot.

We sit there, both of us staring forward. His silence is killing
me and I fight a scream, dropping my head to my lap and tun-
neling my fingers into my hair.

"Sara, what happened to being careful and telling us where
you're going?"

I look at him blankly, his words so unexpected that I can't
process them.

"I went to the coffee shop to be near you, because I was
worried about you. Then you walked in with Alvarez, whom I
don't trust."

I glare at him. "Alvarez is my job. Just my job. You need to accept that—just like I've accepted that there's nothing between you and Ava." My voice softens. "But you're right; I should have told you where I was going. I'm sorry to make you worry."

"Damn it, Sara." He twines his fingers in my hair and lowers his mouth one hot breath from mine. "You are the reason I take my next breath," he whispers. "Why can't you see that?"

His question steals the last of my anger. I soften against him, my fingers curving around his jaw. "Let's go home, baby." He kisses my forehead. "I have something to show you."

Chris threads his fingers with mine as we walk into his apartment. When we go down the hallway, he opens a door. "This is what I did this afternoon. I wasn't giving you a chance to change your mind about moving in."

I walk inside to find stacks of boxes, and the small collection of furniture I'd had at my apartment.

"I snagged the key from your key chain. I had the movers bring everything so you could decide what you wanted to keep, and I paid your lease off." He pulls me close, and his touch *is* home. "From this point on, what's mine is yours, Sara."

I hug him, pressing my ear to his chest, and I don't want to let go. Though he's generous with "things," not *everything* that's his is mine. For only he owns the pain of his past—and just like mine, it's eventually going to catch up with us.

Twenty-five

The next morning, I'm at the bathroom mirror finishing my makeup just before Chris and I head to a breakfast meeting with Kelvin. We'll be discussing Alvarez and the reference to the possible counterfeit art I've found in Rebecca's work journal. Kelvin has also promised to set up an alert that tells him if Ella books any form of travel. It's little comfort, but it's better than nothing.

I am zipping up my purse, ready to head into the bedroom, when Chris appears behind me and sets a black American Express credit card on the counter in front of me. I stare at it in stunned disbelief and then start shaking my head.

"No." I snatch it up and turn to him. "I don't want this. I don't want your money."

"This makes sure you'll have anything you need or want you until we can go by the bank and set you up an account."

"No, Chris, I'm not taking this." I don't want to be like my mother, taken care of by a man. "I want to earn my own money. I *have* to earn my own money."

He cups my face. "I want to take care of you."

My fingers go to his wrist. "Just love me. That's enough."

"This *is* me loving you. Please. Take the card."

I wet my lips and struggle with the demons of my past this conjures. "Just the card for emergencies. No bank account."

"Sara—"

"Just the card. That's a compromise, Chris—and only for emergencies."

He hesitates with obvious reluctance but finally gives in. "Just the card."

His willingness to give me this space means even more to me than I had realized up until this instant. I rise up on my toes and touch my lips to his. "Thank you, Chris."

He cups the back of my head. "For what?"

"Being you." *And letting me be me.*

Friday comes with a symphony of reasons for me to smile as I walk into Diego Maria's, the place Chris and I went for our first date. Chris and I have slipped into a routine, a relationship, that has me walking on clouds. He takes me to work and picks me up each day. We enjoy dinner *at home,* some concoction we attempt to create together, and call Dylan, who has been faring decently, according to Brandy, on speakerphone. Chris then disappears into his studio, losing himself in his painting until the wee hours of the night, when he wraps himself around me and we sleep. Together. In *our* bed.

I wave at Maria as the door chimes shut behind me, and

I note the unfamiliar worker helping her in place of her son Diego, the co-owner of the restaurant. I join Chris at the window table he's claimed as his new place to sketch during the day.

"Hey, baby," he says, standing up to greet me. The raw sex appeal of his blond hair and contrasting black jeans and a black T-shirt with an AC/DC emblem on it wreaks havoc on my senses.

"Hey," I say, letting my fingers tease the wispy strands of sexy blond hair at his nape.

He flattens his hand on my back and pulls me close, kissing me soundly before skimming my jacket from my shoulders and holding my chair for me.

"Any word from Blake and Kelvin on Rebecca?" I ask once I'm settled, placing my portfolio by my chair and my purse on the back.

Chris claims his chair across from me, his lips twisting in a grim line. "Nothing new worth reporting on Rebecca or Ella."

I'm discouraged by the never-ending stream of tidbits that turn to dead ends. "I can't find any more notes about the counterfeit painting Rebecca mentioned in her notes, either."

"On a positive note," Chris interjects, "I did get a call from your father."

Straightening, I prepare for the blow sure to come. "What? He called you?"

Chris slides his hand over mine. "Relax, baby. I said on a *positive* note. Everything is fine. He assured me that Michael has been dealt with—after calling my banker, of course."

"Dealt with? What does that mean?"

"*Contained* was the word your father used. I didn't ask for details. I have Blake running security records on Michael and keeping a tab on him, to be safe."

"Contained," I repeat tightly. "Yes. Well, he's quite good at containing people."

Chris brings my knuckles to his lips and kisses them. "You okay?"

I nod. "Yes, I'm fine." I glance at the counter and notice that Diego still isn't there.

Chris reads my expression and says, "He left for Paris to hunt down that exchange student he had the fling with."

"He's going to be heartbroken if she turns him away," I say sadly, having heard from Maria that the woman didn't feel as passionate about Diego as he did her. "I tried to talk him out of it."

My cell phone rings and I remove it from my purse and glance at Chris. "Ricco Alvarez," I tell him before answering.

"Ah, Bella, speak to me," Ricco says, which is exactly how he started the call he'd made to me two days before. "Tell me you have good news for me."

"I'm sorry, Ricco. Rebecca hasn't called into the gallery and no one has heard from her."

He sighs, and the sadness of the sound reaches through the phone. "Please do what you can."

"I will." I've barely issued the reply when the line goes dead.

I settle my phone on the table and Chris arches a brow. "That was quick."

"He only wants one thing. Rebecca. He's just so damn obsessed with her, Chris."

"Blake and Kelvin have a man on him, watching him for suspicious activity."

"I don't think he hurt her. I think he really loves her. He's like Diego, chasing the ghost of what will never be."

"Or chasing a mistake he's trying to cover up," Chris warns. "Don't let your big heart get in the way of being cautious."

"I know. I'm being careful."

Maria appears with our regular order. I chat with her a moment about Diego, and I can tell she is worried about her son.

When she leaves, Chris studies me for a moment. "It's our scars that define us, Sara. Diego has to live life to appreciate life."

"Yes." A knot forms in my stomach at the idea that I still don't know how deeply Chris's scars define him.

Chris tips back his beer and then reaches for a fork. "Eat, baby. The food is getting cold."

I nod and shove aside my worries and he tells me about Paris, continuing his diligent effort to convince me to take another leap of faith and go with him.

Our plates are removed and I reach for my portfolio. "I want to show you something." I flip it open. "These are the art pieces I have picked out for that property Ryan has me working on."

I spend the next fifteen minutes showing him each one of my prize finds. I glance up to find myself captured by his tender stare. He brushes his knuckles over my cheek. "You really love what you do."

"Yes. This is a dream for me. But I . . . I know it doesn't have to be at Allure." It is the first time I've alluded that I might go to Paris with him.

He goes very still. "What are you saying?"

More and more, I think Paris is my way of peeling back the remainder of Chris's layers. "It means I belong with you."

We stare at each other and I can almost feel the depths of our bond weave deeper into my soul. "Yes," he says softly. "You do."

The waiter interrupts us by bringing the check, but the moment isn't lost. I cast Chris a coy look. "I was wondering if a certain brilliant artist took special requests."

"When being called brilliant by a certain sexy-as-hell woman who happens to share my bed, most anything is possible."

My cheeks heat as I think of what has been possible in our bed, namely the leather straps he'd installed on the headboard to tie me up and torment me with pleasure. "Yes, well. I finally get to go to Ryan's property tomorrow and see firsthand how my treasures will look. I was hoping you might come with me because"—I flip to a picture of a wall inside the property, and turn it to him—"I dream of this spot displaying a Chris Merit San Francisco skyline. You could donate the money, and I'll—"

"On one condition." He isn't looking at the picture. He's looking at me. "You sit for me and let me paint you."

In the past, the idea was intimidating, and I told myself it was because Chris is famously talented, but it was more. It was what his brush captured, and the secrets I worried he'd reveal. I search his face now, and I see that awareness there. This is about trust, about me believing he can see the worst in me and still love me. And maybe, just maybe, if I put that kind of trust in him, he will do the same with me.

"Yes. I'll sit for you."

. . .

At midafternoon I finish helping a customer and return to my office, where I discover a box sitting on my desk with a card. I recognize Chris's writing immediately. Peeling open the card I read, *For tonight. Open alone with the door shut. Chris.*

I trace his signature, the crisp, precise letters created by the same hand that crafts masterpieces that sell for millions.

Amanda pops her head in. "It came a few minutes ago." She bites her lip. "Can I see what it is?"

"Ah, no. That's not a good idea."

Her face lights up. "A naughty gift." She sighs. "I want a sexy, famous artist to send me naughty gifts. I'll shut the door for you."

I break the tape sealing the red box and laugh when I find a pink paddle and a pair of butterfly nipple clamps inside. My lips curve and heat shimmers a path through my body, but this gift makes me feel so much more than desire. He hasn't let what he learned about Michael affect us. If he had, I don't know what I would have done. I need the escape Chris gives me, the way I know I can just let go with him and he will never hurt me. And that's the true gift.

It's an hour before closing time at the gallery and I've spent the afternoon walking on more of those clouds, anticipating my night with Chris, when my cell phone rings. I glance at the number and I don't know why, but the instant I see it, I go bitterly cold inside. "Dylan?" I answer, holding my breath as I await his young, cheerful voice.

"Sara."

The pained whisper of my name from Brandy's lips spirals

through me and tears pool in my eyes. I know what she is going to tell me. "No. It can't be."

"He's gone. My baby is gone."

"I . . ." I say the dreaded words. I can't help it. "I'm sorry. I'm so very sorry, Brandy."

"You need to go to Chris. He didn't take it well. I . . . I just . . . go to him. He needs you."

"Yes. Yes." Oh, God. Chris. "I am. I will."

She sobs and heaves in a trembling breath. "Call us and tell us he is okay."

"I will."

I swipe at the tears pouring down my cheeks and dial Chris. He doesn't answer. I dial again and again. "Amanda!"

She rushes into the office and her eyes go wide. "What's wrong?"

"Call Diego Maria's and see if Chris is there," I tell her and I'm already dialing Jacob.

"Yes. Okay."

Jacob answers. "Is Chris there?" I ask.

"No, Ms. McMillan. He's not been in all day. Are you okay?"

"There's been an emergency. If he shows up there, call me."

"Are you safe?"

"Yes. It's not me I'm worried about. It's Chris. Just call me if you see him." I hang up as Amanda walks back into the office. "He's not there."

"Do you have the number for the coffee shop?"

"Yes. You want me to call?"

"No. Just get me the number."

She darts away and buzzes my desk. I dial the number and a man answers. "Is Chris Merit there?" The answer is no. "Is Ava there?" The answer is also no. My stomach roils. I hunch over my desk.

Mark appears in my doorway. "Dylan, the cancer patient Chris and I are so fond of"—I suck in a breath of air—"he . . . he . . ." I can't say it.

"That explains it then."

"Explains what?"

"Why Chris is at the club."

My world spins and then crashes into a million pieces and I start to shake, tears spilling like waterfalls from my eyes.

"Ms. McMillan," Mark snaps sharply, and somehow he is standing over me and I don't remember him moving. "Pull yourself together, get your purse, and come with me."

I have no idea why but his command is so compelling that I almost robotically reach for my purse and force myself to my feet, using the desk for stability. I can't make it any further. I wobble and sob.

Mark wraps an arm around my waist and catches my chin, forcing my gaze to his. "Ms. McMillan." His thumb swipes away my tears. "I warned you Chris was fucked-up. You accepted that. Did you not?"

"Yes. But—"

"There are no 'buts' today. Today you accept how he deals with pain, or you don't. Choose now."

"I'm trying. I just . . . I thought . . ."

"Don't think. It will get you into trouble. You've made this choice long before now. Accept his way even if you don't understand it, or walk away."

I wet my parched lips. "I accept," I whisper.

He sets me away from him. "Then let's go."

"Where?"

"To my club."

Twenty-six

Mark and I don't speak during the twenty-minute drive. He seems to understand that the tiniest thing might send me into an eruption of tears again. I rest my head on the soft leather seat of his Jaguar, watching the lights and stars flicker by the window. I dig deep inside myself to reopen the black pit I'd buried my emotions in before finding the journals, before finding Chris. I need that place I'd hoped to never go to again, to survive this, and I wonder now if I should have ever left it behind.

Slowly, I harness a thin veil of composure that is momentarily threatened when I spot the gates of the massive mansion that is Mark's club deep in the elite Cow Hollow neighborhood. Will I find Chris with another woman? I can handle a lot but these two things, I don't know if I can.

We park in front of the long stairwell and a suited security guard wearing an earpiece opens my door. I don't move. I can't move.

"Ms. McMillan."

Mark commands me to look at him. This time his Master routine doesn't work. I stare straight ahead. I am clear-minded enough to wonder about his motives behind bringing me here, despite being grateful he's given me the chance to face this thing with Chris regardless of the outcome. But Mark's motive could be an effort to tear me and Chris apart—or a true worry about an ex-friend he still feels some connection with. I'm not sure it matters. The outcome of this night will be determined by me and Chris and no one else.

"I'm not going to like what I find, am I?" I finally ask.

"No."

The hard, cold honesty of that one word sets me in motion. Whatever awaits me inside, I just want to know. I step out of the car, and despite leaving my jacket at the gallery, I welcome the cold night air that lets me feel anything but the ache burning through me. I slide my purse over my shoulder. My cash and credit cards give me an exit route if I need one, and I'm shocked I have this clarity of mind. I've found that deep hole, or at least the edge of the void that I know too well.

Mark rounds the car and cups my elbow, murmuring something to the guard I don't even try to hear, before he leads me up the stairs toward the double red doors I'd entered only once before. They open as we approach and another suited man greets Mark.

Cotton seems to gather in my mouth as we step inside the mansion, onto the expensive Oriental rug. My gaze sweeps the towering ceilings and expensive art and décor surrounding me, and I almost laugh at the façade of proper decorum.

Mark motions to the winding staircase covered in red carpet rather than to the hallway to the right I'd once traveled with Chris. There's a second set I didn't notice going down, and they become our path to wherever we are headed. We travel downward and the winding path is tortuous and eternal. My heart is pounding in my ears, behind my eyes, pounding and pounding. I cling to the rail, and somehow I've wrapped my arm through Mark's to cling to him as well. I don't remember how we get to another red door. We are suddenly just there. It's wooden and arched, with a huge metal bolt. My stomach knots. Oh, God. A dungeon. Pain. Torture.

Mark pulls me around to face him, holding my arm. "Accept him or walk away."

"Why are you doing this?"

"Because he's dangerously on the edge and I think you can pull him back."

I search his face, looking for the truth in his answer, and I find it. I don't care why he cares what happens to Chris. I just know he does. I straighten. "Take me to him."

He studies me for a long moment, assessing my state of mind, and apparently he approves. Without another word, he shoves the heavy bolt aside and opens the door. The scent of something spicy like incense touches my nose, burning through me like acid fear. I hold my breath as I step forward, blocking it out, and I find myself inside what looks like a concrete holding room, not more than twenty by twenty feet. At least half a dozen lanterns pulse from the depths of massive steel encasements high on the walls.

I draw a calming breath and stare at the huge blank monitor

spanning the wall directly in front of me, much like the one Chris had used to show me a woman being flogged in another part of the mansion. Cold seeps into my bones and I shiver; the sensation of being underground and trapped is almost unbearable.

"Where is he?" I ask.

Mark motions to the wooden door on my left. "In the next room, but I need to be clear. To allow you to intrude on play breaks every code of honor I have for this club. I interfere only if I judge that someone's well-being is at risk."

"What are you saying?"

"He goes too far when he's like this. The report I received upon arriving is that tonight is only different from the past in that he's beyond even his worst extreme."

My nails dig into my palms. "Take me to him."

He walks to the monitor and retrieves a remote control mounted to the wall. "I need to know you can handle what you're going to find before I let you inside."

"Then show me now," I demand, balling one of my fists on my chest, as if that might keep my heart from exploding where it beats furiously.

"The reasons people enjoy our play here vary. Most of us simply find it an adrenaline rush and a pleasurable escape. Chris isn't about pleasure. He's about punishing himself."

"Damn it, Mark, *show* me."

His lips tighten and he punches the button on the remote. The screen comes to life. I hear Chris before I see him, his raspy, harsh breathing. I try to process what I'm seeing. Chris is inside a round concrete cell, shirtless, wearing only his jeans. His arms are outstretched and tied to some kind of poles. He isn't wearing a mask, but the woman standing behind him from a small boxed window at the top of the monitor is. She's in some kind of leather barely-there outfit with high boots, and *oh, God*. I cover my mouth and jump as she lays a harrowing strike of a whip against Chris's back. His body jerks with the impact.

"Harder!" Chris snarls, sweat gathering on his forehead. "Fucking hit me like you mean it, or send someone in who can do the job."

She hits him again. He bucks under the lash and then laughs bitterly. "Are you the pussy or am I?"

The woman pulls the whip back, and I shout, "No! No more!" I dart for the door and yank it open and Mark doesn't stop me. I enter the dungeon's circle from behind Chris and the sight of Chris's welts, bleeding down his back, is almost too much to bear.

"Finally," Chris growls at the sound of my entry, unaware it's me. "A replacement. I hope you're better than she is."

"Cut him loose," I hiss at the masked woman even as I'm rounding the poles to stand in front of Chris. Tears streak his face, torment spiraling in the depths of his bloodshot eyes.

"Sara." My name falls from Chris's lips before he throws his head back and growls in complete, utter anguish.

"Chris." His name is a pained whisper wrenched deep from my soul. I start to cry, trembling as I touch his face, forcing him to look me. He lowers his lashes, refusing to look at me. "Cut him loose!" I shout, because the woman hasn't moved.

I hear Mark speak through some kind of intercom. "Do it."

I wrap my arms around Chris. My broken, beautiful man. "Why didn't you come to me? Why?"

His chest heaves against mine, his words heavy, pained. "You were never supposed to see me like this."

One of his arms goes slack and then the next and we sink together to the ground, where Chris buries his face in my neck and whispers, "You shouldn't be here."

"I belong with you."

"No, Sara. You don't. I was wrong. We were wrong."

His words are like a hand plunging into my chest and ripping out my heart. This is the moment I've feared. The moment when his secrets destroy us if I let them. I press my lips to his. "I *love* you, damn it. We can get through this!"

He cups my head and his breath is hot on my skin. "No. We can't." He pushes to his feet and takes me with him. "Come with me." He leads me to a doorway to our left, directly into a private room. Chris immediately releases me. Reeling, I barely process the hotel-like bedroom, much like the one we'd visited on my prior trip to the club.

He grabs his shirt from I don't know where and yanks it over his head, and I hear the hiss of pain he tries to suppress. He turns away from me, spiking his fingers into his hair and just holding them there.

I walk to him and reach out to touch him but pull back, afraid of hurting him. "Chris—"

He turns to stare down at me, his eyes bloodshot, haunted. "I tried to warn you away," he whispers. "Over and over, I tried."

"I'm still here, Chris."

"You shouldn't be."

I flinch at the venomous tone he's used, but I remind myself this is the pain speaking. "Yes, I should. I *love* you."

His jaw clenches and unclenches and his reply is agonizingly slow. "I'm going to fly out and help Dylan's family."

"I'll come with you."

"No." The word is as sharp as the whip that is tearing us apart. "I need to do this alone."

"Don't shut me out." My voice quakes.

"I'm protecting you."

"By shoving me away? By using everything but me to get through this?"

"I'm going to destroy you, Sara, and I can't live with that."

I can almost hear a locked door closing between us. "Shutting me *out* will destroy me."

"You'll thank me later for this, I promise you. I'm going to have Jacob and Blake look out for you and get you through this Rebecca thing."

Like he has some obligation to *protect* me. "I don't need anyone to get me through anything. Just like you, right, Chris? If we're over, we're over. I'll get a mover to take my things back to my apartment."

"No." He grabs my arm and pulls me to him. "Don't make me fucking worry about you on top of dealing with Dylan. You're staying in the apartment and you're accepting protection until Blake says you are safe, or I swear to God, Sara, I'll lock you in a room and keep you there."

I squeeze my eyes shut, and try to find some cold comfort in the fact that he doesn't want me to leave. That maybe, just maybe, he's clinging to me and us, and this tonight is all his pain talking. "Just go do what you have to do."

"You're staying at the apartment."

"Fine. Yes. I'll stay."

Slowly, his grip on my arm eases and he lets me go. "I'll have a driver take you to the apartment. I'm going straight to the airport."

I fight the pain that makes me want to turn and dart away. He's hurting. He's not himself. "I'll fly up for the funeral."

"No. That's not necessary, and it won't be in L.A. anyway."

"I'm coming to the funeral," I insist, and walk up to him and press a kiss to his mouth. "I love you, Chris. Nothing about tonight changes that." Slowly, I pull back, but he won't look at me. With extreme effort, I turn and blindly walk to the door. I reach for the knob and hesitate, waiting for him to stop me, but he doesn't.

He lets me leave.

I have no memory of how I make it to the front of the mansion. Suddenly I am walking down the steps, and a guy in a suit is watching me expectantly. I don't stop at the bottom. I don't stop for him. I keep walking, and I reach for my cell phone as I tell him, "Open the gate." I dial information. "Connect me to a cab company."

"What address do you need?" the woman on the other line asks.

I grimace as I realize I have no clue and I'm halfway down the winding path approaching the exit. Not knowing where I am is yet again another brilliant move on my part. "I'll call back when I get to a street sign," I say and hang up, noting the closed gate before me.

It doesn't open when I finally reach it and I wrap my hands

around the steel bars and drop my forehead to the metal. It's icy cold beneath my palms. How appropriate, since I'm freezing to death in every possible way.

The sound of a car behind me gives me hope the gates will open and I step aside to find the Jaguar beside me. The window slides down. "Get in," Mark orders.

I consider declining but I just want out of here. I just want out. I climb into the car.

Twenty-seven

"Where do you want to go?" Mark asks, leaving the car idling.

I don't look at him. I stare blindly out of the window and give him my apartment address. I don't care that I have no furniture. Chris has his way of dealing with things and I have mine. The idea of returning to Chris's place, which was supposed to be our place, is unbearable tonight. I'll face it tomorrow.

"Sara," Mark says softly and I turn to him. "Are you okay?"

"Not yet. But I'll find a way to survive. I always do."

"You don't need to be alone. I have a spare bedroom and I live a few blocks from here."

"No. I'm not going to your place. Thank you, but I need to be alone."

He considers me for a moment and puts the car into drive. Numbness begins to form within me. I remember this sensation when my mother died. The absolute nothingness of what I felt, and I welcome it, recognizing it as my mind's way of surviving.

Twenty minutes later, I break the silence and direct Mark to my building. "You can just let me out here."

"I'm walking you to your door."

I sigh inwardly. I won't win this battle and I don't have a fight left in me anyway.

He parks and we walk to my door. I turn to him. "Thanks for the ride."

"Let me have your phone."

I don't ask him why. I just hand it to him. He punches something into it and returns it to me. "My address is in your contacts. My offer stands indefinitely. If you need me, my door is open."

I don't question his motives because I am not in a state of mind to judge much of anything. "I appreciate that."

He studies me. "I'm waiting on you to go inside safely."

I dig into my purse and drop my head to the door. "I don't have my key."

Mark leans on the door to face me, his jacket unbuttoned, and I'm struck by how proper he is even now. How in control, and I envy that in him. "Come home with me," he says. "Let me take care of you tonight."

I lift my head and stare into his silvery gray eyes, and part of me wants just to feed off that control he has, to make it my own. But no. If Chris knew I'd gone home with Mark, even to stay in a spare bedroom, it would destroy him. Or maybe it wouldn't. I choose to believe he loves me enough that it would. "I won't do that to Chris."

He studies me a long moment and his expression is as un-readable as ever. "Where to, then?" he asks, pushing off the door.

"To Chris's—" Realization hits me and I push off the door and dig into my purse, and jackpot. I have Ella's key. I hold it up. "My neighbor's apartment. She's out of the country." I motion toward her door and slide the key inside, and thankfully, it opens. I flip on the light and I turn to Mark. "Thank you again."

"You're sure you're okay here?"

"Yes. Very."

He hesitates. "Call me if you need me."

"I will."

I watch him round the corner before I enter Ella's apartment and shut the door. I lean against it, taking in the fluffy blue couch and oversized chairs to match, remembering wine and pizza and long talks with Ella. She should be home next week, if she plans to teach this semester. No "should" about it. She has to be back home. She has to be all right.

Something inside me snaps. I shrug off my purse and start searching for anything that might tell me she is okay. I dig through papers, drawers, cabinets. I find nothing. Not even photos of her and David. Not a mention of him or Paris or a wedding. Nothing.

I end up in her bedroom, and I sink onto the soft white down comforter of Ella's bed. My mother is dead. My father is an asshole who wouldn't care if I was dead. Dylan is dead. Ella is lost. Chris is lost. Everyone I dare to love disappears.

I tuck a pillow under my head and curl into myself. Alone is the only safe place to be. Alone hurts so much less.

I told him I can't do this anymore. I can't be what he needs me to be. He told me to let him do the thinking. Let him decide what

I can be. He then yanked my skirt up and buried himself inside me. Once that man is inside me, I am lost. But maybe that is the problem. I am lost.

I jerk awake out of a dream of one of Rebecca's journal entries, my gaze sweeping Ella's small bedroom, the shadow of the deep night hour surrounding me. The sound of pounding jolts me again and I scramble to the end of the bed. Door. Someone's knocking on the door. Hope flares inside me that it might be Chris.

I rush to the door and start to open it but common sense finds me at the last second. "Who is it?"

"Blake."

I drop my head to the door. Damn it. Damn it. Damn it. Damn it.

"You gonna let me in?" he asks after several seconds.

"How did you know I was here?"

"Mark thought this would be a good place to look for you."

Of course. Mark told him. Sighing in resignation, I open the door and find him leaning on the jamb, hand over his head, his long dark hair falling haphazardly from the tie at his nape. "Chris sent me looking for you. He's worried because you're not at his place."

"Is he here?"

His lips thin and he shakes his head. "He's in L.A."

"Right," I squeeze out. "What time is it?"

"Two in the morning."

"I don't want to go back there tonight."

"You're safer there."

"Right," I say again. "Because I'm in danger from some unknown someone who might have killed Rebecca. Only we can't find her, or Ella, or any proof of any of this."

He studies me, his brown eyes sharp before softening. "Let's go back to Chris's, Sara. It'll give us all peace of mind."

I consider arguing, but what's the point? At least Chris cared enough to find out I wasn't home. At his place, I silently correct myself. Chris made it clear I was to stay there only *until* the Rebecca mystery was solved. In other words, his place was never my place.

"Fine," I concede, and I grab my purse and close up Ella's apartment.

After we get into his car and pull onto the road, I ask, "Where do we stand on Rebecca?"

He fills me in, and when we pull up to Chris's building, I am comforted and disturbed by how thorough Blake is in his work and how absent Rebecca remains.

The doorman opens the passenger door for me. "Sara," Blake calls, halting my exit.

"Yes?"

"My wife is coming in for the weekend. She works with Walker Security. You could do whatever women do together and talk through things. Maybe you'll remember something helpful."

In other words, I'll have a bodyguard I don't want. "I'm working. You enjoy being with your wife." I step out of the car and walk past the night security guard, glad Jacob is gone. I don't want to see the concern in his expression that might send me back over the edge.

I take the elevator to Chris's floor and when the doors open to his apartment, I don't move. Only when the doors start to close do I catch them and enter the apartment. The familiar earthy scent of Chris is everywhere, yet he is nowhere.

I sleep on the couch and wake up to walk through my morning routine like a zombie. I wear a solid black dress with black hose and heels. The safe in the bottom of the closet catches my eye and I sink to my knees and tug on the door. It's still locked, of course, and I don't have the combination.

A few minutes later, I stand in the kitchen, unsure what to do with myself, and dare to try to call Chris. Each ring is like a blade stabbing me in the heart until his voice mail sounds. I don't leave a message this time, either. I dial Brandy and get her husband. The funeral won't be until next week, because of some kind of research testing. It's in North Carolina. He'll have Chris get me the details.

In the lobby, I find Jacob. "I want my car."

"Ms. Mc—"

"I want my car, Jacob."

His eyes narrow sharply. "Mr. Merit—"

"Isn't here."

"You do know you have to remain cautious."

"Yes. I'm aware, but I still want my car."

He gets my car and I settle into the seat, wishing I'd never left the safety of what I knew behind. Everything is broken. I am broken.

I don't even remember the drive.

The first thing I find when I arrive at work is a white envelope with my name scribbled on it in what I think is Mark's handwriting. I sit down and tear it open to find my commission due of fifty thousand dollars, signed by Mark. There's a note attached.

Ms. McMillan:

Under the circumstances, I cut the check early. There is peace of mind and freedom of choice to having money in the bank. After last night, I thought you might need some. If you need to take time off for the funeral, it's yours.

Bossman

While I appreciate the money, I can't help but think of the irony of his words considering how I'd earned the payment. I hold the check to my forehead and relive the wine tasting and the moment Chris had confronted Mark and demanded this commission for me. *"I came here tonight to support Sara. I expect her to get the commission off my sales."* When I'd asked him why he'd done it, he'd said it was so Mark wouldn't gobble me up and destroy me. Then he'd kissed me for the first time, and I was his from that point on. "And I still am," I whisper, folding it and sticking it in my wallet. The problem is, I don't think he's mine. I don't think he ever truly was.

It's a daunting, gut-churning thought that has me sitting at my desk, unable to think of what to do with myself. *No.* Sitting at Rebecca's desk. Who am I kidding? This is her life, her world. I am an intruder who owes her more than stealing her job. It is this thought that sets me on fire. I shut the door and start digging through everything in her office. Opening books, folders, magazines, and I hit a jackpot. Flat against the shelf, hidden behind other books, is another journal. I pull it out and start to read. A few pages into it, I realize she's used it to detail an investigation into the fraudulent art she believes Mary has delivered to Riptide. There are notes about Ricco Alvarez evaluating the pieces. I do a quick specific Google search of Ricco Alvarez and discover he's considered an authentication expert in certain types of art. There are no indications in Rebecca's notes of him looking at the art in question.

I dial Ricco. He answers immediately. "Bella—"

"Meet me at the coffee shop."

"Fifteen minutes."

Adrenaline rushes through me like wildfire and I flip through the records Mark gave me for Riptide to find the pieces Rebecca has listed in her notes. They sold right after she left, or rather, disappeared. I shift from the paper reports to my computer and print details on those pieces and the new ones Mary has listed for the next auction. I slip them into my briefcase, snatch my purse and coat, and, already standing, I dial Mark's office. He doesn't answer.

Heading to the hallway, I pause by Amanda's desk. "I'm meeting a client next door. Is Mark in the gallery?"

"No. He won't be in until after lunch but he told me to tell you he canceled your meeting with Ryan for tonight. He thought you might want to choose the date to reschedule."

I hate how appreciative I am of this news. I have dreamed of this job, this life that has now become a little piece of hell.

Mary appears at the opposite side of Amanda's desk. My cheeks heat with the certainty she is somehow involved in

Rebecca's disappearance. "Call me if Mark gets in before I get back, please," I say to Amanda, and rush to the door, eager to talk to Ricco.

Entering Ava's shop, I inhale the scent of coffee and sweets and manage an awkward wave in her direction. Ricco is already here, and I settle at the table across from him, trying not to look at the table Chris always sits at. But I do. I look as if he will magically appear, and I swallow the emotions his absence stirs.

"Did you locate a number for Rebecca?" Ricco inquires urgently.

"No. Sorry. But I am following up on something she was working on. Did she ask you about a couple of counterfeit paintings?" I pull out my folder and show them to Ricco. "Did you look at these for her?"

"Oh yes. I remember Rebecca mentioning her concern but nothing beyond a verbal inquiry. She never got me what I needed to evaluate the work."

"What exactly would you need?"

"I can begin with digital photos but ideally I'll want to examine the actual work."

"How much per item?"

"I don't charge. I feel it decreases my credibility."

I slide the folder over to him. "I have details for each work and digital photos. Two of the four pieces are in the Allure Gallery. Two are not. Please. Will you look into them for me?"

"This is related to Rebecca's worries?"

"Yes."

"Do you think it has something to do with why she disappeared?"

Disappeared. The word hangs in the air and I remind myself to be cautious. Have I just made a mistake? Could he be involved with Mary? "Doubtful," I reply. "I don't think she went very far with this."

His eyes narrow and his answer comes slowly. "Very well, Bella. I'll look into it." He scoops up the folder. "Shall I walk you to the gallery?"

"No. Thank you. I'll stay a bit."

I watch him leave and consider calling Mark, but hesitate. Not for the first time, I wonder if Mark could be involved. The first two pieces Rebecca questioned sold for large sums of money. I dial Blake instead.

I tell him what I have discovered and hear only silence on the other end before he says, "You do know I am a former ATF, and art theft and counterfeiting operations is one of our specialties, correct?"

"I didn't really put that together in a two-and-two kind of way."

"Well, now I've done it for you and yes, I believe there is something going on and I am dealing with it. You, however, are not supposed to be asking questions. I repeat, we are aware of the situation and PS: I'm handling Ricco Alvarez."

"Is Mark involved?"

"Mark Compton is a lot of things, but as far as I can tell a thief isn't one of them. I'm not prepared to rule out all possibilities quite yet, though."

"Do you . . . do you think Rebecca got close to this and someone . . ."

"I have nothing to connect her disappearance to the art scam but it's a logical link. In other words, stay out of this. If I had my way I'd put you on a plane to L.A. to be with Chris."

If I had my way, I'd be on a plane to be with Chris, too. I end the call and dial Chris again. He doesn't answer. I clutch my phone and wonder what kind of clubs they have in Los Angeles. I wonder what he will do to hide from his pain and I wonder who he will do it with. I dial Brandy and get her husband, only to learn that she's highly sedated and a mess. I hang up and certainty fills me. Unless Chris invites me he will be upset that I show up and Brandy will be upset because he's upset. It's clear that the life I'd convinced myself was mine never was. I can't even properly grieve a brave young boy without feeling like an intruder.

Defeated, I gather my things and start for the door but draw up short when Ryan and Mark walk in. The two of them together are pure testosterone in their perfectly fitted suits, and complete contrasts with their dark and light hair. The masculine beauty they ooze is almost a crime, and downright blinding to us normal humans.

"Hey, sweetheart," Ryan says to me, and gives me a once-over that is thorough and somehow manages not to be obnoxious. "You look gorgeous."

His natural charm pulls a small smile from me. I think it's the warmth in his brown eyes, so unlike the hard glint permanently etched in Mark's. "Thanks, Ryan, but I know I'm far from it today."

"Is the black dress an indicator you are flying out to L.A.?" Mark inquires.

"No. As of now, I'm not going." It hits me that Ava will tell Mark I was with Ricco. "I came over here to meet with Ricco again, but it's still a no-go for his business. I guess I'm a glutton for punishment."

"Yes," Mark agrees wryly. "I do believe you are."

Inwardly, I bristle at his reference to Chris, and I'm fighting a snippy "he's my kind of punishment" when the door chimes behind us. Avoiding incoming bodies, Ryan steps closer to me at the same time Mark does. I end up smashed against Mark, staring up into his piercing gray eyes. My pulse skyrockets and I step backward. "I should get back to the gallery."

Mark's lips quirk. "I don't bite, Ms. McMillan."

"Somehow, I doubt that's true." It's out before I can stop it.

Mark arches an arrogant brow and Ryan laughs good-naturedly. "Oh yes. I do love a woman with some bite of her own. But before you run off to the gallery, Sara, the art you ordered for the demo unit came in. If you come back to the property with me, you can help direct the maintenance team to place it where you want it."

I cast Mark a questioning look. He motions me onward. "Go. See the art you loved enough to buy and make us all money by completing the deal. It'll make you feel better. I know it will make me feel better."

The only thing that is going to make me feel better is hearing from Chris. "Then I guess I'm going to the property. Should I follow you, Ryan?"

"Sure." His hand settles casually on my shoulder, a bold touch when he barely knows me, but he's a friendly guy. "Let me just get some coffee for the road. You want some?"

"More caffeine is always on my to-do list," I joke, then turn to head to the counter only to find that Ava is no longer here. It strikes me as odd, albeit for no identifiable reason. Even odder, it's an impression that I don't shake until I'm at Ryan's property, directly over the ocean, inside the elegant apartment with a wall of windows much like those at Chris's apartment. I walk over to the white marble fireplace, which contrasts with the deep mahogany floors, and stare at the blank wall above it. I intended the wall to hold a Chris Merit original. It's as empty as I am.

Twenty-eight

Six days after Chris's departure, and only a few days until the October 1 start of school for Ella, I am climbing my office walls, willing both of them to call me. It's Thursday and nearly noon, and for the first time all week, I try to truly prepare myself for this breakup with Chris. I even dress in my old clothes, a simple black skirt and red silk blouse. Arranging to have my things moved back to my apartment is inevitable. I'd rather do it now than have Chris return and do it for me.

Feeling more like the kept woman my mother was to an absent man, I am eager to escape the confines of the gallery. Out of worry for Chris's peace of mind, I do as I have been for days, and report to Jacob before heading to the deli three blocks down the road. Once there, I order an egg salad sandwich and find a back corner table and shove my food aside. I can't eat. I haven't been able to eat since Chris left.

The bell on the door chimes and I look up to find Mark and

Ava walking into the deli. The way she's looking at him scorches me from clear across the restaurant. I feel sorry for her husband, trying to compete with Mark. He doesn't have a chance.

Mark's gaze lifts and collides with mine. He whispers something to Ava and steps away from her, and for a moment I see a spark of something that looks downright evil on Ava's face. Whoa—that's new. I think I've sensed this in her, but seeing it is a jolt of reality. She hates me.

Mark joins me without asking, sitting directly across from me at a table more for one than two. "You plan to eat that sandwich or watch it like TV?"

"Ah, now there's that sense of humor I thought you reserved only for e-mails and text messages."

He doesn't laugh. "You look thin." He shoves the sandwich toward me. "Eat."

Surprisingly, he's been quite the doting daddy for a Master who wields a wicked whip, but he's right in this case. I've dropped five pounds I didn't have to lose, but regardless of his good intentions, I truly am not in the mood to be pushed. "I don't want to eat and don't order me around like I'm your submissive. I'm not."

"Ms. McMillan—"

"Sara," I snap, on edge, and irritated that I feel like we've created a friendship this past week and he still can't use my name. "Why can't you call me Sara like you call Amanda, Amanda?"

He gives me one of those unreadable, impossible intense gray stares. "All right then, *Sara*. I'm worried about you."

"Don't be."

He leans in closer. "What can I do?"

"Nothing. Nothing that you haven't already. I know you convinced Ryan to let me decorate the lobby of the property. It helped. It kept me busy and I do appreciate that."

"Ryan's fond of you. We have to milk it for all the business we can."

"Right." I give a laugh. "It's always about money for you, isn't it?"

"Money is power."

So Chris once told me. "And we both know how much you like power."

His brows lift. "Do we?"

"We do," I assure him.

He leans back in his seat and his lips twitch. "Well, as long as we have that settled." He pauses, his mouth tightening, and I sense the subject change before it comes. "Have you heard from him?"

"No." I try to laugh without humor but it comes out as more of a strangled sound. "I guess I didn't do a very good job of getting through to him like you thought I would." I rub at the tension in my shoulder. A burning question constantly on my mind presses me to take advantage of having Mark's rare casual mood and full attention. "Why, Mark?"

"Why what, Sara?"

"Why do you both need that place?"

He appears undaunted by the question. "I told you. It's different for everyone, and Chris and I are as night and day as it comes. He wants to punish himself. The pain is who he is. It controls him."

"And you?"

That steely glint I know well appears in his eyes, and I watch the man transform into the Master who is intensely, impossibly provocative, able to seduce a room just by existing. "Nothing controls me but me. I am who I am and I enjoy every moment of it, and so do those who enter my domain. I make sure of it." I am captivated by his stare, lost in this man who is all power and sexuality, but even more so by the idea of having such confidence and control myself. He seems to sense this or perhaps he can easily read my expression, and he leans in closer, softening his voice to a seductive purr. "I would never put my pleasure, or my pain, for that matter, ahead of your needs, Sara."

I am sure that his vow is meant to lure me deeper under his spell, but it doesn't work. It smacks me in the face with possibilities I don't want to consider and jerks me into defensive mode. I sit back sharply. "He doesn't do that. Chris doesn't put himself ahead of me."

"What do you call what he's done, Sara?"

"He's trying to protect me."

"And how does that protection feel? Because you aren't eating and you aren't sleeping. If that is how he protects you, he's failed."

"Like you failed Rebecca."

He shocks me by visibly flinching, proving again that he is not without a weakness where Rebecca is concerned. "She wanted what I don't have to give, what I never promised."

"Which is what?"

"The façade of love. The same poison that leaves your sandwich sitting here uneaten. Think about what this fairy tale of love you've created is doing to you. When you're ready to get rid of that spiteful emotion, I'll show you how." He pushes to his feet. "We have the open house tonight at the property. We leave at six forty-five. I'm driving."

It's me who flinches as he walks away.

I'm pleased to score a large late afternoon sale, but it delays Mark and me from departing the gallery at the time planned, and we arrive at the open house with only forty-five minutes left before it ends. At the front door of the thirty-floor high-rise on the oceanfront, Mark maneuvers the Jag under the front door over-hang and two valets open our doors. When Mark rounds the ve-hicle to join me, his hand settles a bit too possessively on my back.

The lobby is crowded, warmed by a gas fireplace framed in stone, and furnished with clusters of rich brown leather chairs and several paintings I personally selected. People mill around everywhere, drinks in hand. Mark and I make our way through the visitors, mingling and prospecting for new sales. Ryan finds us quickly, looking stunning in a striking red silk tie that con-trasts with his pin-striped suit as dark as his neatly groomed raven hair.

He takes my hand and kisses it. "You look lovely, Sara." He leans in near my ear. "Far better than any of the many master-pieces here tonight."

My cheeks heat with the compliment I don't deserve, con-sidering the expensive dresses and suits being elegantly worn by the guests. "I should have changed."

"Nonsense," he says. "You look marvelous. Why don't we head upstairs to the demo unit? There are a number of guests there you can impress with your knowledge of art."

Inside the twentieth-floor apartment, I spend the next half hour happily chatting with guests and I try to lose myself in the thrill of discussing the art I've chosen for the project. It's a difficult task, since the Chris Merit cityscape I purchased from a local resident for my blank wall is a constant reminder of him.

When the crowd clears I find myself alone, seduced into deep thought by the dimly lit elegant space and soft music humming in the background. I find myself dreading the empty apartment awaiting me. "It's a wrap," Ryan announces, and I turn to find both him and Mark walking toward me. "The lobby is clear and we've locked up here."

Leaning against the mahogany railing spanning the middle of the ceiling-to-floor window, I feel a charge in the air—the sensation of being prey to not one lion, but two, as they each stop beside me, sandwiching me between them.

"The night was a success, Ms. McMillan," Mark says in praise. "You've proven to be quite the asset."

Even the caged animal I have become these past few days, more now than ever, hungers for this man's compliments, and I tell myself it's about my job and nothing more. "I've tried." My voice comes out shaky and affected, and I can feel how losing Chris has made me revert backward, angry at how easily I still fall prey to a need for approval from men like Mark and Michael.

Ryan brushes my hair over my shoulder, and despite the gentleness of the touch, it's too intimate, and I tense, jerking my gaze to his. "Poor Sara," he murmurs. "You have such pain in your eyes."

"I'm . . . I'm fine."

"No," Ryan insists gently. "You're not. I've watched you bleeding emotionally all week."

"You have to let him go."

Mark proves his ease at stirring my defenses one again, and I turn to him, finding him closer than I'd thought. My thigh brushes his and I feel it like a second jolt. "No," I choke out. "I can't." I back up and Ryan's hands go to my waist. I'm that caged animal again, a deer caught by two predators.

Mark claims the space I'd created and his legs press to mine. "You can't or you won't?"

The urge to bolt is stilled when Ryan leans in, his chin nuzzling my hair as he whispers, "He let go. You have to, too."

I'm shaken by how right he might be, and how wrong I burn for him to be. "It's too soon." *It's too soon.*

Mark's hands settle on my shoulders, branding me. "I refuse to watch you hurt like this one more day. Let go, Ms. McMillan."

He leans in, his head slowly lowering, the punishingly sensual line of his mouth nearing mine. "Think about it," he urges softly. "To feel nothing but pleasure. To expect nothing more."

Ryan's thumbs stroke my waist. "To stop hurting," he adds.

The heat of Mark's breath teasing my cheek, the spicy, powerful scent of him overwhelms me, and for just a moment I am weak enough to want what these two men offer me. Chris doesn't want me. He has all but kicked me out of what he'd called my home. *Stay until the Rebecca thing is over.* Just thinking about it slices through my very soul.

"Just let go," Mark murmurs, his fingers settling on my cheek at the same time Ryan slides his hand to my stomach. Warmth spreads through me and then transforms, twisting and turning inside me, spiraling into the acid depths of darkness, to a place I remember too well. A place Michael took me two years before.

"No!" I shove against Mark. "No. No. *No*."

"Ms.—"

"No, Mark. Let me go." Ryan's hands slide from my body and a bit of relief washes over me, but Mark is still touching me, somehow holding my arms. "Let go!"

They both step away from me as if burned, and I dart from between them in a rush of adrenaline. I all but run to the exit stairwell and start down the stairs. Ten floors down, I regret the walk, but I keep moving, despising what Mark and Ryan have stirred inside me. How they've tried to steal what hope I have left for Chris and me. How I was almost weak enough to let them convince me I could do no better than submitting to their control.

Reaching the bottom of the stairwell, on shaky legs, I draw a calming breath and exit, promising myself I will not lose it until I'm alone, when I know I am already a volcanic mess, burning alive from the inside out.

I manage well enough until I step onto the automatic door sensor and Mark appears beside me. "Sara—"

"Leave me alone, Mark."

"I'll take you to your car."

"No. I don't need a ride."

"I was trying to help," he says defensively as we step outside. "I *can* help."

The instant I see the valet area is clear of people, I whirl on him. "What happened up there shouldn't have happened." Anger radiates from deep in my soul, lacing my words. "It can't happen again. *Ever.*" Urgent to get away from him, I turn to my right and stop dead in my tracks to find Chris standing there.

"Chris," I gasp, my gaze hungrily drinking in the sight of him in all his leather and denim glory. His presence is a sweet relief, filling empty spaces, allowing me to breathe again.

He glares over my shoulder at Mark. "What just happened that can't happen again?"

"You're ripping her to shreds, Chris," he replies with unmistakable contempt.

Chris's green eyes sharpen and he takes a threatening step around me and toward Mark. I jump in front of him, pressing my hands to his chest to stop his progress. Touching him is heaven. "No. Don't."

His lashes lower, his eyes resting on my face. "What happened, Sara?"

Mark answers before I can. "What happened is that she's melting away to nothing over you, asshole."

Chris's head lifts, the fury deep in his eyes as he fixes them on Mark again. "We both know what this is about and I suggest you don't go there."

"You suggest," Mark repeats with disdain. "You're good at suggesting what you can't do yourself."

Chris starts for him again and I wrap my arms around him. "No. Please."

The two men stare at each other, Chris's chest heaving under my hand. "Walk away, Mark," Chris warns. "Walk away now before I don't let you."

"Mark, please," I plead over my shoulder.

He hesitates. "If you need me, Sara, you know how to find

me." I hear his footsteps and Chris remains stiff, on edge, until I assume Mark is gone.

Chris's attention slides to me for an instant, his fingers untangling my arms from around him, banding my wrist as he starts walking, all but dragging me toward the Harley parked near the door. "Chris—"

"Don't talk, Sara. Not now. Not when I'm this pissed." He stops at the bike and shoves a leather jacket my size at me. I stare down at it. He bought me a jacket? "Put it on, Sara."

"I'm wearing a skirt. I can't ride the bike."

"Get on, or I'll rip the damn thing to put you on this bike." I put the jacket on. He shoves a helmet at me. "And this."

The instant I place it on my head, he tugs me forward and I yank my skirt up, sliding my leg over the bike. Chris shackles my wrists and pulls them around him. I begin to panic. I've never been on a bike. What if I fall off?

He revs the engine, rolls backward, and then in a roar of escalation we are on the highway, the cold ocean air blistering my bare legs. Chris speeds up and I bury my face against him. We travel the twisting roads, and he speeds up, faster and faster still. He won't slow down. He won't stop. He's going to kill us.

Twenty-nine

"Terrified and furious" doesn't begin to describe my state by the time Chris brings the bike to a screeching halt just off the coastline, in the midst of twining trails and massive trees with towering trunks dimly lit by moonlight and stars. My heart is in my throat, my breath heaving, and my legs frozen to the bone.

He frees my hands and I scramble off the bike, stumbling and yanking off my helmet. "Are you crazy!" I scream, tossing it away and shoving the mess of my hair out of my face. "Were you trying to kill us, or just punish me, Chris? Have you not punished me enough?"

"Who's punishing who?" he demands, setting his helmet on the bike and advancing on me.

My hands go up and they shake with the volume of adrenaline and emotion pulsing through me. "Stay back. Just stay back. I can't believe you just did that to me."

He grabs my arm and turns me, pushing me against a tree,

my fingers digging into the bark, his hips against my backside. Anger and arousal and a sense of needing him ignite all at once within me. "Did you fuck Mark, Sara?"

"No!"

His hand slides up my waist, under the jacket, and over my breast. I squeeze my eyes shut against the delicious roughness of his touch I don't want to react to. Not when he's angry, not like this.

"Did he touch you here?" The question is gravely spoken by my ear, accusation etched in its depths, and I struggle to remember how I'd feel if I'd seen him with Ava.

"No. Chris—"

"Did you tell him no, Sara?" He yanks my skirt up, his hand framing my hips as he arches his pelvis against me.

"Yes," I pant, impossibly alive with his touch, arching into him, the thick pulse of his erection nestled against my bottom. My body doesn't care how angry and hurt I am.

He tears my panties. "Did he do that?"

"No," I breathe out.

His hand curves around my hip, his fingers gliding into the slick heat of my sex. "Oh yeah, baby, already dripping for me. Or did he get you ready for me?"

"Enough!" I shout, driven to my limit by his crassness. I shove ineffectually against him. "Let me off this tree, Chris."

"Not until I'm ready." He squeezes my breast, strokes the slick, sensitive flesh between my legs, and I moan uncontrollably.

"Did you moan for him, too?"

That's it! I elbow him hard in the side and he grunts, loosening his grip enough for me to twist around to face him, shoving against his chest for more space. "Have you not hurt me enough?" I demand, yanking my skirt down over my exposed, cold backside, and I blast him with everything I've felt these past six days.

"When is it enough? When, Chris? When you've totally ripped out my heart? I didn't fuck Mark, but I could have. You said we were *over*. And damn you, you made me believe home was with you, then the first time life gets rough, you snatch that home from me and tell me I can stay *until* the Rebecca thing is over. Like I'm at a hotel. Do you know how that felt? Do you know how much it hurt me?"

For several beats we just stand there, staring at each other, the moonlight revealing the same anger carved in his face that I know must be mine. An anger I watch transform and soften the amber speckles in his green eyes, turning them to the gray of shadows and torment. His hands go to the tree, framing my face. "Sara." My name gusts from his lips like an ocean wind, and he buries his face in my neck, the earthy male scent of him I've missed so desperately washing over me, filling my senses.

My arms wrap around his neck, my lashes lowering. His arm circles my waist, holding me close. "I'm sorry," he whispers, his tone dark and tormented. "I'm so sorry, baby." He cups my face, staring down at me. "I'd bleed for you, Sara. I would never intentionally hurt you. Never."

"You shut me out, and—" My throat constricts. "I was supposed to be there with you. We were supposed to go through this together."

"Losing Dylan"—he hesitates, seeming to battle within himself before he continues—"it brought back old demons I thought I'd dealt with." He buries his face in my neck again, as if he can't bear for me to see his face. "Do you know *how I felt* when you saw me like that?"

Anguish pours off him and into me and my hands settle on his head, cradling him against me. "I love you, Chris. I can deal with anything except you shutting me out."

"You don't know that."

A heavy weight of doubt settles in my heart, and I wonder if we can make it through this. "*You* don't know that," I whisper. "You don't trust me enough to believe in me, in us."

He lifts his head, letting me see the shame in his eyes, exposing what he's tried to hide. Shame I understand all too well and would never wish on Chris. "You have no reason to feel what you're feeling right now. Not with me," I say.

"There's a part of me that lives in the belly of hell. You don't belong there. I can't take you there with me." His forehead goes to mine. "And yet I can't stay away. I can't let you go."

"Don't," I breathe, my hands press to his chest, the muscle flexing beneath my touch. I wish I could pull the pain from within him, heal him the way he does me. "Don't let me go."

"I'm not," he vows, framing my face to stare down at me, his voice sandpaper rough as it shivers down my spine and into my soul. "I can't, and I can only pray you don't wish I would have." He claims my mouth, and it is as if he is claiming me again for the first time. I offer all that I am to him.

His tongue presses past my lips and teeth, finding mine and stroking, and I feel him everywhere, the heat of how much I need him burning away the cold night. Everything fades away but the two of us touching, kissing, melding our bodies together.

I am blinded by passion, by the relief of his return, by his body next to mine. Time stands still and somehow my blouse is gaping, my bra open, and I'm pressed against the tree with Chris suckling and licking my nipples. My skirt is at my hips and I stroke the thick ridge of Chris's erection, nearly desperate to feel him inside me, craving the connection I thought I'd never experience again.

"Chris—" I pant and yelp, the bark cutting into my back, penetrating the haze of desire overcoming me.

"Ah. The tree." Chris pulls me from the tree, kisses me hard on the lips, and then shrugs out of his leather jacket, spreading it on the ground. He skims my jacket from my shoulders, spreading it on top of his. I shiver in a gust of wind and he takes me down to the ground, his big, warm body blocking out everything but him. Protecting me. He's always protecting me, even from himself.

Our breath mingles, teasing me with a kiss yet to happen, with the depths of passion I feel for Chris expanding within me. Still, he doesn't kiss me. He caresses my skirt up my hips again, his touch leaving goose bumps on my bare skin that have nothing to do with the night air and everything to do with the man. I reach for his waistband; that craving for him inside me reignites, becomes urgent. He echoes my silent plea, shoving down his pants, and I moan with the feel of the hard length of his cock thick between my thighs.

On his elbows, he pins me in a sizzling stare as he enters me and it's as if my soul sighs when he is finally buried deep in the depths of my body, stretching me, filling me.

"I thought I'd never be inside you again and it almost killed me." His voice trembles with a vulnerability that means even more than his confession.

He begins to move, a slow, sensual slide of his cock followed by another, watching me, me watching him, and we are making love, impossible and breathtaking lovemaking. We sway and meld together in a sweet, arousing dance, but it's not the harmony of our bodies that reaches deep and claims me, it's what passes between us as we stare at one another. He is as much a part of me as skin and bone, and it terrifies and completes me.

Chris dips his head and touches his lips to mine, teases my tongue with his, trails his lips over my jaw, over my shoulder, to my nipple. Every lick and taste, and tease, is tender, gentle, a contrast to the hardness of the past week and the man who'd been tied to those poles in the club. Suddenly I need him to know that I see both, I love both.

My hand slides into the silky long strands of his blond hair. "Chris," I manage hoarsely through the delicious friction of his tongue against my nipple, my sex clenching around his cock. "Chris."

His mouth comes down on mine, harder now, more demanding, a raw, hungry need in him rising to the surface. "You belong to me," he growls. "Say it."

"Yes. Yes, I belong to you." His mouth finds mine again, demanding, taking, drawing me under his spell.

"Say it again," he demands, nipping my lip, squeezing my breast and nipple, and sending a ripple of pleasure straight to my sex.

"I belong to you," I pant.

He lifts me off the ground with the possessive curve of his

hand around my backside, angling my hips to thrust harder, deeper. "Again," he orders, driving into me, his cock hitting the farthest point of me and blasting against sensitive nerve endings.

"Oh . . . ah . . . I . . . I belong to you."

His mouth dips low, his hair tickling my neck, his teeth scraping my shoulders at the same moment he pounds into me and the world spins around me, leaving nothing but pleasure and need and more need.

I am suddenly hot only where he touches, and freezing where I yearn to be touched. Lifting my leg, I shackle his hip, ravenous beyond measure, climbing to the edge of bliss, reaching for it at the same time I'm trying desperately to hold back. Chris is merciless, wickedly wild, grinding and rocking, pumping.

"I love you, Sara," he confesses hoarsely, taking my mouth, swallowing the shallow, hot breath I release, and punishing me with a hard thrust that snaps the last of the lightly held control I possess. Possessing *me*. A fire explodes low in my belly and spirals downward, seizing my muscles, and I begin to spasm around his shaft, trembling with the force of my release.

With a low growl, his muscles ripple beneath my touch and his cock pulses, his hot semen spilling inside me. We moan together, lost in the climax of a roller-coaster ride of pain and pleasure, spanning days apart, and finally collapse in a heap and just lie there. Slowly, I let my leg ease from his hip to the ground, and Chris rolls me to my side to face him.

Still inside me, he holds me close, pulling the jacket up around my back, trailing fingers over my jaw. "And I belong to you."

The unexpected vow does me in. Tears spring from my eyes,

trickling down my cheeks. "I thought . . . I thought . . . I can't go through this again."

"Shhh," he murmurs, kissing away the droplets clinging to my cheeks. "We're together now."

I shake my head, rejecting an answer that promises only one moment in time. "I have to know that the next time you get like that, we deal with it together, no matter what that means, Chris. I *have* to know."

"I won't get—"

His denial spikes through me and I try to push away from him, but he holds me. "Sara, wait."

"You *will* go there again. You will. I'm not about to pretend otherwise. It's all or nothing, Chris. All the dark, hated places you go, you go with me. You have to trust me enough to love that part of you as much as I do the rest."

"You don't know what you're asking."

"It's not a question. It's not even close to a request. This is how it has to be." His lashes lower; his struggle is palpable, and I soften instantly, hurting as he hurts. My fingers find his hair, stroking tenderly. "Let me love what you hate. Let me do that for you."

He presses his cheek to mine, his whiskers a welcome rasp on my cheek. "God, woman. I can't lose you."

I close my eyes and whisper, "I'm not going anywhere."

For a time, we huddle together, neither of us ready to move or to leave, almost as if we both fear that the real world will steal this newfound rein we hold on our future. And then we start to talk about Dylan, about the nightmare that has been Chris's week, until the chill of loss collides with the chill of the night, and we can stay no longer.

Chris helps me to my feet, and I do the best I can to clean up and pull myself together. Remarkably, my heels are still on my feet, but my skirt has not weathered the reunion well. I have a rip up the side, and as I try to close my blouse, several buttons have gone astray. "I'm a mess. I can't walk into the building like this."

"I never let the valet park my bike. We'll head in through the garage." He hands me my helmet and his voice softens. "Let's go home, baby. *Our* home."

And I dare to believe that it really is. I dare to bet on us again.

Chris and I are walking toward the elevator, our fingers laced, my shoes dangling from my free hand, when Jacob steps out of the elevator and heads toward us with determined steps. "So much for my discreet entry," I murmur, appalled at my ripped skirt and thankful the leather jacket I'm wearing is zipped.

"Something wrong?" Chris asks as Jacob joins us.

"I was about to ask you the same," Jacob comments, giving me a once-over.

"Sara's first trip on a motorcycle was eventful," Chris replies.

Jacob looks like he expects more of an explanation, and when it doesn't come he casts me a puzzled look before glancing at Chris. "Blake's been trying to reach you."

Chris checks his cell phone. "So he has. Any idea what it's about?"

"Mary and Ricco were arrested trying to leave the country."

"What?" I gasp.

"Mary and Ricco?" Chris repeats, sounding as stunned as I feel. "Are you sure?"

"Completely," Jacob assures us, "but beyond that I know

nothing. Apparently, Sara asked some questions and spooked Ricco. Blake wants to explain it all himself. He said to call him since you quote 'won't answer the damn phone.'"

Chris punches in Blake's number. "On it," he promises, and we step onto the elevator.

I desperately try to make out the conversation, but Chris mostly listens. It drives me insane. "And Rebecca?" Chris finally asks.

Yes! What about Rebecca!

"I see," Chris replies to whatever Blake says. "Yes. Not a problem."

"Well?" I demand as we enter the apartment and he ends the call.

"Let's talk while we start a hot shower." He laces his fingers with mine and leads me toward the bedroom. "Turns out Ricco was not only jealous of Mark and Rebecca's relationship, but furious that Mark took advantage of Rebecca. He wanted to bring down Riptide as payment for hurting her. Mary went along for the ride for the money and because she was angry Mark didn't give her more opportunities."

"Is Rebecca involved?" I ask as we enter the bathroom.

Chris removes his boots and opens the shower and turns it on. "Not according to Ricco and Mary."

"Then where is she?"

"That's the big question. Ricco insists Mark had to have done something to make her run."

"So, do the authorities think she's in hiding?"

"They don't know where she is, but if Mary and Ricco, or Mark for that matter, know, I'm confident Blake will find out."

"There's still a concern that Mark is involved?"

"Blake doesn't think so. He thinks Mary and Ricco know where she is, and that they'll break under questioning."

"I just can't believe Ricco knows where she is. But then, I wouldn't have believed he was a part of this, either."

Chris scrubs his jaw. "You and me both. I don't have a high opinion of Ricco but I didn't have this low of one, either. Oh, and Blake wants you at the police station tomorrow to go on file formally with what you know."

"Right." I grab my purse off the counter and remove my phone. "I guess I should text Mark and tell him I won't be in." Chris's shift in mood is instant, his expression turning stormy, his jaw clenching, and I quickly add, "Maybe not ever again."

He goes still. "What are you saying?"

"That I want all or nothing so I have to be willing to give the same."

He closes the distance between us, his arms caging me against the counter, searching my face. "You'd give up Allure for me?"

"Yes." It's a decision I didn't fully realize I'd made until this moment, but after tonight it's inevitable and right. "But I need my own career and independence. Those things are important to me."

"I'll support you in any way I can, baby."

"But not by doing things for me, Chris. Me earning success because I'm me. I need that."

"I understand." He brushes my hair off my shoulders, his fingers resting on my neck in that familiar way I've missed so much these past few days. "We're going to make this work this time."

The conviction in his voice makes me believe him. "Yes, we will." I text Mark and drop my phone to the counter, not caring what the reply is. Not when Chris's fingers are tugging at my blouse.

He slowly strips away my clothing, tenderly kissing my shoulders, my neck, my lips. We step under the blissful heat of the hot shower, washing away the chill of the night, and with it the bitter cold of all we have been through these past few days. Resting my head on Chris's chest, being in his arms, I feel as if I've been lost and found again. But Rebecca is still lost, and I fear the worst for her.

Thirty

⁓

Chris and I spend several hours on Saturday at the police station, and the Rebecca mystery is no closer to being solved. I have a bad feeling about her that I can't shake, and this fans the flames of my need to find Ella. I go ahead and file a missing person's report and contact the French consulate. After that, Chris and I go home and we don't leave the apartment the rest of the weekend. We just revel in being together, making love, and watching movies, though we take a trip to the gym, where I just about die re-creating my much-neglected treadmill routine.

Monday morning, we reenter the real world. Chris goes with me to the school, and despite expecting the worst, I am crushed to discover Ella is a no-show. Afterward, we discover she hasn't paid her rent. We pay it for her and then stop by the police station to update the report with what we've discovered.

In an effort to cheer me up, Chris convinces me we should head out Tuesday morning to his godparents' Sonoma property and attend an art exhibit in the gallery next door. Katie is thrilled, and truth be told, so am I. The feeling of family and belonging is a welcome one. By eight that evening, Chris and I have had dinner, he is painting in his studio, and I am packing for the trip. Chris has yet to unpack from L.A., so I open his suitcase to begin pulling out what isn't needed.

After I remove the dirty clothes, my hand settles on a small, clear bag of the paintbrushes he autographs, and I stop. There was one of these in Rebecca's keepsake box—but he said he barely knew her. Why would she have kept one? I pull one of the brushes from the bag and stare at it with a frown.

Chris appears in the doorway. "Do you know where I put—" He pauses. "What's wrong?"

I get up and go to the closet. "I have a question for you." I flip on the light and drop to my knees in front of the safe. "What's the combination?"

"What's going on, Sara?"

"You'll see in a minute. The combination?"

He tells me the numbers and I dial the lock. Yanking open the door, I grab the box I'd found in Rebecca's unit, retrieve the brush inside, and hold it up for Chris to see. "Why does Rebecca have your paintbrush in her keepsake box?" Then I grab the torn photo and pop to my feet to show that to him, too. "And do you know anything about this photo?"

He sighs. "The picture was taken at a charity event, with me and Mark. That was before he and I had a falling-out."

"Over Rebecca?

He nods. "The night after the charity event, I was at the club when a buzz was going on about Mark and his new sub, and how she'd cried through a public flogging. I confronted him and told him he'd pushed her too far. He told me to butt out, that he was Master of the club. Since he wouldn't listen to me, I tried to warn Rebecca away from him."

I suddenly feel a déjà vu. "Like you warned me."

"*Not* like you, Sara. I barely knew her."

"But you wanted to protect her, like you wanted to do me."

"Look, I know those journals make you relate to her, but she was nothing like you. She was just a kid, and Mark couldn't see why that mattered, but it did. She was happy with him that night at the gala, a schoolgirl in love—before he stole that innocence from her. When I warned her off him, she was furious. I'm not surprised she tore me out of the picture. She felt the same way about Mark as your mother did about your father."

"She kept your brush," I say flatly.

He shrugs. "I have no idea why. Maybe because it reminded her of that night with Mark."

I let that sit, then I nod. I can accept that answer, but not his silence before now. "So why wouldn't you tell me this before? I asked you directly if you knew her. We've been looking for her together, Chris."

"I told you I barely knew her, and that was the truth."

"But you knew her better than you made me believe," I say, trying to keep the accusation from my voice, but it's hard. I don't understand his silence. "You didn't tell me you'd seen her at the club, and there were plenty of chances for you to speak up."

"When you asked me about her, I didn't want you to know the club existed. I didn't want you in that part of my life."

His words hit me hard. I am still raw from him shutting me out of the funeral and his life. Suddenly, I realize this ache inside me isn't so much about Rebecca as it is about the realization that Chris is still keeping me at an emotional distance, never really letting me inside his life. I am here with him but I am never fully present the way I want to be.

I try to move past him. He blocks me. "Let me pass, Chris."

"Sara—"

"I need to think, Chris. I need space." And I do. I don't understand what I feel, but it hurts. I hurt and I've hurt for weeks on end. I'm tired of feeling this way.

He hesitates and then backs into the bedroom. I walk past him and snatch up my purse. "Where are you going?" he demands.

"I told you: I need some space."

"No. You need to stay here and we'll talk this out."

"I can only assume you've told me everything there is to say now. Unless there's more I don't know?"

He visibly flinches. "No. There's nothing else. That's it."

"Then we're done talking. I need to take a drive and think."

"I didn't want you to know about the club, Sara. Right or wrong, that's my honest answer," he pleads.

"I know. The problem is that everything you tell me is because you're *forced* to tell me—not because you *choose* to tell me. You never fully trust me."

"That's not true." He runs a rough hand through his hair and he looks as tormented as I feel. "It's *not* true."

"It's how I feel. It's what I feel right now." He's been all about secrets from day one, and I chose to ignore the danger they might present. I chose to look the other way because I'm so damn in love with him. I walk toward the door and he steps in front of me. "Stay."

"Keeping me here right now is the worst thing you can do, Chris. It'll make me feel trapped. I've felt that way too much in my life. Don't do that to me."

He steps aside.

I start walking, part of me wanting him to stop me, even though I'll be furious if he does. And part of me thinks his not stopping me is so out of character that it scares me. He let me go before, after I found him begging for a beating. No, that's not right. He'd downright pushed me away. I haven't fully healed from that and right now, I'm afraid of what I don't know and how it will tear us apart, like the club discovery almost had. I'm afraid it's going to happen again. I can't help it. I need him to fight for me now, no matter how wrong of me that might be.

He can't win by letting me go or keeping me here—and neither can I. Maybe we never *could* win together. We were destined to shred each other inside and out. Destined to end up right here, where we are tonight.

At the front of the building, I order my car brought up to me. Once I'm inside it I sit behind the wheel, unsure of where to go. I want to be with Chris, but the secrets he keeps, on top of the rawness of his withdrawal this past week, eats away at me.

He didn't trust me to go through the loss of Dylan with him. He didn't trust me to tell me about Rebecca. No, about the club. He hid that from me for as long as he possibly could. What else is he hiding and unwilling to share because he still thinks I can't handle it? I've poured my heart out to this man, and now I've given up my job for him. I had put all fear aside and gambled on us. When will *he* fully gamble on us? Will he ever?

My phone rings and it's Chris. I decline the call. The doorman knocks on my window and I jump. He mouths, "Are you okay?" and I wave and pull onto the road. I don't know where I'm going; I just drive.

An hour later, I end up at Mark's white mansion in the same Cow Hollow neighborhood as his club. I have no idea why I am here. Honestly, I have nowhere else to go. And Mark really is my one real connection to both Chris and Rebecca, who have both become a huge part of my life. Both of whom I now feel like I am losing.

Besides, Mark is all about facts, not the emotions I am letting control me right now. Just hearing him tell the same story Chris has told me about Rebecca might give me new perspective about why Chris's silence on the subject bothers me so much.

I grab my purse and shove open the door. Motion detectors flicker to life and doors identical to the ones at the club become visible, sending a frisson of unease through me. I press past it and ring the bell. I shiver, telling myself it's because I've hastily forgotten a jacket, not because of my location. It doesn't work. Nerves flutter through me and the frisson becomes full-blown doubt. I'm about to make a mad dash for the car when the door opens and Mark appears, looking like a Mark I've never seen. He's barefooted and his normal, finely groomed blond hair is rumpled. The perfectly fitted suit I've become accustomed to him wearing has been replaced by a white T-shirt and faded jeans.

His gaze sweeps my jeans and T-shirt, clearly finding my attire as striking as I do his. One blond brow lifts. "Ms. McMillan. What a surprise."

"Isn't it?" I ask, sounding as awkward as I feel. "Am I interrupting anything?"

"Nothing that can't wait."

He motions me forward and I hesitate, remembering the room called the Lion's Den at the club, and that caged feeling I'd had in the demo unit. But I want answers. I need answers. I draw a breath and step onto the pale ivory hardwood floor and into a narrow hallway, too close to Mark for comfort.

"Is everything okay?" he asks.

"Yes. No. I just need to ask you a few questions about . . . Chris."

His eyes narrow. "Chris?

"And Rebecca."

"And Rebecca," he repeats, and I catch a flash of consternation in his gaze that quickly fades. "I'm not sure how they connect but I'm intrigued enough to see where this is going." His chin lifts to urge me forward. I just stand there, frozen in place, his gray eyes sharp as he watches me. Oh yes, I feel like I am in the lion's den and want out. "Staying or going, Ms. McMillan?"

Answers, Sara. You want answers. "Staying. I'm staying." My feet move. That's progress. One step into the den is closer to one step out.

The massive living room I bring into focus a few feet down the hallway is exactly what I expect of Mark. Rich, rich, and rich in every way. An obviously expensive chocolate brown leather couch is framed by two oversized matching chairs. A fireplace is to the left, and above it a painting I recognize as a Motif. Two sculptures are to either side of the fireplace, and I have no doubt they were done by famous artists, though I am not knowledgeable enough to be certain.

Mark steps to my side, intimidatingly tall and close. "Let's sit."

I walk forward and choose the solitariness the overstuffed chairs allows me and perch on the edge of one, setting my purse beside me. Mark sits on the arm of the couch facing me, automatically assuming the position of dominance.

My throat is ridiculously parched and my pulse starts thrumming wildly, afraid of what may be another Pandora's box.

"Yes, Ms. McMillan?" he asks when I've apparently let too much time pass.

A heavy breath escapes my lungs. "I need to know what caused you and Chris to come to bad terms."

He considers me a moment. "What did he tell you?"

"I'd rather hear it from you."

"Why is this important?" His voice is crisp.

"It just is."

"That's not a good enough answer."

Of course not. That would be too simple. "Was it over Rebecca?"

"Is this about the police investigation?"

"No, it's not that. I . . ." I almost tell him about the storage unit but think better of it. "She's just become very personal to me and I came across some of Rebecca's items, and there were keepsakes from a charity event that she and Chris—"

"They weren't involved. Not even close. In fact, she came to dislike him quite a lot."

"I didn't think they were involved, but what made her dislike him?"

"He saw her as a young kid who needed a daddy more than a Master."

This explains why Rebecca had scribbled out Chris's name in her work journal. "And you didn't agree with him?"

"No. I didn't agree with him. I saw a young, intelligent, beautiful woman with the world in her hands."

There is a softness to his voice I've never heard, and not for the first time I believe he had feelings for Rebecca. Maybe not love, but he had an attachment I once thought him incapable of feeling for anyone. "Where is she, Mark?"

"Contrary to Ricco's insistence that I know that, I don't."

"What the fuck is she doing here?"

I jump at the sound of Ava's voice and stand up, turning toward a hallway to my right. Ava is standing there, eyes ablaze and wearing nothing but an oversized T-shirt. Ryan is behind her, bare-chested, in a pair of dress pants.

"I tried to stop her, Mark." He reaches for Ava and she turns and throws punches at him, tearing her nails down his cheek. "Holy fuck, Ava!"

"What the fuck is she *doing* here, Mark?" Ava screams, and she looks wild, insane.

"Ava, I told you to wait in the bedroom," Mark warns sharply. "*Go back* to the bedroom."

"So you can fuck her and then come back and fuck me like you did that bitch Rebecca?" She bolts forward and Ryan tries to grab her, but he misses. My heart jackhammers as she closes in on us and I'm not sure where to go, what to do. She's running toward us, no—me, and I start backing up.

Mark grabs me and shoves me behind him just as Ava crashes into him. She starts thrashing around, trying to reach me. Before I escape, she grabs a chunk of my hair and twists it in her hands. Pain splinters through my scalp and I scream with the force of her grip.

"Enough, Ava!" Mark barks, and I feel a painful jerk before I am suddenly free. I stumble backward, hit the table again, and this time I end up on top of it with a hard thud that rattles me to the bones.

"Fuck you, Mark!" Ava screams in pain, and I can see Ryan's hand wrapped around her hair, yanking her backward. "You did this to me with that bitch Rebecca!" Ava screeches. "You're not doing it to me again."

I roll to the floor and land on my hands and knees.

"I'll kill that bitch," Ava hisses. "I'll kill her."

"Get out of here, Sara," Mark orders. Kill me? Was she serious? Mark grabs me and pulls me to my feet. "Sara! Get the fuck out!"

I don't need to be told again. I run out of the room and for the door, and I don't even shut it behind me. Ava is screaming from inside, wild, insane. I'm running so fast I smash into the side of my car, heaving in air. I reach for my purse. Oh, God. Oh, God. No! My purse and keys are inside. Pressing my hand to my forehead, I try to think what to do, but there is too much adrenaline rushing through me to think straight. I start to pace, willing myself to calm down. Neighbor. I have to walk to a neighbor and call Chris for a ride. There isn't another option. I start to run down the drive.

Behind me I hear the garage door creak open and I turn to be blinded by headlights that start moving toward me. I edge to the side of the driveway, but the lights follow me. I cut across the lawn, and I don't have to look back to know the car is still behind me and it's close—too close. Desperately, I dart behind a massive tree and stumble to my hands and knees as the car blasts into the trunk with a loud crash that echoes through my bones.

I hear my own breathing. I hear shouts. Mark and Ryan, I think, but I can't make them out. I scramble to my feet and run toward the voices, bringing both men into focus as they head for me as well. The car door opens with a groan behind me and I turn to walk backward as Ava pushes out of the car, holding a gun on me.

"Stay where you are, bitch!" Ava screams, blood gushing from her temple.

I freeze at the venomous look on her face, at the certainty she is insane and will pull the trigger. "Ava!" Mark shouts from somewhere just beyond my shoulder, and he must have taken a step forward because Ava hisses at him, "Stay where you are, Mark, or I'll shoot her right here and now. Get in the car, Sara."

Ryan says nothing. I don't know where he is, but I hope he's not here and he's getting help. It's our only hope.

"*Get in* the car, Sara," Ava orders.

I can't get in the car. I can't. I know if I do I won't get back out alive.

"Now!" she screeches.

I swallow the panic threatening to overcome me, trying to be logical, trying to think of a way out of this. She won't hurt me. There are witnesses. People will know I left with her. None of it is true. She's crazy. That's what it comes down to.

She fires by my feet and I jump, and Mark shouts. I move toward her out of fear she will shoot again at me this time. I'm one step toward her and I hear the sound of a motorcycle before I see it. Ava hears it too and reacts by turning the gun toward the sound. The motorcycle comes into view and I know it's Chris. It has to be, and all I can think is that she's going to shoot him. Instinct kicks in and I run for Ava, but the gun goes off before I get to her. The bike and Chris go flying and crash into my car. I reach Ava and jump her from behind and try not to think about Chris dead and bleeding. Just get the gun. I yank her hair and do the only thing I know to do. I bite the shit out of her arm. She screams and twists and we go down to the ground with her back to my chest, but I have what I want. The gun flies through the air and I can hear the sound of sirens fast approaching, but I lose my hold on Ava. She rolls off me, going for the gun.

I grab her shirt, which is all she's still wearing, and she kicks me hard in the face. Pain jolts me and I lose my grip on her shirt. She scrambles away and somehow I rise to my hands and knees to follow. At the same moment I see a bloodied Chris grappling with Ava for the gun. Her hand touches the gun and terror for Chris shoots adrenaline through me.

"Chris!" I scream, and slam my fist into Ava's head. She falls to her side with a yelp.

Ryan comes out of nowhere and grabs me, pulling me back. Mark yanks Ava against him and she screams bloody murder, fighting against him like some kind of possessed person, blood pouring down her face.

Chris comes to his knees, and he has blood pouring from a gash in his head, too, but he's got a steady hand on the gun and it's pointed at Ava as he shouts at Mark, "Get that bitch out of here or I will shoot her!"

Mark drags Ava away from us and police cars screech into the drive. "Don't move!" a police officer screams at Chris, holding a gun on him. "Drop the weapon."

My eyes meet Chris's and hold as he drops the gun and I feel the short distance between us like punishing desert miles. He had secrets he kept from me. I went to Mark for answers. Police swarm the yard, blocking my view of Chris, separating us. We are worlds apart, damaged beyond our bodies, perhaps beyond repair.

Swarms of EMT and police officials surround us and I cannot see Chris, but I am assured he is fine. I don't feel like he is fine. I don't feel like anything will ever be fine again. It's only after Ava is taken away, and I see Chris talking to police across the lawn, that I can breathe again. Only then do I let myself be ushered to an ambulance to be checked out.

It's there, with a kindly older gentleman with salt-and-pepper hair checking my vitals, that Chris finds me, as he appears at the door looking battered and bruised. The idea that he could have died tonight to save me, because I came here, overwhelms me.

"How's your head?" I ask, noting the rather large bandage on his forehead.

"I need stitches but I'll live." He flicks a glance toward the EMTs. "How's she looking?"

"Bruised up but she'll live, too."

Chris and I stare at each other, and my heart twists at what passes between us, with the certainty we are still worlds apart. The EMT clears his throat. "I'll be right back," he says and quickly exits the vehicle, clearly reading our need for a few moments alone.

Chris climbs into the ambulance and sits down next to me. "Blake called. Ava confessed to killing Rebecca."

My hand balls between my breasts with the impact of this news. "How? When?"

"We have no details, thanks to an attorney who arrived and shut her up, but I suspect we will in the next few days. The private eye you had the encounter with at the storage unit turned over some journals he took from the unit. He's had some past trouble and wants no part of being connected to a murder. He seems to think they'll be helpful."

"More journals," I say. "More people reading Rebecca's private thoughts. Like I did."

"Because of you, she can be properly put to rest. And Ava can be put away before she hurts someone else—like she almost hurt you tonight."

I turn to him, wishing away the space between us. "You saved my life."

His reply is slow, his expression shuttered, closed off from me the way he is. "Yeah, well, this time I got protecting you right. Apparently I haven't done so well in other cases."

"That's not true. I just—"

"Had to hear the truth from Mark because you didn't believe it from me. I know. I get that."

"You didn't tell me about Rebecca until I discovered it on my own."

"I get that, too, but what I can't seem to get is the fact that you were willing to take his word over mine." He scrubs his jaw and rests his elbows on his knees. "You say I shut you out when life gets hard. Well, you seem to run to Mark."

"No, Chris. It's not like that. Not even close to that."

"You want honesty, Sara. I'm giving it to you. I knew you'd go to him. That's why I let you leave the apartment so easily. And I swore if you went to him, it was over between us."

I am weak all over, trembling from the possibility that he means this. "No, Chris. Mark has nothing to do with us. It hurt that you hadn't told me everything about Rebecca, and I was still raw over last week."

"I know. I know, Sara. We are just so damn good at hurting each other."

"What are you saying?" The question comes out barely there, my voice lodged in my throat with my heart.

"I don't know what I'm saying. I know I died a thousand deaths tonight when I thought Ava was going to shoot you. I would have died for you tonight; that's how much I love you."

"But sometimes love isn't enough," I say, repeating his words from back at the club. "Is that where we're at again?"

"I'm not sure I'm the one who has to answer that question this time, Sara. I think you do."

"What does that even mean?"

"Excuse me." I look up to find a police officer at the back

of the vehicle and will him away but it doesn't work. "Ms. McMillan, if you're up to it, we'd like you to come inside to answer some questions."

"Of course. Now?"

"That would be the preference."

Chris climbs out of the ambulance and offers me his hand. I slide my palm in his and warmth spreads up my arm, but the space between us, the damn space, is thick and cold, and I fear it is becoming more impenetrable by the second. I don't want to leave him. I want the people to go away and leave us alone.

The EMT reappears and eyes Chris. "We're ready to roll on to the hospital, if you are?"

"Yeah," Chris says. "I'm ready." His eyes meet mine and hold a moment. "I'm going to get my head stitched up."

"I'll go with you."

"You need to answer the questions they want answered, and get tonight behind you and us. Stay here. Do what they need you to do."

I cling to the word *us,* but I know how broken we are. I know how close we are to losing each other, how abnormal it is for Chris to not insist on being by my side for this. My throat constricts. "Right. Okay." I turn to the officer. "I'm ready." I don't look at Chris again since I know that if I do, I won't walk away. For the first time since meeting him, I wonder if he might be relieved if I did.

Thirty-one

An hour after Chris left for the hospital, I'm done with the police questioning and I step outside Mark's house. A flicker of movement draws me to the shadowy area of the yard, to the tree Ava had crashed into, and I find Mark resting against it. His head is bowed low, his arms resting on his knees, and it's clear this isn't the composed, controlled Mark I've come to expect.

After a moment of hesitation, I join him and settle onto the ground beside him. His head lifts and I'm shocked at what he allows me to see. Pain. Torment. Blame.

"She came back because I asked her to," he tells me.

"What?" I ask, but then it hits me what he means. I remember Blake saying Rebecca came home and just disappeared.

"I called Rebecca while she was on her vacation with the guy she took off with, and told her to come back. That things would be different. She told me no." He shoves a rough hand into his hair and curses. "I thought she shut me out. I never even knew she came back into town. I brought her back here, and Ava did God knows what to her. I'm the reason she's dead."

"Don't do this to yourself." I go to my knees to face him. "You didn't do this. You aren't responsible for what Ava did."

He fixes me with a haunted stare. "I am. You don't know just how fucking responsible I am. I threw Rebecca and Ava together at the club. I included Ava in play. I—" His voice breaks off and he looks away sharply. "Rebecca was . . ." Seconds tick by and abruptly he is staring at me again. "I caused this, and I almost did the same thing to you. I would have, if not for Chris. You and I both know it's true. Go home, Sara. Get as far away from me as you can."

The order is rough and razor sharp, but I don't move. I want to help him. "Mark—"

"Go home."

I know then that he has to deal with his demons in his own way, like I've had to deal with mine. I push to my feet and stare down at him, but he isn't looking at me and I know he won't again. I walk to my car. Once I'm inside, I start the engine, but I'm not sure what to do with myself. Chris had said he'd vowed we'd be over if I came here tonight. Did he mean it? I've heard nothing from him, but I love him too much to have much pride right now.

With nerves fluttering in my stomach, I try to call him. The rings radiate through me, one after another, until I hear his voice mail and hang up. I feel that same pinch in my chest that I did last week when he'd shut me out. He's angry and hurt and I'm not anymore. I'm uncertain and confused.

I'm not sure how tonight landed where it did, and as I start driving, I find myself searching for answers where it all seemed to start. I end up at my old apartment and go to Ella's unit, the place where I first discovered Rebecca. I walk to the bedroom, drop my purse on the bed, and lie on the mattress to stare at the ceiling. Thanks to Ella and Rebecca, I dared to be me, not the shell of a person I had settled for. And because of them, I found Chris.

I roll to my side, exhausted beyond belief. I want to go home, I want to see Chris. I want to talk to him about all I am feeling, but we are broken. So very broken. I don't know how to fix us. I don't know if he wants to fix us. Maybe I shouldn't want to fix us. But I do. And I don't care if that makes me foolish. I dig my phone from my purse, shut my eyes, and will it to ring.

"Sara." I blink awake to the sound of Chris's voice and find him standing above me.

I sit up in a haze, afraid I'm still dreaming. "Chris?" I scoot to the end of the bed, relieved he is indeed here, hope filling me that we still have a chance.

He squats down in front of me, but he doesn't touch me. "I thought you'd be here, when I didn't find you at home."

"I couldn't go home when you weren't there. I tried to call you."

"They made me turn my phone off at the hospital, and you haven't been answering yours since I turned it back on." He cuts his gaze away and I sense the struggle in him, and dread fills me before he turns back to me. "Look. Sara." Again he hesitates, and I hang on the moment until he continues. "I'm leaving for Paris at ten in the morning."

My shoulders slump, pain spiraling through me. "You're leaving?"

"Yes. I'm leaving."

"No. Don't."

He studies me a long moment, searching for something I hope he finds. "Come with me. We'll find Ella and we'll try to find us again. I've thought about this for hours. I've held things back, and maybe tonight wouldn't have happened if I hadn't. If you want to know exactly who and what I am, Paris is where you will find out. I've always known that but I wasn't ready for what that means until now. And I'm not sure you ever will be. You need to think long and hard on that before morning."

"My passport—"

He reaches into his pocket, then pulls out my passport and tosses it on the bed. "It came while I was out of town." He pushes to his feet and he still hasn't touched me. Why won't he touch me?

This is too sudden. My head is spinning. "Chris, please. Let's talk about this."

"No. No talking. No in between. All or nothing, Sara. I'm offering that to you, and you have to decide if you really want it. There's a reservation in your name with American Airlines. I'll be on the plane. I hope you will be, too." He walks away and the door opens and shuts behind him.

He's gone, leaving me with confirmation of what I've already sensed in him. There is more to his pain than I know, more secrets to be revealed. He's left me with another one of his tests, and I have only a few hours to answer. Not knowing what secrets he holds, am I willing to take this risk with him?

Thursday, August 2, 2012

I told him good-bye today, but he didn't believe I meant it. His lips curved in that sensual way they do, and he murmured wicked promises of pleasure in my ear. But this time those promises weren't enough. He looked shocked when I told him that pleasure was the façade he used to hide from love. I saw something deep in his eyes, a flash of torment. And I knew I was right, that there is more to him than he allows me to see. I'm not blind anymore, though. I know now that I'm not the woman who can reveal the man beneath the Master. I'm simply a part of his journey and he of mine.

Ah, but there is a part of me that hopes he will miss me. That maybe we will find each other again someday. I didn't dare see him again, or touch him again, for fear I'd be weak and change my mind. I left him a handwritten note on his desk, and said all there was left to say. "Good-bye—Love, Rebecca"

Turn the page for an exclusive sneak peek
at Lisa Renee Jones's spicy final installment
to the Inside Out trilogy

Revealing Us

Available September 2013 from Gallery Books

The elevator opens and he waits for me to enter, and I do. With fast steps, I rush inside and whirl around to confront him. He stalks forward, and this time he doesn't avoid looking at me, his expression etched with pure determination and some raw, dark emotion I cannot fully name. I don't get the chance to try.

Before a word is out of my mouth, and I have many intended, the bags he's holding hit the floor and he has pressed me back against the wall. My purse tumbles from my arm and his powerful thighs encase mine; his hips mold my hips. I gasp with the rough tangle of his fingers in my hair and the blaze of his eyes as they capture mine. I am angry with him. I am aroused. And when his mouth claims my mine, his tongue slicing past my lips with a delicious lick followed by another, demanding my response, I am at his mercy. My fingers curl around his T-shirt and I eliminate the tiny space between us, molding myself against him. He owns me and, considering how the past thirty minutes have gone, this terrifies me, but I'm all in with him. I decided that long ago. I am his to command, moaning with the taste of him, sultry and male, on my tongue.

His hand sweeps up my side, fingers flexing over my ribs, palm covering my breast. My nipple tightens in anticipation of the tug that follows and I moan, my need to touch him almost unbearable. I reach for his shirt, intending to push beneath, but he doesn't let me.

His fingers close around my wrist and I know he is in that dark place, where he doesn't let me touch him—but I am in a dark place, too, on edge, ripe with my anger and unwilling to be submissive to him. Challenging his silent message of control, I reach for his shirt with my free hand, and he shackles my other wrist as well and tears his mouth from mine. Our eyes lock, the sound of our heavy breathing filling the air, and the motion of the elevator I didn't even know was moving sways our bodies. The floor vibrates slightly beneath our feet and I sense that the doors behind him slide open, but still we stand there, staring at each other.

"They don't get to tell you who I am," he says. His voice is a rough growl, low and tight. "I do. I tell you and I show you, so you get the truth—not their fabrication of it." A muscle in his jaw flexes. "Understand?"

My anger and fear dissolve instantly. He's not pulling away from me. He's angry that Amber and Tristan might taint my view of him, when he's already convinced I'll hate him before this discovery process is over.

"Do you understand?" he demands again when I apparently don't answer fast enough.

This time I don't fight the bark of his order, understanding the desperation beneath its surface. "Yes. Yes. I—"

His fingers tangle in my hair again, tugging my head back in that deliciously rough way he does. His dark side calls to me and I no longer fight answering.

"Do not go there without me again." His voice is gravelly; raw like the emotion I've seen in his face and tasted on his lips.

"My going there wasn't what you think it was."

His eyes flash with disapproval. He is not pleased, or accepting of what I've said, and his mouth closes down on mine, punishing, controlling. His tongue thrusts and tastes before he repeats his words, his fingers stroking my breasts, teasing my nipple. "Do not go there again without me, Sara."

"I won't." The words come out a hoarse groan as his hand strokes a path up and down my side, and back over my breast. His touch is heavy, the air thick, and I'm certain he isn't convinced. "I won't go back without you."

His fingers curl around my neck and he stares down at me, searching my face with such intensity, it feels as if he's seeing straight to my soul. And I welcome it. I welcome him. Seconds tick by, and I have no idea what he sees or doesn't see in me, but he drags my mouth to his and kisses me.

The silky hot stroke of his tongue is a shot of adrenaline and desire that spikes through my body and creates a tingling sensation from head to toe. I shudder with pleasure and drink him in, tasting the bittersweet hunger in him, the anger and torment. I burn to touch him beyond where my fingers rest on his chest, to feel hard muscle flex beneath my fingers.

But control is his outlet of choice when there is no whip, no pain. And I am no longer angry, no longer rebelling against his demands. No longer fighting his need for an outlet I have long ached for him to know he has with me, in me.

I tremble with the caress of his hand over my waist, traveling to my hip, and curving around my backside to firmly pull me hard against his thick erection. His palm skims upward to the small of my back and flattens, molding me even closer. I moan into his mouth and he groans in response, his tongue delving deeply, hot with growing demand, with a palpable urgency. And his hands are everywhere, touching me, stroking me, caressing me, driving me wild. Before I know what's happening, he's shoving my jeans down my legs. I blink and my boots are gone, and I'm half-naked in an elevator with the doors locked open.

He turns me to the wall and his hands slide, slow and firm, possessively down my waist and over my hips. Feeling his gaze rake over my body, I am wet and weak in the knees. He cups my cheeks from behind and steps forward, pressing his lips to my ear. "Tonight I want to spank you, but I won't. Not when it would be punishment. I won't ever do that to you. But don't think that means I won't want to."

I understand him. I don't know how or why, but deep in our souls, we connect, and I know what he is doing. He's showing me a hard exterior, but all I see is vulnerability, a need that tonight has sparked: to show me a darker, more dangerous side of himself and have me not run for cover.

"You can't scare me away," I tell him, "so throw all the words you want at me. I'm still here. I'm still not going anywhere. And in case you forgot, I liked it when you spanked me."

His hand finds my stomach and then presses deeper between my legs, until his fingers tease my clit. "Maybe this time I'll tie you up and flog you."

"Do it." His fingers stroke into the silky wet V of my body, and I am panting, barely able to speak, but I somehow finish my challenge. "The more you push me, the more I push back."

He nips my earlobe and I can feel him unzipping his pants. "So you say," he murmurs.

"So I *know*." Throwing caution to the wind, I press on, trying to unleash the pent-up energy that he always bottles until it explodes. "Only one of us is running. Only one of us is afraid of what I have yet to discover."

The air crackles and his hand goes to my waist, fingers flexing into my flesh, and I revel in knowing I've succeeded in taking him to the edge.

"You think I'm running?" he demands.

"No. I think you're trying to make *me* run so you can blame me if we fail."

His cock presses between my legs. "Does that feel like I want you to run?" He drives hard inside me without any prelude. "Does *that*?" And then he is thrusting, reaching around me to meld his hand to my breast, holding onto me. He thrusts again, burying himself with a fieriness that outreaches pure physical need.

Oh yes, I have made him angry, and I am glad. I want this side of him—I want all of him. And damn it, he just keeps trying to deny me. He keeps trying to hold back, and keeps trying to make me run.

I press my hand to his on my breast, holding him there and wanting to never let go. Pleasure splinters through me with each thrust of his cock, each moment he's buried deep inside me. Sensation after sensation begins in my sex and rushes through all my nerve endings. I am lost in how he feels, how I feel, and I arch into him. My muscles clench around him, and then I can't breathe—my orgasm takes me by surprise, enveloping me, consuming me. I rise to the top of it far too quickly and come down far too hard and fast, but just in time to feel him shudder, his body tensing with his release. He stills, burying his face in my neck, and his body slowly relaxes. For several moments he holds me there, and I'm not sure either of us breathes. I'm not sure what to say or what to do next.

Abruptly, he pulls out of me, and an unusual sense of utter emptiness washes over me. As I start to turn, he's already headed out of the elevator. I stare after him, knots tightening in my stomach.

Maybe I pushed the wrong buttons.

Maybe I pushed him too far or too hard.

Maybe I made a mistake.